THE MAFIA'S
TELEPHONE COMPANY

INSPIRED BY A TRUE STORY

TERENCE D. ROBINSON

Title of Book: The Mafia's Telephone Company

Copyright © 2025 by Terence D. Robinson

Published by Bitterroot Mountain Publishing House LLC
P.O. Box 3508, Hayden, ID 83835
Visit our website at www.BMPHmedia.com

1st edition: 2025

Interior and cover design by Jera Publishing
Editor: Amber Laura M. Young

Library of Congress Cataloguing in Publication Data

ISBN: 978-1-960059-32-1 Hardcover
ISBN: 978-1-960059-31-4 Softcover
ISBN: 978-1-960059-33-8 eBook

Printed in the United States of America

10 9 8 7 6 5 4 3 2 1

CONTENTS

A NOTE FROM THE AUTHOR

The mid-90s were the Wild West days of the telecom industry. Most American families had adopted cell phones. Many dropped their landlines. At the same time, home internet became ubiquitous. Landline phone companies began a transformation to wireless and internet services. Much of this innovation was spurred by the Telecommunications Act of 1996. Companies rushed to merge and implement revised strategies to survive.

Organized crime found pearls of opportunity in the new era. In 1996, a Fortune 500 company sold a small landline telephone company tucked away in rural Cass County, Missouri. Ostensibly, the buyer was a highly regarded business executive. In what could be a scene plucked from The Sopranos, the executive acted as a frontman for the New York Mafia. The Mafia allegedly owned the holding company that acquired the phone company. They used the same frontman to purchase a bank in nearby Garden City.

After acquiring the phone company and bank, the executive and his Mafia associates allegedly used the companies and other Mafia-owned businesses to perpetrate fraudulent internet porn billing schemes on the American public. These actions cost consumers as much as one billion dollars. At that time, it was the largest consumer fraud in history.

The Mafia's Telephone Company is inspired by that true story. The people and companies described in this novel are fictional. The crimes are realistic portrayals of fraudulent schemes carried out across the United States.

I worked with the frontman during the early '90s, before his involvement with the Mafia. I returned to Missouri in 2005 as a consultant, assisting the group tasked with removing the telephone company from the Mafia-controlled holding company.

Terence Robinson

"The price of anything is the amount of life you exchange for it."
—Henry David Thoreau

PART I

The Deal

When stars die, they recede
with planets and moons in tow.
Disappear into black holes.

When an industry dies, its
companies vaporize. Executives
dispatched to early graves.
Memories suspended, timeless in the void.

WesTel died, the industry survived,
dust and gas from the company live on.
Collapsed inward by gravity, a new planet forms.

I slip into the vortex, reborn.

—Erick Olson

CHAPTER 1

May 1999

THE GARBLED SOUND of their chatter carried through an open window and spilled across the night quiet.

"Gin!" The janitor leaned back in his chair and smiled.

"Again? Man, you're good," the night watchman said. "I've got time for one more hand before rounds."

Like clockwork, the night watchman patrolled the grounds every two hours. He drove the perimeter, checked the hangers, and looked for anything out of place. His next round was scheduled for 2:30 a.m.

They played cards in the breakroom of an otherwise deserted corporate airpark in the early morning hours. Gerald Carter smiled. He listened through his earpiece and watched them through binoculars from his rental car parked on a seldom-used service road across the tarmac. He had staked out the facility for ten days and planted a transmitter in the breakroom. Gerald expected the two would be distracted by their nightly game at this time.

"I don't know why you bother. Never anyone out there," said the janitor.

"Except the time I caught them kids screwing in daddy's jet." They both laughed at the memory.

At precisely 2 a.m., Gerald laid down his binoculars and stepped from his rental car into the cool salt-laden ocean air. He leaned against the door and applied pressure until he heard the latch click. Darkness cloaked the tarmac on this moonless night. Security lamps positioned high in the hangar gables washed the buildings in an ominous yellow glow.

The former Navy SEAL stroked the deep scar on his cheek, a wound he suffered from a failed mission in Libya. The scar transformed a face with handsome features into an unsightly mask. The strong jaw, sandy hair, and deep brown eyes—lost in the shadow of war. Only Gerald survived the attack, which cast a cloud of suspicion over his medical discharge. Heroes were expected to die on the battlefield with their comrades. Bright flashes and loud booms still sent him back to Libya.

Gerald rehearsed the job's choreography in his head—each step crucial to his success. He closed his eyes and considered every move. Mentally prepared, Gerald dropped to his good knee in silence. Dressed in black, he slid on his belly into the dew-covered tall grass and crawled to the razor-wire-topped chain-link fence. The early morning sounds of the outdoors were disturbed only by the muted rustle of leaves beneath him and the distant sound of highway traffic a half-mile away.

Gerald cut the fence with wire snips, rolled up the metal fabric, and secured it with zip ties. Sliding through the opening, he disappeared into the shadows and limped one hundred yards to the Lear 45. He lifted himself halfway into the empty wheel-bay cavity and used a small screwdriver to open a service panel. The cramped space smelled of oil and jet fuel. Unzipping his backpack, he removed a package half the size of a cigar box. After Gerald secured the box in the recess with black duct tape, he flipped the altitude sensor to the on position. Holding a penlight in his mouth, he struggled to reattach the cover. Nearly finished, the final screw slipped from his hand and fell to the tarmac.

"Shit."

Gerald dropped to the ground on all fours and frantically scanned the asphalt with his flashlight and searched for the screw. He found it in a crack and poked at it with the screwdriver. The tip struck the screw and lodged it deeper. Gerald unsheathed his tactical knife and tried to drive the blade under the screw but failed. After a hectic minute, he checked his watch—2:25. *Time's up, got to go.*

Gerald made his way back to the fence, crawled through the opening, and rolled the wire back in place. His war-injured leg ached by the time he reached the vehicle. With the headlights turned off, Gerald drove away slowly. Fifteen minutes later, he arrived at the Charleston International Airport. He returned his rental car and found a quiet spot in the terminal to make a private cell call to Chicago.

"Mr. Acosta ... it's done."

"Any problems?"

"No, wire the balance." Gerald disconnected the call.

CHAPTER 2

One year earlier—May 1998

DISCOURAGED, ERICK OLSON waited impatiently for a break in the storm. He was returning from lunch and needed ten seconds to jump from his Porsche, sprint through the flooded parking lot, and into the main lobby of WesTel Corporation to finish out his last day. But the Seattle rain fell relentlessly that first day of May, refusing to grant him passage.

A strong wind out of the northwest drove sheets of water against the office building windows as if to cleanse them of memories held within. Heavy clouds hung low in the sky, producing a half-light determined to lure even healthy souls into the depths of depression. Erick's chest tightened. He fought to claim a breath. *God, I hate the rain.*

"Screw it," he muttered under his breath.

Erick climbed out of the car and folded the collar of his trench coat up, tight against his neck. Holding his briefcase above his head like an umbrella, he dashed toward the door through puddles and wind-driven rain.

For the most part, the WesTel HQ building had emptied of employees. The building facilities staff, as well as a small contingent of accountants and support staff, were still on the payroll. Office machines and furniture had been auctioned off the previous week. Crews from the winning bidders wandered in and out of vacant offices. Erick watched them remove equipment and dismantle office cubicles to the music of power drills and the idle banter of men who made a living with their hands. They filled the building with the sounds of opportunity, but not for Erick. The stuff would be resold and redeployed to another location for another business enterprise. Perhaps the new owner's luck would run stronger.

"Excuse me." A young, clean-cut guy in his twenties stood in the open doorway to Erick's office waving an envelope. Erick didn't recognize the kid. He motioned him in.

"What can I do for you?" Erick ran bent fingers through his mop of unruly, blond hair. Staring at the kid, Erick wondered if he was looking for a job.

"Sorry, no one was up front. I'm looking for Erick Olson."

"You found him. What've you got?"

The guy handed him an envelope. "You've been served."

"What the hell!" Standing from behind the desk, towering over the kid now, Erick held his chiseled chin out and glared down his nose. "What is *this*?" Erick's steel blue eyes cut into the guy.

"Sorry, I only serve 'em. Best of luck to you." He turned and was out the door in a hurry.

Erick reclaimed his seat and opened the envelope. He read the first page. Betty had filed for legal separation, the first step toward divorce. The date for an initial court appearance had been set.

"Damn it all."

He spun around in his over-size executive chair a dozen times, as a child might—let the moment flow through him. His feet stopped kicking the floor, and the chair slowly rotated to a stop, facing the rain-battered window. A sharp pain stabbed hard at his gut, then rose to his heart, where it squeezed out any remaining thought Erick held to reconcile with Betty. All hope was lost, and he sat alone, helpless to save his marriage.

Erick knew the summons was coming. He just didn't expect it today. Betty had never forgiven him for the affair with Sara. He had been on the interview team and pushed to hire the young attorney, rationalized at the time—a lawyer is a lawyer, might as well bring on an attractive one. Erick recognized now how wrong that was. Not long after Sara started, he bedded her for the first time on a business trip.

He had wanted to work something out with Betty. Clearly, she thought not. Erick's shoulders fell, and he slumped in his chair. A sense of hopelessness ran through him. He cupped his face in his hands and leaned over the desk. Erick knew Betty was too good for him, and there would be no second chances; in his life, there rarely were.

The rain continued falling through the afternoon, and the sky darkened further with the onset of evening. Erick spent most of the day in his office dealing with financial documents as he did on every other workday. A cardboard box sat on his desk half-filled with personal effects and career mementos commemorating his success. He held a small marble plaque in his hand and ran his thumb over its smooth surface. In silence, he read the inscription engraved on the brass plate:

Presented to:
Erick Olson, "The Financial Wunderkind"
For outstanding performance on the
1983 Whitman Telephone Acquisition

That was fifteen years ago. Reading the plaque, Erick didn't feel much like a *Financial Wunderkind*. He often second-guessed the bloody fight he waged with Local Telephone Exchange Corp. over its unsolicited offer to acquire WesTel. He wondered if his tendency to argue to the point of alienating even his most vocal supporters arose from a genetic weakness in his personality. His college football coach kicked him off the team because of the same behavioral tic. He had fought it his entire life. Like a boxer who leads with his chin, Erick couldn't control his mouth.

Despite Erick's objections, WesTel had been sold to Local Telephone Exchange Corp. The Seattle office was being closed, and the surviving employees were being relocated to Texas. Erick recognized the fight he waged centered on him losing his CFO title. Initially, LTE offered him a senior VP position in finance, but his strong resistance to their takeover plans burned that bridge. He would leave the company with a hefty severance package designed to suppress any thoughts of litigation.

The LTE management team didn't need to worry about Erick fighting the severance. Erick needed the cash. He owned a fabulous mansion north of Seattle in Mukilteo, a yacht, and a Porsche—all mortgaged to the hilt. Erick spent every penny he earned supporting an affluent Seattle lifestyle. It wasn't clear how long the severance would last; his monthly nut was twenty-thousand dollars. If not for his WesTel stock options, which soared in value in response to the LTE acquisition, Erick would have little cash beyond his severance. It was possible the stock options would provide the means for Erick to buy his own phone company.

A cold sweat ran down Erick's back. *How can the Financial Wunderkind be so competent with corporate finance and have a personal balance sheet under such duress?*

The sound of Betty's footsteps pierced the depth of his thoughts and unwillingly pulled him to the surface. His soon-to-be ex-wife stood in the office doorway—the last person he wanted to see today. In the light reflected from her eyes, he saw his failure as a husband—a man—and abruptly shifted his focus to the window, grimacing.

"Penny for your thoughts?" she asked.

It was the final day in the life of WesTel, and nearly all of the remaining employees wore jeans and sweatshirts. Betty wore tight designer jeans and a tattered Washington State University sweatshirt with sleeves pulled up to her elbows. Her shoulder-length blonde hair was pulled back in a ponytail, and gentle hazel eyes peeked out from beneath her bangs. At five-six, she wasn't particularly tall but slender with long legs. He still saw the eighteen-year-old sorority sister he met at the beginning of their freshman year at WSU.

"Your guy dropped this off." Erick held the summons in the air, waving it. He bit his lip.

"Yeah, sorry about that. The court required someone other than me to deliver it. You knew it was coming," she paused, her face turning contrite. "Look, Erick, you'll always be an important part of my life. It just ... just doesn't work for us—this whole marriage thing."

"Whatever." Erick shifted his gaze to the box on his desk, the pain too acute to look Betty in the eye. It wasn't as though Erick hadn't tried to reconcile. He had tried. It didn't matter what he did to try to fix their relationship. Betty had made her mind up. A hint of a smile broke on his face. *At least we'll be friends, I guess ... and if we find a company to buy, we'll be working together.*

"If you have a minute, I wanted to talk with you about Amy Summers." Betty walked to the guest chair in front of Erick's desk and sat down.

"What about her?"

"She's got an outstanding offer from LTE for a manager position in their Dallas finance department. It's a great opportunity for her. I spoke with Amy, and she said she may turn it down to work with you. Well, us, but mostly you."

"She doesn't want to move to Dallas. It's too far away from Seattle and her elderly grandmother. I guess they're really close."

"Erick, she's only a kid—totally infatuated with you. You've got this light that draws girls in. God, I should know. Don't drag her along with you in pursuit of this *hope* of buying a company." Betty's tone was sharp, her eyes narrowed.

"It's what she wants to do. It's what I want. Hell, it's what you want, to buy a phone company of our own." He thought for a moment about the young financial manager. She was a gorgeous half-Japanese woman assigned to the WesTel acquisition team. He hadn't picked up any social cues indicating an interest in him. He wondered if he hadn't noticed because of his relationship with Sara or if perhaps he was growing old. Erick's face blushed, flattered Amy might be interested in him romantically.

"You should cut her loose. It's the right thing to do. You're perfectly capable of handling the financial aspects of an acquisition without her help." Betty stood and walked toward the door.

"Her minor in software engineering will be useful once we close on a company and begin to rework the enterprise software systems," Erick said. He stroked his chin and wondered how advanced Amy's programming skills were.

"Look, we both know you can hire consultants to work the software issues," Betty said with a bite in her tone.

"I'll talk to her." Erick had no intention of setting Amy free, but he did need to settle on an arrangement if she would be working with him to buy a company. He jotted down a note to call her later that evening.

CHAPTER 3

May 1999

ERICK OLSON BIT into a foot-long sandwich in a Subway Shop near his Seattle area home. The Swede's cool, steel-blue eyes focused on Amy Summers as she picked at her salad across the table from him. Nearly forty now, Erick wished he had the discipline to go with a salad. He had added a pound a year since graduating college, and most of the extra fifteen pounds had landed in his waistband. She ate like a bird. Not yet thirty, her exotic half-Japanese look turned heads. A tiny ball of fire, she weighed barely one-hundred pounds.

A year had passed since he, Betty, and Amy began working together to acquire a phone company of their own. They were close to making a bid to purchase Whitman Telephone Company from LTE, the enormous corporation that had acquired their former employer. The small company was located near Erick's hometown of Colfax, Washington, in Whitman county. Deep in thought, Erick's eyes drifted away from Amy, and his face fell slack.

"Erick, what's on your mind?" Amy asked, breaking the silence. Her full lips parted in a smile. She toyed with a cherry tomato rolled in her tongue. The light glistened off her shoulder-length jet-black hair.

"I was daydreaming." Blood rushed to his face. He glanced at her, quickly averting his eyes to the tabletop.

"About what? You're blushing," she teased.

Erick's cell rang. "Hold that thought." He reached in his coat pocket for his cell phone, relieved by the distraction. It was Pat Mango from LTE on the caller ID. Pat ran the financial aspects of the auction of Whitman Telephone for LTE. "Hey Pat, what can I do for you?"

"Have you seen the news today?" Pat said in an urgent tone.

"No, we've been working. Having some lunch now."

"There was a plane crash in Charleston this morning … The LightPoint team was on it," Pat's voice cracked, "they're all gone … gone."

Erick's heart caught in his throat. He knew the team well. "What? How?"

"They don't know the cause yet. The control-tower reported the plane disappeared from their screens. Witnesses said there was an explosion, and the plane fell into the ocean."

"This is terrible," Erick broke in. An intangible emptiness filled him. He stood and shuffled aimlessly toward a window, his legs like iron pegs.

"The crash is under investigation."

"Isn't that routine?" Erick made it back to the table and fell into his seat.

"Yeah, I suppose it is."

"How many were on it?" Erick poked at his sandwich with his finger.

"Six employees and two crew."

Erick stared at the table in disbelief; he tugged at his lower lip with his thumb and index finger.

"Sorry buddy, I know you were friendly with them," Pat said.

The restaurant door opened, bells hung to announce arriving customers sang a shrill-pitched off-key note. A group of construction workers walked inside, talking loudly, and gave Amy the once over. No longer hungry, Erick pushed his sandwich away. His thoughts drifted half-heartedly back to the Whitman deal.

"Is the deal off?" He made an unconvincing attempt to refocus the conversation back on business, if only momentarily.

"That's partly why I called. We still have other bidders, including you. As you might surmise, LightPoint dropped out. We spoke with our leadership back east and tried to slow the process down. They want the Whitman auction to move forward on schedule."

"Okay. I appreciate the call. Take care. We can talk more when I'm in Dallas next week." Erick laid down the phone and slumped in the booth.

He gathered himself and looked up into Amy's probing, almond eyes.

"What happened?" she asked, her brow furrowed.

"A jet carrying LightPoint's acquisition team went down."

"That's awful, Erick … What about the auction? Will they delay it now?"

"No. Pat said corporate wants to move forward." Erick gazed out the window. A cold, early May rain danced on the sidewalk. He allowed the pain of the families his friends left behind to flow through him like a river of sorrow.

After lunch, holed up in his study, Erick and Amy poured over financial documents provided by LTE, trying to establish fair market value for the Whitman asset. The plane crash and images of the victims kept invading Erick's thoughts.

Like most homes in the gated enclave north of Seattle, Erick Olson's eight thousand square foot mansion rose from the bluffs as a monument to his career success. The architect had been inspired by the Cape Cod Style and designed the expansive structure with an exterior sheathed in weathered-cedar shingles and white trim. Oversize windows framed magnificent views of Puget Sound and the snowcapped Olympic Mountains range beyond.

Doodling on a yellow legal pad at his desk, Erick made a note to call Farmers Bank about his loan application. The bank's general manager had assured him they would issue a commitment letter this week but he hadn't heard a word in a while. This worried Erick greatly.

Erick kept an eye on Amy as she worked on her laptop by the fireplace, seated in a leather club chair. She wore her alma mater, University of Washington sweatshirt, and shorts. Her bare legs were outstretched, feet up on the stone hearth. The firelight glowed on her skin and made it look satin smooth. Amy played tennis frequently, and her legs were firm.

"Are you ready for the call with Flores?" Erick asked, pushing the legal pad aside.

"Sure, I'm ready." Amy laid her laptop on an end table and moved to a chair across the desk from Erick.

He wasn't looking forward to the call with the LTE Vice President. The company had tasked David Flores to run its contractor diversity program and handle the sale of non-strategic customer telephone lines. The Whitman asset had been determined surplus and non-strategic. The Fortune 500 Corporation had a long list of demands for groups bidding on its Whitman property. Contractor diversity appeared to be the newest addition to the list.

Erick placed the call to David's direct line on speakerphone. He was a master multi-tasker and adroit at compartmentalizing feelings and emotions. Still, Erick was having trouble focusing on the call. Just when he thought he had tucked the plane crash away in some remote recess of his brain, it would seep back into his present. No matter how hard he fought, he couldn't escape his memories of the people who lost their lives. They continued to rise to the surface of his mind like bubbles in a flute of champagne.

"David here."

"Hello, David, Erick Olson, and Amy Summers in Seattle."

"Good to hear from you, Erick. I hope it's not too rainy out there."

"You get used to it," Amy said.

Erick gave her a half-smile. He was drowning in the Seattle gloom. "Spoken like a true native."

"So Erick, are you running this acquisition effort from your home in Seattle?"

"Well, a bit north of Seattle, but yes, we are. Amy and I set up shop in my study, and Betty works from a spare bedroom down the hall."

"It's really neither here nor there, but I've always been fascinated by the struggles entrepreneurs face starting a business."

"It's not nearly as sexy as the business press would have you believe." Erick checked his watch. Time was a wasting.

"I don't want to take up much of your time, but I would like to spend a few minutes talking about diversity. This has really become a hot-button issue with corporate. We're under enormous pressure from the Feds to use more women and minority-owned contractors."

"Amy's half-Japanese, does that count?" Erick's comment dripped with sarcasm. He winked at Amy. She scowled in return.

"That may fall short, given it's not her money at play."

"If you're intent on selling assets to minorities, why'd you send me the package?" Erick's blood pressure rose.

"Think about it, where are we going to find minority buyers with access to capital *and* industry experience? We need at least two bidders to run an auction. The more, the better."

"Are you suggesting I gather an investor group that fits your diversity definition?" Erick's frustration rose.

"It would strengthen your bid. It could be more of a structural thing, say an independent board having some level of investment in the deal."

"Let me think about how I can address your concern. I'm raising the required equity through a limited-partnership with forty investors. That's really not congruent with an independent board of directors." Erick detested the idea of giving up any control of *his* company.

"Alright, you give it some thought. We can talk more when you're out here next week to complete your due diligence. Keep in mind, anyone you select will need to be closely vetted."

"Well, I wouldn't let anyone invest in this deal," Erick rolled his eyes.

"Of course. Are you coming alone next week for due diligence, or will Amy and Betty be joining you?"

"It'll be Amy and me this trip. Betty will be in Spokane working with our lawyer."

"Then, I suppose, I'll look forward to seeing the two of you next week."

"Look forward to it. We'll see you then," Erick hung up the phone.

Erick scratched ideas on his yellow pad during the call. Near the bottom of the paper, he had drawn three boxes.

Amy leaned forward and looked at the pad. "What are the boxes for?"

"An idea for structuring the deal." Erick pointed his pencil toward the bottom of the sheet. "We could have two corporate entities." Laying his pencil on the box labeled Whitman, he said, "Rather than the limited partnership purchasing the phone company directly, Whitman Communications would serve as the operating company and acquire the Whitman asset from LTE." He shifted his pencil tip to the box labeled LP. "The limited partnership would own shares of Whitman Communications." Moving his pencil to the third box, "Our directors would each own one share of Whitman Communications stock as individual shareholders.

"The LP will own ninety-eight percent of the Whitman Communications stock, allowing me as General Partner to control matters coming before the shareholders for a vote. Decisions such as appointing a board member, appointing corporate officers, changing bylaws, or selling the company require a vote of the shareholders. We will control all but the two percent owned by our directors.

"The seven board members, including me, will provide governance for Whitman Communications over company procedures and policies. Operational matters." Erick paused for a minute while Amy looked over the rough corporate family tree. "Think it might work?"

Amy looked up from the yellow pad, "Clever, the directors are equity owners and sit on our board, but you have them on a tight leash." She smiled at Erick. "That's why you're the *Financial Wunderkind*."

CHAPTER 4

AMY LEFT ERICK'S mansion early and stopped by her grandmother's Queen Anne home in Seattle to change clothes. She pulled on a pair of skintight jeans and a navy pea coat over a white, long-sleeve polo.

Amy arrived early at the quaint coffee shop in the Seattle business district, ordered two beverages, and took a small table by the window. Amy's college roommate, Alison Kendrick, worked for Murphy Avery, CPAs. The firm had brought her to town from Spokane for audit training. The two women were meeting for coffee to catch up on their busy lives.

Amy waived to grab Alison's attention when she stepped into the coffee shop. Best friends since second grade, Amy didn't get to see her friend nearly enough.

Alison wore a navy pantsuit with a long silk scarf around her neck. Shoulder-length auburn hair fell with a soft wave over the collar of her suit blazer. The two friends wore the same size and shared clothes frequently during college. Amy stood as Alison made her way to the table, and they held each other in a long embrace. Alison's inquisitive brown eyes lit up, and she opened a huge smile, exposing her gums and a crinkled ski-jump nose.

"You look great, Amy. How have you been?"

"I'm terrific, really busy, but I guess that's good. How are you?"

"I'm fine. Murphy has me traveling so much it's hard to meet anyone in Spokane. But other than that, it's all good."

"I got your favorite, Chai Tea Latte." Amy handed her a Grande and dropped back into her chair. The accounting firm had the reputation of working its young accountants excessive hours. Amy thought her friend looked tired.

"You're the best, Amy." She sat in the vacant seat and sipped her tea. "How's Grandma? I haven't seen her since Christmas."

"She's worse, didn't even recognize me last time I visited in the nursing home, thought I was her sister in Japan. I'm afraid of losing her, Ali." Tears formed in the corner of Amy's eyes. *I need to make it back to Japan again to visit the rest of my family.* The only family she knew in the states was her grandma.

"I'm sorry, Amy. You know she'll always love you."

"Yeah, but it's hard. Grandma raised me. I owe her so much." Alison handed her a tissue, and Amy wiped her eyes.

"Tell me how work's going. Has Erick found a company to buy?" Alison turned the conversation in a new direction.

"We're working on one now," Amy said, shifting her eyes away from Alison. "I can't say much. You may have a client looking at the same deal."

"Did you hear about the LightPoint plane crash? They're a client of ours, a real tragedy."

"Yeah, Erick got a call from someone he knows with ties to the company. Erick knew the people on the plane." She thought back to how the news of the crash had devastated Erick. He had shown a softer side she had never seen in him before.

"One of our partners is close to Paul Banta, the CEO. Sounds like it may have been sabotage," Alison said.

"Hard to believe with such a plain vanilla company." Amy picked up her tea with a trembling hand and took a sip. The LightPoint team was traveling to visit LTE when the plane exploded. The LightPoint group was working to place a bid on Whitman, the same as Erick and Amy.

"I know, scary—right?" Alison grimaced.

The two sat in silence for a minute as if to pay respect to the people who perished on the plane. An articulated Seattle Metro bus rounded the corner and rumbled past their window, billowing diesel exhaust in its wake. Amy looked out and scanned the streets and shops through the light rain.

"How's the severance holding up?" Alison asked.

"Fortunately, I live in Grandma's house rent free. I figure I can last another year, maybe two, before I have to find a regular paycheck. Hopefully, we'll close on a deal by then." Amy lowered her gaze to the table.

"And how's Erick? Are you still crushing on him?" Alison asked. Her smile opened wide.

Amy blushed and looked up at Alison. She knew Alison took great pleasure in teasing about her romantic interests.

"You are, come on, girl, I need details. Does he know?" Elbows on the small table, Alison leaned forward until their faces nearly touched as though sharing a secret.

Amy looked back at her friend with eyes that pleaded for her to stop. "He doesn't have a clue," she whispered.

Erick's interest never seemed to be more than collegial, which tore at the fabric of her heart. Amy had thought Erick was about to kiss her once when he leaned into her while standing next to his car. She felt the warmth of his breath on her cheek and the smell of his cologne as he bent over her to open the passenger door. Excitement tingled in her fingertips and lips. She closed her eyes in anticipation of the moment. As he brushed past her, she blushed in embarrassment over misreading his intentions. The disappointment still stabbed at her confidence.

"Then take the lead, girlfriend." Alison leaned back in her chair. "What's the problem? Is he shy?"

"I think he's hurting. His wife left him. I don't want to be a one-night stand," Amy said, toying with her coffee cup.

"Give him space. You can't catch his heart in a jar. He'll see the light. He'll see it in your eyes—like I do." Alison sipped her tea.

Amy's mind drifted back in time to when she was eight years old, living with her grandmother, a year after both of her parents died. They had spent a warm summer afternoon catching butterflies in a net on the front lawn. She had delicately transferred each specimen into a mason jar with air holes pounded in the metal lid.

"Amy, you must decide which to set free and which to keep," Grandma said.

"But I love them all," Amy pleaded.

"The butterflies won't survive confined in a jar. If you love them, you must set them free. Trust that they will come back again to be near you."

Amy did love the creatures and removed the lid from the jar. She said goodbye with tears in her eyes as they flew in a colorful parade from her glass container toward the clouds.

CHAPTER 5

FBI SPECIAL AGENT Richard Monroe watched the late-afternoon Chicago traffic building on Roosevelt Road through his eighth-floor office window. A half-eaten pizza rested in a white grease-stained box on his desk next to a six-inch-thick case file. His stomach ulcer burned. The smell of peppers and onions had turned rancid. He ran thick fingers through his thinning gray hair and wished he could join the commuters passing his office on their way home for the evening.

Monroe turned his attention back to the case file. If he could build a successful case against the Ferrari Crime Family, he would go out on top. Retire with a clear conscience, knowing his work had made a difference. He felt close. Somehow, Monroe needed to establish the money flow between Ferrari's Chicago operation and Spokane.

The file included dozens of complaints from Visa credit card customers claiming porn sites they visited had offered free trials but charged their cards nonetheless. It appeared the culprit was a small billing services company in Spokane, owned by Michael Romano, a suspected associate of the Ferrari Crime Family.

"Knock, knock, Agent Monroe?" Jesse Walters, an analyst in the Chicago field office, held up a sheet of paper.

"What have you got there?" Agent Monroe asked, not pleased with the interruption.

"I've been researching our bombing incident data base. I came across something interesting."

"Go ahead."

"We knew there were similarities to the bomb used to blow up the motel propane tank in Peculiar, Missouri, ten years ago and some known Ferrari events in the past. I ran a query against our database, looking for any common elements. Turns out I uncovered one." Walters stepped into the office, grinning.

Monroe dropped the report he was reviewing onto his desk and sat up straight, "You've got my attention. Please continue."

"Agents interviewed all of the Missouri motel guests in order to determine why they were in town that day. There was a group of four employees from WesTel Communications out of Seattle working on a possible acquisition of the local telephone company. The group was led by Erick Olson, a Vice President with WesTel at the time. As I said, the company was based out of Seattle but has since been acquired by LTE Communications in Irving, Texas."

"Alright," Monroe said, not certain where the conversation was headed.

"The plane that blew up in Charleston earlier this month had been chartered to fly the LightPoint Communications acquisition team to Dallas to work on a deal with LTE. Apparently, LTE is selling a small operation in Washington State called Whitman Telephone Company. I checked with folks at LTE regarding other groups trying to buy the company. Turns out Erick Olson is also leading an effort to purchase the Whitman company." Walters dropped the piece of paper with his findings on Monroe's desk. "That's a pretty big coincidence."

Agent Monroe leaned back in his chair and rubbed his neck, "Damn big. Good work, Walters. Keep poking around. Try to figure out what's so special about these small telephone companies. Find out where Olson's employed now and where he lives."

Agent Monroe stared out the window, befuddled. For the life of him, he couldn't see why Ferrari would be interested in a highly regulated landline telephone company. And he couldn't fathom a phone company executive like Erick Olson being involved with the bombing of businesses. Dots were starting to connect, but they made no sense.

CHAPTER 6

ERICK AND AMY'S airport limo arrived at the Las Colinas Four Seasons Resort Thursday afternoon. Situated between Dallas and DFW International Airport, the Irving, Texas office complex hosted campuses for the corporate headquarters and subsidiary operations of many Fortune 500 companies. Tenants landed in the low-cost area en masse like lemmings falling from a cliff. LTE had moved its telephone operations headquarters to the park in 1989. During the LTE merger transition with WesTel, as Chief Financial Officer, Erick spent weeks in Las Colinas, helping the LTE group absorb WesTel. The Four Seasons had become his second home.

Erick scheduled an informal business dinner with Amy and two former WesTel colleagues—Mike Swenson and Pat Mango. Mike and Pat accepted senior-level roles with LTE and were assigned to the Whitman divestiture team. The LTE executives were privy to confidential information on the deal, which had not been disclosed to the bidders. Erick hoped to loosen the two up with a few drinks and pry some of that intel from them.

Pat and Mike picked Erick and Amy up at 5 p.m., outside the hotel lobby. Pat's dark hair and closely trimmed beard had turned gray. Still a beanpole, he seemed older than his thirty-five years. Mike, on the other hand, looked the same. He wore his light-brown hair cut short, nearly to a military crew cut, with whitewalls around the ears.

Pat pulled the car up to the valet parking stand in front of Morton's Steak House and tossed his Mercedes valet key to a kid barely old enough to shave. The four walked through the ten-foot-tall, hand-carved mahogany double-doors and approached the hostess stand. They appeared to be an odd group. Amy wore jeans and a purple blazer. Erick wore business-casual khakis, a Ralph Lauren Polo golf shirt, and Gucci loafers. Pat and Mike were dressed in Nordstrom's tailored business suits and button-down white oxford shirts.

Erick's eyes wandered to the profile of a blonde sitting alone in the waiting area. She wore a red silk blouse and a grey skirt slit high on one side. Her shapely legs were crossed, revealing skin up to mid-thigh. She flashed him a warm smile. He caught sight of Amy in his peripheral vision as she shuffled away from him toward Mike and Pat.

"Erick, how are you?" the woman said and rose from her chair.

Erick recognized Sara Wilson the moment he saw her smile. He felt the shiver of love foregone run through him, leaving his heart empty. In the waning days of WesTel's existence, the LTE General Counsel offered her a senior legal position in Dallas, which she accepted.

"What a pleasant surprise, Sara. They didn't say you'd be joining us." Erick held her in a warm embrace. She hugged him lightly. The warmth of her body set him at ease.

"Erick, I should have mentioned Sara was free this evening, so we invited her to join us. She provides legal support for the Whitman team," Pat said.

"Well, this is terrific," Erick smiled broadly. He wondered if she had taken up with someone new since moving to Dallas. She'd be a hell of a catch for some Dallas urban-cowboy.

"Do you have a reservation, Sir?" asked the slightly overweight forty-something hostess. She wore a too-tight short, black skirt and white blouse squeezed around her ample bosom.

Pat stepped forward. "Yes, under Mango for five."

"I have it here. Please follow me."

She picked up five menus from behind her stand and led them through a hallway to a secluded table near a stone fireplace. The walls were covered in dark, felt-textured wallpaper. Heavy floor-to-ceiling draperies muffled the conversations of other diners. The smell of sizzling beef and garlic filled the room.

No sooner were they seated than a waitress appeared and offered to take drink orders. Erick ordered his usual gin and tonic, and Mike and Pat ordered imported beers. Sara and Amy each ordered a glass of white wine. Pat spoke with the server and had the kitchen prepare a platter of appetizers for the group, including prosciutto-wrapped mozzarella, bacon-wrapped sea scallops, and Ahi tuna.

The room was warm, but a chill hung over their table, introducing an awkward silence. The LTE folks at the table had been Erick's close work friends a year earlier, but he sensed a bit of distance in their countenance and how they interacted with him now. Then it struck him hard. All they ever really held in common had been WesTel, and that company was dead. The familial bond of a common employer had been lost. Suddenly, it seemed to Erick that his friends would be unlikely to share any information about the other bidders with him.

"So tell me straight, guys. What's the level of interest in asset sales these days?" Erick asked.

Sara and Mike turned their cautious eyes to Pat, poker-faced.

"It's high, Erick, very high," Pat said but didn't sound convinced.

They're giving me the corporate BS line, Erick thought.

"There are lots of displaced telecom executives running around the country looking to buy assets. Some of them well-financed," added Mike.

"How much interest in the Whitman property?" Erick wanted to know how many groups he was bidding against.

"I think we had a dozen or so groups looking at it initially. A few decided not to pursue the opportunity, and then, of course, LightPoint dropped out," Pat said.

Erick slouched in his chair. "I'm still processing the crash. Any news?"

Pat frowned, "We hear informally NTSB believes it was foul play."

"What motive would there be?" Erick had faced intimidation tactics and veiled threats with acquisitions in his past. Yet, such actions were rare in this business sector.

"We may never know," Pat said.

The server reappeared with their drinks and offered to take dinner selections. Mike and Pat ordered aged sirloin steaks with asparagus, fully loaded baked potatoes, and small side salads. The women chose dinner salads topped with grilled chicken. Erick selected the nine-ounce bacon-wrapped filet mignon, asparagus, mashed potatoes, and a side salad.

Erick shook his head deliberately and took a deep swallow of his drink, "What's going on with David and this diversity thing?"

Pat sat up at the table and spoke in a whisper. "It's a corporate power play. The Feds are demanding that government borrowers use more minority and women owned subcontractors. A lot of LTE debt is financed through government programs, so we're sort of tied up in those policies. It would be viewed favorably if you could pull together a group of minority investors and involve them in the company in some manner."

A busboy passed their table, pushing a cart filled with chattering dirty plates and glasses. Erick watched it roll slowly by.

Sara had been uncharacteristically quiet until now. "Look, it's a bit more complicated than that. We must vet these investors thoroughly to ensure we know who they are. Make certain no skeletons pop up."

"Once it's sold, why would LTE care?" Amy shot back.

Erick glanced at Amy, caught off guard by her sharp tone.

Sara rolled her eyes as if speaking to a child. "LTE will have an ongoing contractual relationship with the new owner of the Whitman asset for both administrative functions and network operations." Sara paused and sipped her drink. "In some parts of the country, organized crime has found a toehold in our industry. We can talk more later, but suffice it to say, for now, it's a serious matter, and we need to know the background of the people we're working with."

"We certainly don't want to re-experience our western Missouri debacle," Erick said and faced Pat.

Pat looked at Amy. "This was before you joined WesTel, Amy. Have you heard the story?"

"I don't think so." Amy sat up tall in her chair.

Pat started, "About ten years ago, LTE offered to sell a subsidiary phone company a bit south of Kansas City, Missouri."

"Yeah, in Peculiar, Missouri, if you can believe that," Sara said.

"We joked about the name of the little town, but it was a damn strong company," Mike said.

"Anyhow, the four of us were out there on a due diligence trip reviewing the operations and financial statements. We were staying in a little rat-hole motel." Pat stopped talking and took a swig of his beer. "We're having dinner in a café across the street from the motel, and the goddamn motel propane tank blows up, setting the two-story building on fire. I mean, we're sitting in the café watching the flames move toward our rooms."

"We got lucky. It was a thousand-gallon tank. The explosion took out the rooms Sara and I were originally booked in," Erick said. He reached for the appetizers and picked up a scallop with his seafood fork. "When we checked in, there had been a cancellation which allowed them to put the four of us together at the other end of the building."

Mike shook his head, "Lucky break."

"No kidding," Sara added.

"So we're sitting there halfway through dinner and can hear the fire and police sirens coming. Erick jumps up and says, 'We have to get our stuff!'" Pat pushed back his chair and stood to reenact the moment. "The four of us ran from the café and across Main Street to our rooms with the waitress chasing us."

"I guess she thought it was an executive-level dine-n-dash," Sara said, laughing.

"We blew by the front desk clerk, grabbed our bags from the rooms, and tossed them in the trunk of the rental car," Erick looked at Amy. Her face showed concern but not worry.

"What did you do?" Amy asked.

"What Erick always does," Mike said, shaking his head slowly from side to side. "Found a new motel and moved the ball forward."

Sara turned in her chair and leaned closer to Amy. She gave her a tight-lipped smile and narrowed her eyes as if telling a ghost story. "But the scary thing was, and we didn't find out until later, the explosion may have been a message. Rumor among the Missouri Telephone Association was the Kansas City mob was trying to find a way to buy the damn phone company."

"No way," Amy said. She shifted her gaze to Erick; her face had lost all color.

"No, I'm serious, and organized crime is still active in the industry. Not in a large way, but there's evidence they're finding ways to participate." She retreated and turned back to the table. "I hope Erick's paying you well. This can be a dangerous business." Sara winked at Erick.

Erick sat his empty wine glass on the table and cut his eyes to Sara, "That's enough, Sara."

"It's eight o'clock, Erick. Do you want to swing by the hotel for a nightcap?" Pat asked.

"Thanks for the offer, but I have some work I still need to get to this evening," Erick said.

The entrance to LTE's Las Colinas campus welcomed visitors at the end of a long, winding cobblestone driveway, richly landscaped on both sides with a lush green carpet of lawn and an assortment of native shrubs and seasonal flowers. The picture-book setting sparkled and smelled spring-time fresh in the morning dampness left behind by the irrigation system. Rolling slowly down the enchanted driveway, images of Dorothy following the yellow-brick road into the Emerald City filled Erick's mind.

Erick approached the reception desk and asked for David Flores. A stiff-looking woman wearing a grey business suit and oversized glasses entered the reception area through a locked door moments later. She carried a mousy appearance, with her brown hair cut short in a boyish style.

"Mr. Olson?" She demanded

"I am, and this is Amy Summers." He gestured with his hand toward Amy.

"I'm Mary Repass, David's assistant; it's a pleasure to meet the two of you. Please follow me. I'll take you to the conference room."

They followed her down a hallway to a four-story atrium. Dozens of employees walked with apparent purpose from one meeting to another on every level. Their leather shoe heals struck the tile flooring and filled the space with a sharp chorus of clickety-clack. The employees chatted in furtive, muted tones as they moved along, weighed down by briefcases and overstuffed three-ring binders. Many shot curious looks at the two escorted strangers. Erick and Amy wore large visitor placards hanging from their necks by a blue sash emblazoned with the LTE logo—branded as outsiders.

The sound of movement and muffled conversations heightened Erick's self-awareness. He missed working for WesTel and the camaraderie of being on a winning team. He drew in a deep breath as the reality of his mission settled in. He and Amy would take on the LTE beast alone. *It's me and Amy against the world.*

Mary placed her badge against a keypad. The door buzzed, and Erick heard the subtle click of the electric lock being released. The three entered a common area shared by several conference rooms of varying sizes and purposes. Erick recognized Pat Mango speaking with a group of men he didn't know, standing next to a refreshment bar with soft drinks, water, coffee, and pastries.

"David, this is Mr. Olson and Ms. Summers." Mary had engaged a distinguished-looking Hispanic middle-aged man standing at the coffee service. He had deep brown eyes, heavy eyebrows, and a narrow, closely trimmed Zoro-style mustache. Erick glanced at his hip, half expecting to see a sword, and mused to himself that a horse might be tethered outside on the emerald lawn.

David extended his hand, "Nice to finally meet you two in person."

A title like VP of Diversity Programs smelled transitional to Erick. The guy was probably being forced into retirement. Still, Erick needed to win David over to walk away with the Whitman prize.

"Likewise," Erick shook David's hand.

"Amy, it's a pleasure," David said, extending his hand, which she accepted.

David stepped closer to Erick and asked, "Have you had time to consider the diversity element of this deal we spoke about last week?"

"Of course, I have my lawyer in Spokane pulling some names together as we speak. It would have been nice to know about this diversity issue early in the process. We're approaching the deadline for making an offer on Whitman, and introducing a new group of players onto our ownership team complicates things somewhat."

"Well, it's good to hear that you're on top of it, Erick," David said, "I'd hate to see your bid fail for something that seems fairly simple to accommodate."

Erick bit the inside of his cheek and held his tongue.

"Good morning, David, Erick, Amy," Pat said, breaking awkwardly into the conversation.

"Morning," Erick said.

"Good morning, Pat," David said. "If you'll please excuse me, I must take care of something back in my office. Erick, it was good to meet you."

"Was everything up to snuff at the Four Seasons?" Pat asked.

"Yes, indeed. It's one of my favorite places to stay," Erick said.

Sara joined the small group holding a coffee in one hand and a pastry in the other. "Erick, how are you this morning?"

"Tired, I was up late last night reviewing the purchase agreement for this deal," Erick said, furrowing his brow.

Sara smiled at Amy and said, "Good morning, Amy."

Amy smiled in return and greeted Sara.

"Pat, if you'll excuse me, I need to make a phone call about my potential board of directors before we start digging into operational and financial issues," Erick said. He stepped into a vacant conference room and closed the door. He pulled out his cell and called his Spokane lawyer, Skip Britain, on his private line.

"This is Skip."

"Hey, Erick here, I read the draft purchase agreement last night. Have you gone over it yet?"

"Most of it. I should have something for you next week when you visit Spokane.

"Have you thought about directors for my board that meet the seller's diversity profile?"

"I've been working on that with my Chamber of Commerce contacts. Betty's here, and I was reviewing a few potential candidates with her when you called. She brought the list the two of you put together, and I have some additional names to recommend. I should have something for you in a few days."

"Thanks. They'll have to pass a background check and make an investment in the company. The management group here at LTE seems concerned about organized crime buying their way into the telephone industry. I don't share their concern, but we must ensure our directors are squeaky clean."

"How much will they need to invest?"

"I estimate it will be fifty-thousand dollars per director for one share of stock."

"Alright, I'll keep that in mind as I compile the list."

CHAPTER 7

MICHAEL ROMANO FOLLOWED Tony Ferrari off the elevator into an oak-paneled reception area with plush burgundy carpet. Romano wore his black hair over the ear and collar. At thirty-nine years old, there was a hint of gray beginning to show—soon, it would be salt and pepper. Too much Italian food and too little exercise had left him obese.

Romano had operated the Ferrari Family's Spokane billing and advertising business for nearly twenty years. The previous owner ran into financial trouble and borrowed money from a loan shark in Chicago. The owner fell behind on his payments, and the Ferrari Family bought the note. Tony Ferrari took the business as payment and relocated his nephew Michael to Spokane to run the operation.

Michael tried to read Tony's mind but came up empty. They breezed past the receptionist and turned toward Tony's office. The hallway smelled of cheap perfume.

"Morning," Tony barked at his secretary, who rose from her desk and followed them into Tony's office. She struggled to keep up, dressed in a dark-gray pencil-skirt and four-inch heels.

"Good morning, Mr. Ferrari." She chomped a mouthful of gum. "Nice to see you again, Michael." She took Tony's Armani suit coat and hung it on a wooden hanger in a small cedar-lined closet. Romano pulled off his suit jacket and laid it over the arm of a chair.

Tony grunted, and his secretary scurried away. He ran a comb through thick, slicked-back hair. The gray hair and extra fifty pounds made Tony look older than his sixty years. He had been a good-looking man in his forties, but the added weight had found its way to his face. A double chin obscured what was once a strong jawline, and his puffy cheeks made him look portly.

Weight gain hadn't affected the sizzling intensity of Tony's green eyes. His eyes changed color with different moods and lighting. They had earned him the nickname 'Green Eyes'. Subordinates dreaded being held in their grasp. Romano watched Tony walk across the room to the window of his sixteenth-floor office and face Lake Michigan.

Michael dropped into a guest chair in front of the polished walnut desk. Moments later, Tony eased into his oxblood leather seat, picked up the *Chicago Tribune,* and seemed to scan the headlines. Michael stared out the window and waited in silence.

A few minutes later, the secretary's voice squeaked over the intercom, "Mr. Ferrari? I have Mr. Acosta here for your 9:30."

"Send him in," Tony demanded.

"Morning, Boss ... Michael." Joe Acosta served as Tony's chief business advisor. Joe's short stature, painfully thin build, long face, and bald head gave him a haggard appearance. Around forty years old, he wore round, wire-rim glasses that hid non-descript grey eyes. Acosta favored two-thousand-dollar custom-tailored suits. He held an undergraduate degree in finance and an MBA.

"Have a seat, Joe."

Joe sat next to Michael in the empty guest chair across the desk from Tony. "I wanted Michael to join us. Some of this affects his Spokane operation."

"That's timely, Boss," Joe said.

Romano remained quiet, not sure of their agenda. He didn't relish the thought of Chicago messing with his business in Spokane.

"Joe, what have you found about the missing money," Tony asked.

Acosta drew a deep breath and exhaled slowly. "I brought in a forensic accountant one of the families in New York uses a lot. We know *what's* happening, but not *who* yet. It's basically a sophisticated siphoning operation. We have over one-hundred-sixty trusts and LLCs here and overseas, each with its own bank account. To keep the money clean and untraceable, we're running funds between entities constantly, hundreds of millions a year." Acosta shifted nervously in his seat. "Boss, someone's pulling off one-half of one percent as an administrative fee each time cash runs through two of the accounts. One in Belize and one in the Caymans. That works out to fifty grand for every ten million passing through those accounts."

"You said we don't know who's behind it yet? Do we know where the money's going?"

"Yeah, a numbered account at another bank in the Caymans. It's not ours."

"Shit, this won't stand!" Tony's green eyes burned into Acosta.

"It won't, Boss. We're closing in. Just a matter of time. When we find the *who*, we'll eliminate him and reclaim the money."

"Okay, good update," Tony paused. "How's the Visa plan going?"

"I got it worked out. I need to have you sign some papers and we'll get it done." Joe crossed his legs and plucked a piece of lint from his handcrafted Santoni wingtips.

"What's goin' on with Visa," Michael asked nervously.

"Hold on a bit, Michael," Tony said. "We're making some administrative changes." Tony turned to Acosta. "So we'll start processing the porn charges through a bank in Central America?"

"Guatemala."

"And that's gonna fix it?"

"It should. When the marks call to complain about the free trial, the South America fraud division will have to deal with them. The South American group is not nearly as good at detecting fraud as the North American group."

"What about Spokane Community Bank?" Tony asked.

"We'll still run all the credit card payments through them as a Merchant bank."

"So my part, running the charges through Spokane Community, stays the same?" Romano interrupted.

"That's right, Michael, no change on your end. Joe, we got a lot invested in that bank ... Start thinking about a plan-B, in case this Central America play doesn't work out."

"Sure, Boss."

Tony faced Joe and leaned into the desk. "Is the film production keeping up?"

For a moment, Romano relaxed in his chair and pictured the young women making adult films three floors below.

"Yeah, Global's picking up three or four girls a month, mostly runaways. It's probably not the kind of work they were expecting in Chicago," Joe chuckled. "But they're paid well, and we take good care of them. Bobby's got it under control."

"He still testing the merchandise?" Tony asked. He pulled a pack of cigarettes from his desk drawer.

Cancer sticks gonna get ya, Green Eyes, Romano thought to himself.

"I think that's part of the audition." Joe looked at his shoes and crossed his arms over his chest.

"Sick bastard. Remind him I don't approve." He pulled a cigarette from the pack and shook his head in disgust.

"Michael." Joe cut his eyes to Romano. "We're expanding the internet porn subscription business. We got a major publisher on board to run our free trial ads in their magazines. And we have a new concept where the subscriber can video chat live with one of the girls. The guy can ask her to do different things he wants to see."

"That is somethin' new," Romano chuckled.

Acosta leaned toward Romano. "We need to have Angela work up some ads. I'll send you the different price points we're looking at. It'll take several months to get things rolling."

"Okay, I'll get with her when I'm back in the office," Romano said.

"Let's talk about Whitman Telephone. Listen up, Michael, this affects you." Tony leaned forward in his chair and lit the cigarette. Dirty-white smoke drifted toward the ceiling. "Can we use Spokane Community Bank to make the purchase?"

Romano straightened his posture and leaned forward to hear clearly.

"The bank's clean. We can use it for the Whitman deal," Joe said.

"What's Whitman?" Romano broke in.

Tony's green eyes locked on Romano, the cigarette hanging from the corner of his mouth. He pulled it out and tapped the ash into a crystal bowl. "It's a telephone company we're trying to buy down by Pullman, Washington. You know the area?"

"Sure, it's where WSU is, south of Spokane, a bit."

"That's right, Michael. Once we get the company, your operation will work with it," Tony said.

Romano's pulse quickened, "Will I be runnin' things?" He had no idea what would be involved in running a telephone company.

Tony drew on his cigarette and let out a long, slow exhale, clouding the air between them. "No. We'll have a legit manager. There's too much regulatory oversite. We have some plans on how to leverage our internet porn business through the phone company. With Joe's help, I want you to find more ways for our Spokane operation to work with Whitman," he paused. "This is a big deal, Michael. Listen to the guidance Joe gives you. We'll need time to grow into the business community. It may take a while."

"We have a group of former Illinois Bell executives fronting our bid for Whitman," Acosta grinned and bit his lip. "There's a guy in Seattle bidding against us. His name is Erick Olson. Used to work as an executive in the telephone industry. We're working to get in front of his bid. I'll let you know more on that later."

Romano nodded his head. He figured it wouldn't be difficult to put pressure on the manager running the phone business when the time came.

"Joe, one more thing. I got a call from Rickie at the Boys and Girls Club. They need seventy grand for an afterschool tutoring program. I'd like to help 'em out." He drew deep on his cigarette and focused his green eyes on Joe.

"The whole seventy?" Joe's eyes darted around as though making financial computations.

"All of it."

"I'll take care of it today."

Michael Romano reclined in his office chair in Spokane the next day. His five hundred dollar custom-made Jojayden loafers were propped up on the desk. After lighting a cigar, he tapped an oversized diamond pinky ring on the wooden arm of his office chair.

The desk phone rang, and Michael reached for it. "Romano."

"Michael, it's Joe. I've got the name of the lawyer Erick Olson's using for his bid on Whitman. His name is Skip Britain."

"Britain, really? We've used him quite a bit," Michael said. "We got leverage on him."

"I thought so. Call him. This may be our avenue to get in front of Olson's bid. Word on the street is Britain's putting together a list of possible board members for Olson to use. We need to have him put Angela on the list."

"I'll talk to him." Michael hung up the phone and leaned back in his chair again. It seemed like a pretty big coincidence that Olson used Skip Britain as his lawyer, but Spokane wasn't that big a city. There weren't that many large law firms in town to pick from.

He dialed the lawyer's cell phone.

"Skip Britain."

"Michael Romano, here. I need you to do something for me."

"What is it?"

"Erick Olson's a client of yours, right?" He rubbed his hand over the five-o'clock shadow on his cheek.

"Yeah, why?"

"He's bidding on a phone company in Whitman County—"

"I can't discuss client business," Skip interrupted.

Romano grinned. *So ya gonna go and get ethics all of a sudden.* "I hear you're working on a board of directors list for him. Chicago has some input."

"What do you want me to do?"

"We need you to make sure Angela Michieli's on the board," a closed-lip smile broke across Michael's face. He enjoyed applying pressure to people.

"I have some influence with Erick, but ultimately, it's his decision," Skip sounded uncertain. After a brief pause, he continued, "He has people in mind."

Romano threw his feet off the desk and leaned forward in his chair hard—his obese two-hundred-fifty pounds shook the floor when his feet landed. His round, cheeky face turned a deep shade of red. "Don't bullshit me. He's looking to you for help. Find a way—got it?" His bass voice boomed across the phone line.

"I'll look into it," Skip said in resignation.

"You do that. I'll send the particulars." He hung up the phone hard and crushed his cigar into an ashtray.

CHAPTER 8

July 1999

ERICK SIPPED COFFEE on the lakeside deck of Betty's childhood home in Coeur d'Alene, Idaho. From his hillside perch, surrounded by towering Larch and Grand Fir evergreens, the thirty-foot tall window walls of cottages across the lake reflected the morning sun and sparkled like diamonds in a necklace. Lake City, as the small town was affectionately known, was Betty's hometown—born and raised.

Betty stepped onto the deck and glanced at her watch. "Looks like we've already slipped back into lake time."

In lake time, everything ran a half-hour or more behind.

"Right," Erick said. "People sort of get-to-it when they get-to-it." He didn't see it as laziness, but more a way of life like living on a Caribbean island.

It was the Tuesday following the Fourth of July, the start of North Idaho's two-month summer season. Boats pulling water-skiers were already on the lake at play. They disturbed the morning quiet with powerful, throaty engines.

While he enjoyed his morning coffee, memories of the lake from an earlier time flooded his thoughts. Twenty summers before, he stepped onto Betty's family beach for the first time. In the second week of their freshman year at WSU, Betty approached Erick and asked him to be her Biology lab partner. She flashed her well-practiced sorority smile, and he accepted the invitation.

Fresh off the farm, Erick carried a boyish charm and knew how to work it with the girls. He may have come off as a bit of a country hick, but college girls loved it, and everyone knew wheat farmers were loaded. From a well-off Idaho family, she was carefree and exuded fun and laughter. Like most kids raised on the lake, Betty was unpretentious.

Erick invited Betty to a fraternity party midway through their first term. After that weekend, they were inseparable. They married following graduation in a spectacular evening ceremony on her family's beach. At the end of the reception, they boarded a restored 1954 Chris-Craft launch and sailed into the sunset on their way to a new life together. Reliving the memory brought on an unwelcome twinge of sadness, knowing his time with Betty had passed.

He glanced at his phone and realized it was past time to leave. Skip Britain had provided them with a slate of a dozen possible board members, which they had added to their list. Erick and Betty had cut down the final list to six potential candidates. Interviews were scheduled with each of the finalists to ensure they'd be a good fit with the corporate culture Erick and Betty hoped to cultivate in Whitman Communications. Over the past week, they had conducted interviews with five of the prospects. Skip had vetted and prepared written comments regarding each candidate's suitability. The interviews were mainly to get to know them personally and gauge their temperament for the role of governance.

Erick drove west on I-90, toward Spokane, to meet with the final prospect—Angela Michieli. Angela owned Michieli Internet Hosting and Web Design. As he drove, Erick reviewed notes from the other interviews in his mind. Of the six business owners on their list, Michieli seemed to be the one business that would best complement a phone company.

Erick took the Division Street exit and turned north. The street split downtown Spokane in half. The area west of Division bustled with retail businesses and office buildings. Sidewalks were crowded with people as they hurried from one appointment to the next. The blocks east of Division had been left behind. Many of the buildings were in disrepair. Some were boarded up.

Erick turned east off Division onto Main Street. His notes indicated an address of 710 East Main Street.

"There it is," Betty said and pointed toward a pre-war, six-story brick building that appeared to have been a factory at one time in its past.

Erick parked the rental car, and they hurried across the parking lot to the lobby. The marque listed Michieli, LLC, on the second floor.

"I wonder what Romano Enterprises is," Erick said pointing at the marque. "Looks like they've got two floors here." The remainder of the building appeared to be unoccupied.

"No idea," Betty said.

They took the elevator to the second floor. Stepping into the hallway, they faced a heavy oak door, its frosted glass window embossed with 'Michieli, LLC' in gold letters.

"Locked." Erick reached for the buzzer.

The door opened a few moments later, revealing a striking woman of about thirty with shoulder-length dark hair tied in a ponytail. She had unblemished olive skin and a welcoming smile. Erick observed she didn't wear a wedding ring.

"Hello, you must be Erick and Betty. I'm Angela."

Erick accepted her outstretched hand and shook it gently. "Yes, pleased to meet you. Sorry for being late. The time sort of got away from us."

"Hi, pleased to meet you," Betty said, shaking Angela's hand.

"No worries, come on in. We can talk in my office."

They walked into a small reception area furnished with an old oak desk, matching swivel back chair, and two faded guest side chairs. The well-worn hardwood floors were nearly black in color.

Erick exchanged a glance with Betty. *Looks like a ghost ship.* They followed Angela down a long, poorly-lit hallway to a corner office. Erick thought it odd that the dozen office doors they passed were all closed. No sound, no light—nothing.

Angela's office sported the latest in style and furnishings. Painted a warm beige tone, it offered a modern glass-top desk, two comfortable floral upholstered guest chairs, and a sofa against one wall. Tall windows faced south and west, flooding the room with natural light. Angela motioned for them to sit in her guest seats and took her place behind the desk.

"This is a nice space, Angela," Betty said, breaking the ice.

"Thanks, my uncle owns the building. He set me up with one of his contractor friends to refurbish my company's office space. Things have been so busy this is all the progress we've made," Angela paused and surveyed the room. "May I get you a coffee or water?"

"I'm good, thanks, though," Erick said.

"No, thank you, I'm fine too," Betty said, crossing her legs. "May I ask you a question … about your building?"

"Sure, go ahead."

"We read on the lobby marquee that Romano Enterprises occupies the upper floors. Do you know what business they're in?"

"I'm not really sure. Hardly ever run into them." Angela averted her eyes when she spoke.

Erick's intuition told him Angela wasn't comfortable talking about the Romano business or at least wasn't interested in discussing the matter. He wondered why.

"It's so quiet here. If you don't mind me asking, how many people do you employ?" Betty asked. They hadn't seen another soul in the building.

"We have thirty and growing."

"How long have you been in Spokane?" Erick asked.

"I moved my business here from Chicago three years ago. The rent and labor costs back east were killing me."

"I would imagine so," Erick said. "Have you read the file I sent you a week or so ago?"

"Yes, I have. Investing in a telephone company and serving on the board is an interesting opportunity."

"This meeting is mostly for Betty and me to get to know you a bit and talk about what we're looking for in a director," Erick smiled.

Betty leaned forward. "That's right, it's really more of a conversation than an interview."

"Alright, what would you like to know about me?" Angela leaned back in her chair and crossed her legs.

"Let's begin with leadership. You run your own successful company. How would you describe your leadership style?" Betty asked.

Angela looked toward the window in thought. "I'd say I'm a collaborative leader with a sense of compassion. I value the input and opinions of my staff and clients and typically seek their involvement before making any major decisions."

"That's what we're looking for," Betty said. "We need directors that can work well together and with management as we get the company going."

"On a different front, how do you address employee performance problems?" Erick asked.

Angela didn't hesitate. "I value every employee. When I see a performance issue, I try to determine the cause. Is it something distracting at home, or are we not providing needed tools and training? I probe into what's going on and try to understand why. If it's something I can help with through counseling or an investment in tools or training, I'll move in that direction. Sometimes, we'll put someone on a performance improvement plan with specific, measurable goals. If all of the above fail to get the person on track, I'll terminate as a last resort."

"I like it," Betty said. "That's definitely a fair and compassionate approach."

"As I mentioned on the phone, each director must invest fifty-thousand dollars in the deal. Is that something you're prepared to do if invited to join our board?" Erick asked.

"Yes, I have the funds available."

"Good. It's important that our directors believe in the company and have an opportunity to benefit financially as Whitman Communications grows ... you need to know, LTE has engaged Pinkerton Investigators to run a background check on all of the directors. I will instruct them not to do so if you wish." Erick paused. "However, without the background check, you'll be removed from the director slate."

Angela looked Erick in the eye, "The background check isn't a problem."

"Do you have any questions for us?" Erick asked.

"One thing that's not clear is the timing of this deal."

"It's somewhat convoluted and drawn out, Angela. Being the winning bidder and signing a purchase agreement with LTE is the beginning of a long process that will play out over six months or more. We have to arrange bank financing before submitting our offer, which is what I've been spending most of my time on. It's a bit of a struggle working with traditional banks because much of Whitman's revenue is derived from complex rules and regulations.

"Following a signed purchase agreement, we must seek regulatory approval from the Washington State Utilities and Transportation

Commission. That work and getting certain licenses to operate a telecommunications company transferred from LTE to the new company by the FCC in Washington, D.C., could take as long as a year. I'm well-known in the industry and should be able to fast-track much of the process. You would be involved in some of that approval process as a board member."

"Will it require much travel?"

"I'd say two or three trips to Olympia to meet with our Washington State decision-makers. I will likely have several meetings with officials in Washington, D.C. Still, it's not clear at this point if any of my directors would be involved. Is out-of-town travel a problem for you?"

"Not with advance notice."

"Excellent," Erick looked at Betty. "If that's all, then I think we're good here. We'll be in contact with you soon."

"I'll walk you out."

After leaving Angela's office, Erick and Betty caught the elevator down to the first floor.

Erick and Betty left the Michieli parking lot. They drove west across Division and back into the colorful downtown business district. Erick turned his attention to their final meeting of the day—their attorney, Skip Britain. His law offices were located on the twentieth floor of the Bank of America building.

They parked in the garage across the alley from Britain's office building and hurried to the elevator. The glass door to Skip's office suite was marked *Britain and Son, Counselors at Law*. Erick held the door open for Betty and followed her into the reception area.

The office teamed with the sounds of productivity. Erick's ears filled with shards of whispered conversations conducted over complex legal issues between attorneys, a rattling copy machine turning one single copy of a twenty-page document into ten collated copies, and office phones ringing off the hook.

"Good morning, may I help you?" asked the receptionist, sitting at her desk. Her phone station had two-dozen lines, with most of them lit up and flashing.

"Erick and Betty Olson, here for Skip, please." He looked around the reception area. A red leather sofa and two matching side club chairs filled most of the waiting area. Today's copy of *The Spokesman-Review* and the *Wall Street Journal* lay neatly folded in half on a glass coffee table.

Erick and Skip belonged to the same fraternity while undergraduates at WSU. Being two years ahead of Erick, they knew each other, but not well. Erick knew Skip majored in pre-law and headed to the UW Law School following graduation. They had lost touch with one another until the Whitman deal took form, and Erick reached out for legal advice.

"If you would like to have a seat, Skip will be out in a moment. May I get you coffee or water?"

"No, thank you, I'm fine," Erick said, settling into a club-chair. "How about you, Betty?"

"Thanks, but no. I'm good."

Five minutes had passed when Skip strode into the reception area, his blue eyes sparkling. "Hi there, good to see you again, Betty," Skip walked toward Betty with his arm outstretched. "Second visit in as many months ... People may start talking," Skip said, grinning. Betty shook his hand. Turning to Erick, he said, "Erick, it's been a long while," He reached out to shake hands.

"It's nice to see you. You're looking good," Erick said.

Skip looked the part of a successful attorney, complete with a neatly trimmed beard and a headful of wavy dark brown hair. He had put on a few pounds over the years and now carried a bit of a paunch.

Skip led them down a well-lit corridor with offices lining both sides. The doors were open, and the buzz of important activity filled the air. Skip held the corner office at the end of the hall. It was nicely appointed with a Cherrywood desk, credenza, and filing cabinets. Stacks upon stacks of papers and law books covered every surface.

"Wow, nice view of Mt. Spokane," Erick said. The six-thousand-foot, rounded mountain loomed in the distance. The hillside was covered in evergreens except where ski runs had been cut through in hourglass patterns.

"When you get up high like this, you can see forever," Betty said.

Skip lifted piles of reports from the guest chairs facing his desk and motioned for them to sit. "Please sit ... This deal with LTE is fairly complex.

It's moving pretty fast, so I may need to bring a couple of associates onto the team. When we get to the Washington Utility and Transportation Commission regulatory docket, we'll need to add co-counsel in Olympia familiar with those administrative law processes." Skip cleared space on his desk and opened a file folder labeled Whitman Acquisition.

"We expected you would," Erick eyed the two-inch thick file.

"The contracts, limited-partnership agreement, bank financing, stock certificate filing for an unregistered corporate stock issue, all of that we can handle. I marked up the LTE asset purchase agreement making notations as to some wording we may want to consider changing." Skip handed Erick an inch-thick file folder containing the marked-up agreement.

"We'll look this over and get back to you," Erick said.

"When do you have to provide your preliminary price for the company?"

"Next week. I've got Amy working on it now."

"Do you feel good about what you've reviewed so far of the Whitman documents provided by LTE?"

"I do, I do." Erick crossed his legs. "LTE seems overly focused on the diversity issue. This deal requires the FCC to transfer operating licenses from LTE to the new owner. So, if the Feds want more women and minority business owners involved in Whitman Communications, that's what we'll do. We have a viable plan to make that happen."

"How did my list of possible directors pan out?" He tapped his ink pen on a legal pad.

"Good. I combined your list with mine and picked the strongest six prospects to interview in person. We interviewed the final one this morning," Erick said.

"Who was that?"

"Angela Michieli."

"What'd you think of Angela?"

"She should be a good fit, awful young, but seems bright," Erick uncrossed his legs and leaned forward.

"I liked her," Betty said, "seems very confident."

"Yeah, she'll be good for you."

"She shares her building with a company called Romano Enterprises. Know anything about them?" Erick looked Skip in the eyes.

"Heard the name, I think, but no, not really." Skip looked away toward his desk and rifled through some papers.

Erick, rubbed his cheek. *Why does Skip seem nervous?*

"As for the loan, last time we spoke, you thought you would need borrowing of around eighty-five million. Is that still the number?" Skip said.

"It is. We still need to get Farmers Bank to issue a commitment letter. They've given a verbal, but that's it. Seem to be dragging their feet. Actually, the bank manager has been ducking my calls. I'll call him again on Monday and insist he speak with me." Erick said. Skip looked up, and Erick read the concern coloring his face. They both knew if Farmers Bank backed out it would be near impossible to secure an alternate lender quickly enough to satisfy LTE.

"Have you raised the fifteen-million equity through the limited-partnership?" Skip pulled a pack of cigarettes from his desk drawer and lit one up, taking a deep draw.

"Yes, I have written commitments from the group. Including a share for me and one for Betty, we've got forty participants signed on, each contributing three-hundred-seventy-five thousand dollars. I found about half of them at my yacht club on the coast, and the balance are former WesTel executives I used to work with."

"Good. I'll need the names and addresses by the end of next week." Skip leaned forward and balanced his cigarette on the edge of an ashtray. "About the financing, it's concerning that Farmers Bank has yet to issue their commitment letter. It's getting late in the process. Let me poke around a bit and see what lender options we may have if it comes to that."

"That's probably helpful at this moment," Erick said. A tinge of anxiety ran through him.

CHAPTER 9

MICHAEL ROMANO WAITED for his lunch date in his reserved booth at De Rosa's Italian restaurant. The establishment had been a staple of Spokane dining for sixty years. A red and white checkered cloth covered the table, and an open bottle of Pinot Noir rested on top breathing. Classical music in the background turned the small talk of nearby diners unintelligible.

Romano sat with his back to the corner, where two brick walls joined. It's where he always sat. The table provided him with a complete view of the place. He could watch the front door straight down the aisle in front of his table and see pedestrians as they passed by the front windows overlooking the sidewalk and street beyond. To his right, along a windowless brick wall, he could make eye contact with the bartender and keep tabs on any questionable characters sitting on the stools. He knew the barkeep kept a loaded pistol-grip shotgun hidden close by, just in case. It wasn't so much that Romano expected to have trouble in Spokane. It was more his behavior formed growing up with the Family in Chicago. It had become his way—to be alert—many Chicago mob assassinations had been carried out in Italian restaurants.

A cherry-red Audi TT roadster rolled into the parking lot across the street with its top pulled down. Romano watched as the driver parked the car and restored her wind-tousled hair. It was five minutes before noon. As usual, Angela was right on time. He smiled as she jay-walked the busy street and confidently breezed into the restaurant.

Angela Michieli was the kind of woman men threw topcoats over mud puddles for, and you could tell she knew it. *The Spokesman-Review*, the local newspaper, had named her one of the rising young stars of the local business community. She seemed to enjoy the sensation of being someone prominent—if only of local provenance.

Romano waved to her from his booth in the back corner. There was no need to—he was always in the same spot.

The Whitman board of director position Romano sent Angela's way represented a critical opportunity for the Ferrari Family and Romano personally.

"Hi, Uncle Mike." Angela leaned over and kissed him on the cheek.

"Angie, please have a seat. We keepin' you busy enough?" He knew the answer; by Joe Acosta's design, Romano Enterprises was her only client.

"There's never enough time to finish everything."

"That's a sign of a thrivin' business, honey," Romano said, leaning into the table, "How'd the meeting go with Erick Olson?"

"I feel like I had a good rapport with both Erick and Betty." Angela paused, her forehead creased in thought, "I think I made the cut. They said they'd be back in contact with me soon. I have to invest fifty-grand in the deal. The thing is, I'm sensing Olson may be having problems getting his acquisition loan approved."

"That's good news. The phone company's a big deal for us. Green Eyes has tried to get one for a while now. Other bidders keep gettin' in the way. Don't worry about the money. We'll front the dough." He poured a glass of red wine for himself and offered Angela one.

"Thanks." Angela sipped the wine and set her glass on the table.

"How much money they lookin' at borrowin'?"

"I think they need eighty-five million, plus or minus. It doesn't sound like they've finalized their offer price yet."

"Don't say nothin', but this could work out good. Acosta wants to use Spokane Community Bank for the loan. We've been workin' to get in front of Olson's financing effort." Romano stopped there. Angela didn't need to know about the other group Tony had bidding on WesTel or that their effort to finance Olson's bid was a plan to influence the auction's outcome. "Anything else come up?"

"Yeah, they asked about Romano Enterprises being in our building. Saw the name in the lobby. I didn't tell them anything, but it felt awkward." Angela's face tightened, and she placed her hands on the table, palm down.

"Good girl. We need to keep my name out of it, same with Chicago—for the time bein'anyhow."

"Why does Joe want to use our bank for the loan?"

"It'll give us leverage over Olson. The phone company gets millions from government support payments meant to keep phone costs down for people livin' out in the sticks. We can squeeze out more of those payments, but we need control. That's why the loan. It gives us the leverage we need." Romano sipped his wine.

Michael and Angela sat quietly for a long moment, enjoying their wine.

"I got an important project for you, Angie," Romano said, his brow furrowed.

"Sounds serious, Uncle Mike. What is it?"

"Acosta is expandin' the internet porn business in a big way. He's got contracts with all the well-known nudie magazines to run our ads."

Angela pulled a small notepad and pen from her purse and made a note.

"We want you to work up the ads. Same basic program we've been runnin' up to now—only bigger. A lot bigger. We'll reach a lot more people with these new magazine advertising contracts. We'll continue to offer a free thirty-day trial membership to our porn websites. To get access, they'll have to give us a valid credit card to keep on file. Tell 'em the card is needed to prove they're over eighteen. We're already doing this with internet advertising, but now we'll expand into print magazines," Romano grinned.

"And, once we have the credit card, we'll start charging a monthly subscription fee?" Angela said.

"That's right. And in the ads, we tell 'em the charge will show up as 'subscription services' or whatever. Be creative and make up something good. Surprise me." Romano glanced around the restaurant, searching for prying ears.

"How much is the monthly subscription?" Angela finished making a note and looked up at Michael.

"I have a schedule I'll send you. It depends on how many sites they want access to. We do have one new idea that'll cost more. It's a live interaction. The guy subscribes and then gets to have a one-on-one live internet video session with one of the girls. She'll do whatever he asks.

Well, within reason, ya know. That service will be for a premium rate. They'll pay by the minute." Romano swirled the wine in his glass and stared out the window.

"That's sick, Uncle Mike." Angela frowned.

"It's business, honey." Romano looked at Angela. "Spend a week or so on the ads, and let's see what you come up with."

"I'm on it." Angela dropped the pad and pen into her purse and zipped it shut.

CHAPTER 10

MONDAY MORNING, THE Clinton ferry approached the terminal landing, announcing its arrival with two short blasts from an air horn. Raising his head from the document he was reading, Erick gazed out his study window toward the ship. A light rain fell. He watched a fog bank roll over Whidbey Island across the bay.

Erick refocused on the Whitman documents and considered the loan he needed to close it. The time had arrived for Farmers Bank to put their offer in writing. Anxious, Erick glanced at his calendar again, accepting it would be nearly impossible to secure an alternate lender this late in the game unless Skip came through at the last minute.

Erick took a deep breath and checked his email.

Nothing.

Erick lifted the handset on his desk and dialed Farmers Bank. His chest tightened.

"Farmers Bank, may I help you?"

"Robert Miller, please, tell him Erick Olson's calling."

"One moment."

"Erick, good morning. What can I do for you?"

"You're a difficult man to get a hold of, Robert. Honestly, we're getting close to submitting our bid on Whitman Telephone Company. Are you prepared to issue the commitment letter?"

"We have a problem, as—" Miller's voice came across the line as a whisper.

"What problem?" Erick demanded. Blood shot through his arteries and into his head, turning his face red. His mind rose to high alert.

"As you know," Robert continued, "the lending committee signed off—preliminarily. The relationship your family has enjoyed with the bank going back nearly seventy years was largely the reason the committee granted preliminary approval. Because of its size, the loan has to go to the full board as well. Three of my seven board members have visited with me privately. They're concerned with a loan of this size. It would be the second-largest in our portfolio and is not in our core business of agriculture—"

"I thought this was a lock," Erick interrupted again. He stood and paced his study floor.

"I'm afraid there's more. Two days ago, a bomb went off and burned the barn next to our Board Chairman, Lewis Granger's house. He's pretty shook up."

"That's terrible, but accidents happen. What's that got to do with *my* deal?" Erick wandered aimlessly to his study window and watched a car roll off the ferry onto the landing and disappear into the rain. The knot in his stomach tightened.

"The bomb wasn't an accident. There was a warning in his mailbox. The note said we should stick to ag loans."

Erick paused for a moment and fell into a chair by the window, sensing his dream slipping from his grasp. "So where are we on this, Robert? Will the bank make the loan or not?"

"The Board has voted … I'm afraid not. The phone business is too far astray from our agriculture mainstay. We wish you the best, Erick."

"Thanks." Erick's heart sunk, defeated. He shuffled to his desk and hung up the phone.

CHAPTER 11

MONDAY AT 5 p.m., Michael Romano held court in his reserved booth at De Rosa's. He shared a bottle of red wine with Jason Rossi, the president of Spokane Community Bank. Joe Acosta handpicked Jason to run the bank. The two men had attended the same MBA program together.

"So Michael, what's Joe's take on this Whitman deal?" Jason asked.

"The loan will give us leverage over Olson," Romano said. "Plus, he wants some of our people on the board of directors."

"Leverage for what?"

"There's a lot of government money flowing into the company. We might ... could be ... more aggressive with that part of the business." Romano sipped his wine.

"I see," Jason said, rubbing his cheek. "When's Skip supposed to be here?"

"Soon." Romano glanced at his watch and looked toward the door. "I see him. He's coming in now."

Skip strode across the room to Romano's table, exuding confidence.

"Michael, Jason, how's everyone's Monday?" Skip asked.

Michael sat his wine glass on the table, "We're good, Skip. Please sit."

Skip sat next to Jason, across the table from Michael. "So, you wanted to talk about the Whitman loan?" Skip fiddled nervously with his tie.

Romano swallowed down a mouthful of wine. "Bottom line, we'll do the loan. We'll also be takin' an active role."

Skip stroked his beard in thought, "What do you mean by an active role?"

"We'll do the eighty-five mill, but Jason will take a seat on the board."

"Mostly as an observer," Jason added. "We can make it non-voting if that helps."

"I don't think Erick will like it," Skip said.

Romano leaned forward over the table, "Well, then he can go somewhere else. When it's my money, I can't have the other guy unchecked—capeesh?" The lawyer was becoming disrespectful, and that posed a problem.

"Doesn't matter, he's out of options," Jason said.

"You ain't listenin'—" Michael started to say.

Jason leaned into Skip and interrupted, "We expect you to sell this to Olson." His harsh tone left no room for debate.

CHAPTER 12

WALKING BRISKLY FROM De Rosa's toward his car, Skip pulled the cell phone from his suit coat pocket and hastily dialed Erick's number.

"Hey there, Skip, did you get my email?" Erick sounded defeated. "Farmers Bank won't make the loan. They really screwed me over by waiting so long."

"Sorry to hear that, Erick. On a brighter note, I had a meeting with Spokane Community Bank. Jason Rossi, the Bank's president, is interested in writing your loan!" Skip feigned excitement.

"Seriously? This is great news, Skip."

"Erick, it's far from a sure thing, but I feel hopeful. With your permission, I'd like to send the loan package we prepared for Farmers Bank over to Jason for their review. That package should have everything they need to make a go-no-go decision."

"Absolutely!" Erick's renewed enthusiasm shot across the line. "If the bank needs anything further, don't hesitate to call me. Or feel free to have them call me directly. Whatever works best."

"Okay, buddy, let me get the ball rolling. I'll call you when I know more. Hope to hear back by Friday."

"Thanks, Skip. This is the best news I've received in a while."

CHAPTER 13

LATE FRIDAY AFTERNOON, Erick mixed a gin and tonic while waiting to hear from Skip. Four days had passed since Skip called to share the outcome of his meeting with Spokane Community Bank. The lender appeared to be Erick's last hope to finance the Whitman deal.

The original terms floated by Farmers Bank had been favorable, but they were now out of the picture. With his back against the wall, the *Financial Wunderkind* ran complex financial calculations through his head. He attempted to set the benchmark for the most oppressive terms he would accept to close the Whitman deal. His cell phone vibrated—*Skip*.

"Olson here ... what's the good word?" Erick shuddered, recognizing this call might either make or break his dream of acquiring a phone company of his own.

"I heard back from Jason Rossi."

"What will he do for us?" Erick sat on the edge of his seat.

"Something a bit unexpected came up ... the lender wants a seat on your board."

"Isn't that somewhat unusual?" Erick stood from his desk and walked to the window.

"It's not unheard of. Sounds as though they'll accept a non-voting role."

"I can live with that if it means getting the deal done." Dropping back into his chair, Erick wondered why they would want to sit through monthly board meetings focused on operations. "When will they have loan agreement documents drafted?"

"I can send the terms sheet now. The rest will follow early next week."

"Alright, send them over." Erick ended the call. A tight smile broke across his face. "We're going to get this done," he whispered.

The following Tuesday evening, Erick read the final page of the Spokane Community Bank loan agreement and dropped it on his desk. He stared out his study window into the night darkness and watched the illuminated, double-deck ferry approach its landing in the harbor below. The loan interest rate, term, and covenants were all reasonable and in line with his expectations.

Erick reached for the agreement and turned his attention to the paragraph that troubled him most. The bank demanded a seat on his board of directors. A little tickle in the *Financial Wunderkind's* brain warned him this might lead to trouble. He held his head in his hands rubbing his temples, trying to lower the stress.

"Hell, it's a non-voting seat, and I'm out of options. Out of time," Erick said the words out loud. "Damn it all."

"Erick, did you say something?" Betty stood in the doorway to his study. "What are you working on?"

"I didn't realize you were still here," Erick said. He held the bank agreement out to her. "Take a look at this clause in the loan agreement, will you please?"

Betty sat in a guest chair in front of Erick's desk and read the letter.

"The bank wants on our board?" Betty asked with a raised eyebrow.

"Yeah, it sucks." Erick leaned back in his chair and lifted his stocking feet onto the desk.

"That's a tough one. What's the downside?" Betty's eyes narrowed.

"There's a long list of operational and financial covenants in the loan that we will be bound to. Having the bank in the board room will make it hard to have certain difficult discussions when the outcome may affect our ability to meet the covenant metrics." Erick stroked the stubble on his chin and shook his head slowly from side to side.

"The six outside directors we picked, and you will provide governance, well, I suppose it's seven now with the bank. I don't see the bank as much of a problem." She laid the letter on his desk and leaned back in her chair.

"So you think we should accept their terms?" Erick walked to the bar and poured a gin and tonic. He turned toward Betty. "Would you like a drink?"

"No thanks," she paused and seemed to hesitate for a beat, her face painted with worry. "It's the right opportunity at the right time in our lives, Erick. I'm not concerned with having the bank on our board. This is our best chance to buy a company. So yes, I say we do it. Do you have other concerns?"

Erick walked to the window and sipped his drink. "Concerns? Yeah, I'm concerned."

"About the bank?"

"Partly ... Moreover, it's the way this deal came together. I can't quite put my finger on it, but something feels off."

"How so?" Betty asked.

"It's a feeling I can't shake. We started with over a dozen bidders on Whitman, or so Pat Mango said. That number seems to have dropped significantly, almost as though bidders are being run off or seeing something big that I've completely missed. Then the LightPoint plane blew up, and LTE pushed this diversity crap on us. There's a barn fire, and Farmers Bank pulls our loan for no good reason. A few days later, Skip shows up with a new lender that wants a board seat." Erick paced across the room, eyes glued to the floor.

"How well do we really know Skip? Until this deal came up, we hadn't seen him since our undergraduate days eighteen years ago. That's a long time. I mean, can we put our complete trust in him?" Erick had closed dozens of deals for WesTel and had a well-honed nose for things that didn't add up. *What am I missing*? Straining to think of what he may have missed, Erick came up empty. "Do you believe in coincidences?" Erick's eyes met Betty's.

"Sure, they happen all the time, and it's something we need to take seriously. I'm not seeing a pattern, though. I can't connect the dots."

Erick watched cars roll onto the evening ferry for the trip back to Clinton. "Maybe I'm overthinking this. I can't shake the feeling that something's not lining up."

CHAPTER 14

AN EMAIL FROM Skip Britain arrived a few minutes before 2 p.m. the next day. It included an attachment with the final version of the Whitman Communications purchase agreement and bank commitment letter. After printing the documents, Erick held the one-page bank letter and read it carefully.

His heart beat faster. A year had passed since he left WesTel, yet it felt like the culmination of a lifetime of work. His hand trembled while he was holding the single sheet of paper. At last, the funding to buy his phone company was within his grasp. Erick read quickly through the purchase agreement, ensuring all of his final edits had been made. The document was complete, and he stood ready to sign it.

Erick set the documents down and walked to his study doorway. He called out for Betty, "Can you come in here for a minute?"

"I'm in the kitchen. What's up?"

"Skip sent the final purchase agreement. I need to get it signed and over to FedEx. Do you have the director profile documents printed out?"

"Of course." Betty breezed into Erick's study and headed toward the credenza behind his desk. She picked up a folder of papers and handed them to Erick. "There's a profile on each director in here."

"Will you check the FedEx label Skip's office prepared against the LTE Irving, Texas address and make sure it's right? Here's a business card for David Flores with the correct address," Erick handed the card to her.

"Sure, anything else?" Betty asked.

"No, that should do it. I need to stop by the bank to get my signature notarized. There's a FedEx drop box across the street. This needs to go out today. Thanks."

Betty slumped into the guest chair across from Erick's desk and sighed, "How are you feeling about this deal?"

"I think we're golden. Our offer price is strong, we have industry experience, and the LTE people know us. On top of that, we gave them a board with the diversity they want."

"I hope so, Erick, I can't see you chasing many more of these deals. They're time-consuming, expensive, and there are more productive things you could be doing."

"Like what?" He pushed back from his desk in defiance.

"Go to work doing acquisitions again. I know Paul Banta, from LightPoint, reached out and—"

"I'm going to close this deal, Betty, or die trying," Erick interrupted. He would fight the good fight and leave his blood on the boardroom floor but never surrender.

"I hope so. With WesTel gone, I'm feeling detached living here on the coast. If the deal falls through, I want to pull my financial contribution out of this effort to buy a company and move back to Coeur d'Alene. This is our last hurrah."

"Whitman Communications is our company, damn it. Now more than ever, I need you to believe in what we've done here, Betty. For Christ's sake." Erick snatched up the FedEx envelope and left for the bank in a hurry.

CHAPTER 15

WEDNESDAY AFTERNOON, TONY Ferrari, Joe Acosta, and Michael Romano sat at the round conference table in Tony's Chicago office. The smell of stale cigarette smoke and burnt coffee filled the room. Tony took a deep drag on his cigarette. His ashtray overflowed with butts. Romano tapped his foot nervously. *I'm here to listen—speak only when spoken to. I'm here to learn. That's it.*

Tony Ferrari led a bid for Whitman Telephone, fronted by a group of black former Illinois Bell executives. The group was brought together to meet LTE's diversity objective and keep Ferrari's involvement hidden. Carlton Henderson, a prominent industry figure and former Illinois Bell CFO, headed the group.

"What should we have our guys bid?" Tony asked, his green eyes focused on Acosta. He tapped the smoldering ash off the end of his cigarette into the overflowing ashtray.

"Jason says Olson's at one-hundred-million." Acosta leaned back and crossed his legs.

"So what do you think, ninety-five?" Tony brought the cigarette to his lips.

Joe leaned forward, "That should be enough to throw it to Olson."

So that's the game, toss it to Olson and then force him to play along, Romano thought.

"With the five million difference, they may take the auction to two rounds," Tony said matter-of-factly.

"Doubt it, with a five-percent spread between the two bids. That should be close enough. This deal's lunch money to LTE." Acosta's eyes darted around the room.

"Moving into this telephone business is a long game." Tony took another deep pull on his cigarette. "It's going to take time to blend our business into it."

"I agree, could take years. The phone business is highly regulated, sort of like getting into casinos," Acosta said. He shifted his focus to Romano with a look that encouraged Michael to sit up straight in his chair.

"We need to take it slow. Olson will be the frontman. He's clean— that's good. Michael, we don't want you getting involved yet. We don't need anyone screwing the pooch. You understand?" Tony said.

Romano locked eyes with Tony briefly and then shifted his focus to the window, "Yeah." Tony was the boss. There was never any doubt.

"It's going to take months to get the government approvals to close the deal," Acosta said.

"You think Olson will follow the program?" Tony turned his attention back to Acosta.

"If he won't play ball, we'll squeeze him out." Acosta stood from his seat and backed his thin frame away from the table. "With or without Olson, we win, and he loses. Michael, when are you heading back to Spokane?"

"I'm on the Southwest four o'clock flight."

"You've done well on this deal so far, getting our directors on the board and financing the purchase through Spokane Community Bank. Both will be critical elements to our future success. Keep it up. I'll be in touch," Acosta headed for the door.

Tony snuffed out his cigarette and stood, "Good plan, gentlemen, call Henderson."

CHAPTER 16

WORKING WITH AMY in his study the last Friday in July, Erick's cell phone rang. *David Flores* lit up on the screen. He dropped the document he was reviewing with Amy. Heart racing, he reached for his cell.

Erick looked at Amy, "It's LTE, I need to pick up." Amy's eyes lit up in anticipation.

"David, how are you this afternoon?" Erick said, choking on the words.

"I'm good, Erick, thank you for asking. I have some news for you," David paused, "LTE has selected your bid to acquire the Whitman asset."

"Wow!" Erick said in elation. "I wasn't expecting a call so soon. This is wonderful news."

"Congratulations, Erick. As far as next steps, our legal and regulatory team will be contacting you soon. Sara Wilson from Legal and Pat Mango from Regulatory, I believe you know them well. They will work with your group to obtain the necessary regulatory approvals before we can put this deal to bed. Congratulations again. We'll be in close contact, as I'll be running point for LTE until the deal is closed."

"Thanks again, David … I mean, really, thank you." Erick's head exploding with joy, he disconnected the call. Jumping up from his chair, Erick howled, "We won!" and high-fived Amy. She stood, looking more excited than he'd ever seen her. He took her in his arms and hugged her tightly, "We won it," he yelled again, as though she hadn't heard him the first time.

Attracted by the noise, Betty rushed into the study. "What's all the commotion?"

"LTE called. We won the auction! Whitman is ours!" Erick shouted and took Betty in his arms, hugging her.

"I thought it would be at least a month before we heard anything. This is great. We won!" Betty cried out.

"Yeah!" Amy squealed, pumping her fist in the air.

"We need to celebrate," Erick said. "I'm buying!"

PART II

The Scam

In too deep, too late to back out,
they control the business and me.
My dream company a front for the mob.

Victimless crimes as we pilfer federal cash
sources available to rural providers. Well,
the porn billing scam will have victims,

but who the hell cares, I'm too far gone
for any concern beyond the money. Let
the cash flow to the mob and me.

—Erick Olson

CHAPTER 17

July 2000

HOLDING THE INVITATION from LTE in his hand, images from the past twelve months danced in Erick's head. A year had passed since he received the call from David Flores informing him he had won the Whitman auction. In the time following that call, his life had been a whirlwind of activity. He traveled with his board of directors to Olympia, Washington, twice: the first time to meet with the commission staff, the second for a hearing with the commissioners. He also traveled to DC and met with FCC staff and the Washington State congressional delegation to enlist their support in garnering the needed FCC approvals to close the Whitman deal. Erick persuaded the FCC to place the operating license transfer process on the fast track. Generous campaign contributions ensured the support he sought from elected representatives.

Erick dropped the invitation card on his desk. He walked to his study window overlooking the harbor and ferry terminal. The regulators never seemed to share Erick's excitement for the sale of Whitman. That troubled him. Did they not recognize the company's customers would receive better service from a local owner than an impersonal Fortune 500 corporation two thousand miles away in Dallas? A wave of melancholy ran through him, and he winced. *Doesn't matter; they approved the sale, and now the company's mine. Or at least it will be following this signing party.*

Two weeks later, on Friday, July 14th, Erick, Betty, and Amy stood on the pergola-covered flagstone terrace adjoining LTE's executive dining room. A sheaf of legal documents transferring ownership were executed this morning, and it was time to celebrate. The outdoor gathering area boasted views of the Four Seasons championship golf course and the Dallas skyline in the distance. Buffet serving tables and tuxedo-clad attendants lined one side of the terrace. An open bar served beverages at the opposite end. Many of the Company's senior executives attended, including the company president, Harry Black.

Smiling and nodding to his well-wishers, Erick floated from small group to group with Betty and Amy in tow. This was Erick's big day, and he intended to soak it in—bask in the glory. The hot Texas sun beat down upon the LTE campus like fire. Erick felt reborn.

With assets exceeding fifty billion dollars, Whitman's sale would result in no more than a rounding adjustment on the LTE financial statements. Erick marveled at how his acquisition of a lifetime would be so inconsequential to the seller. And yet, LTE had fought hard to claim the highest possible auction price.

Erick watched from across the terrace as Harry Black, broke away from a group of his senior VPs and wandered in Erick's direction. Erick was speaking with Pat Mango and Mike Swenson as Harry approached, well on his way to tossing down his fourth flute of champagne. He'd need to take a cab to dinner tonight.

"Congratulations, Erick, I'm happy this worked out for you," Harry said.

"Thanks, it feels good to get the deal closed." Erick gestured his hand toward Betty and Amy. "I'd like you to meet my partners, Betty Olson and Amy Summers."

Harry took Betty's hand and shook it graciously, and then the same with Amy.

"Partners? Well, you'll have your hands full keeping this guy in line," Harry smiled at the women warmly.

"It's a struggle," Amy said. She let loose a nervous laugh and looked away.

"Ha!" Betty tossed her head back and laughed. "That's an understatement."

"Seriously though, Erick, you've been in this business quite some time now. What opportunity do you see in the landline business? Our strategic plan has us mostly out of the sector ten years from now. We'll likely sell out of the rural areas over the next five."

Several of Harry's subordinate executives joined the small group like football players in a huddle. Erick squared off his shoulders as though challenged.

"I believe there's still a lot of service value we can squeeze over land-lines for the foreseeable future," Erick said, his face serious and confident. "Given the size and scope of LTE, it may be difficult to justify committing a lot of management time on making marginal improvements in an operation the size of Whitman. But, if we work hard and increase revenues by three million a year, that would be a ten percent bump. And would increase the market value of our equity investment significantly. That same three million for LTE is lost in the travel budget."

Dale Jenkins, the VP of Marketing, spoke up, "Yeah, guys like you exist on the crumbs we leave behind, and I don't mean that in a negative way."

"Look, in a lot of cases, I see large phone companies stepping over dollars to pick up pennies," anger rose in Erick's tone. "You could staff up a 'small company' division and make a ton of money. If nothing else, you could sell operations like Whitman for a hell of a lot more if you improved the financials first."

Harry cut in, sporting his most sincere smile, "But why bother? We can sell for market value to guys like you, guys who want their shot at owning a phone company. And hell, for all practical purposes, we've put in play a plan to exit the landline phone business. Spending the time to manage rural landlines is a distraction from our larger goal. For us, it's all about wireless technology now. Best to leave landlines to entrepreneurs like you, Erick. I've got to get back upstairs. Best of luck to you." Harry shook hands with the three of them and headed back into the building.

Erick leaned into Betty and whispered in her ear, "Let's get the hell out of here."

CHAPTER 18

ARRIVING AT THE Spokane airport the following evening with Amy, Erick rented a car in the terminal. Betty would fly in tomorrow from Seattle. The thought of being alone with Amy tonight in Pullman tickled something deep inside Erick. A sly grin broke across his face.

Erick left the interstate, heading south on US 195. He turned to steal a look at Amy. She caught his glance.

"So, what do you think? Ready to start life over in the Palouse?" Erick said with a broad smile.

"Honestly, I never saw myself leaving Seattle, but opportunities like this are rare. So, yes. I guess I'm ready," Amy said.

"You're young, Amy. It's okay to take a flier at this stage of your career. I might add that doing so is a sign of an ambitious woman and one with strong character." Erick sensed a hint of sadness in her tone. Guilt stabbed at his heart for pulling her away from her life on the coast.

"I feel homeless right now. Thanks for inviting me to stay at your place until my apartment's ready," Amy smiled warmly.

"Of course, it's my pleasure," Eric blushed at the thought of them living together. "You know this professor's house I rented is large, plenty of room for the two of us."

"How long's the lease," Amy asked.

"One year, but informally, the professor said he'll be in England for two years, and I can stay into the second year if I like. He wants the place lived in and someone paying the utilities."

"Cool."

Erick turned onto the driveway of his rental home at 9 p.m., as daylight faded to dusk. Completing the paperwork to lease the house the week before, he had the keys in hand. Fumbling for a moment with the house key like a newlywed, Erick opened the front door and led Amy inside.

"Your room is down the hall on the left," Erick said, pointing down a long hallway. "Why don't you get settled, and I'll order a pizza?"

"Sounds good. Order me a side salad, too, please."

Watching her thin silhouette walk down the hall and disappear around the corner, Erick thought: *Yeah, I should get a salad.*

After ordering the food on his cell phone, Erick dropped his bags in the master bedroom and headed to the kitchen. Pulling the refrigerator door open, he was surprised to find a six-pack of beer with a note from the professor. 'Erick, please enjoy the beer. It will surely go bad by the time I return.' Erick placed the bottle of champagne he brought with him from Dallas next to the beer to chill.

Hearing the doorbell, Erick jumped to his feet. "Hey, Amy, the food's here, would you mind finding some plates and silver while I pay the guy?"

"Sure, I can do that."

"Grab a couple cold beers from the fridge, too."

"We have beer?" Amy asked sounding surprised.

"The professor left a six-pack for us."

By the time Erick paid for the pizza and made his way to the dining room, Amy was sitting at the table sipping a beer.

"That was nice, leaving the beer for us. It's what I needed after a travel day," Amy said and smiled. "I noticed a bottle of champagne, too. Are you planning a celebration?" Amy winked.

Erick felt the blood rush to his face, "I brought that, knowing we'd want to celebrate at some point."

He dug into a thick slice of pizza, watching Amy toy with her salad.

"I want you to know, Amy, anytime you feel the need to be with family back in Seattle, I'll find a business reason to send you there for a few days," Erick's tone turned serious. "I know you're close to your grandmother. Anyway, I wanted you to know."

"Thanks Erick. I should be fine. As a bonus, I'll be much closer to my best friend, Ali over in Spokane. She's more like a sister than a girlfriend."

"That's right. She works for a CPA firm, right?" Erick vaguely remembered seeing Alison once when she picked Amy up at his Seattle home.

"Murphy Avery CPAs. She's doing well, made manager this year." Amy picked up her beer and took a sip.

"We'll need a CPA firm for our audit and tax work. Maybe we should give them a call?"

"I'm sure they'd love to work with us. They're big in the independent telephone sector."

The longer they drank and talked, the closer he was drawn to her light. Finishing the pizza, Erick grabbed two fresh beers and led Amy into the study, turned on the gas fireplace, and sat in a club chair facing the fire. Amy sat in the chair next to him and kicked off her shoes. The dancing light from the fire cast a soft glow on her skin. Sitting beside her put Erick's heart at ease, as though they had always been together.

"We should celebrate the first night in your new home, Erick," Amy said, playfully tossing her hair to one side.

"You're right. This calls for champagne! Better yet, champagne in the hot tub!"

"I'm not sure about the hot tub," Amy said, casting her gaze to the floor and feigning modesty.

"Why not," he said, "it's right out this door." He pointed to French doors leading from the study onto the terrace. "Come on, don't be a party pooper," Erick pouted.

"Okay, give me a minute to get ready?" A smile lit up Amy's face.

"I'll meet you outside." Erick stood from his chair and headed to the master bedroom in search of his swim trunks.

After changing into his swimsuit, Erick made his way to the terrace. He removed the cover from the hot tub and turned up the heat. Sitting on a molded loveseat, neck deep in the bubbling water, he popped the cork on the champagne bottle.

Amy stepped from the study onto the terrace, wearing a white terrycloth robe she had found in the bathroom. She seductively dropped the robe from her shoulders. Climbing into the tub in her pale yellow bikini, she sat in the corner across from Erick, maintaining eye contact the entire time.

"This is nice," Amy said, sliding into the water to her chin.

Erick handed her a glass of champagne. "A toast to us, the new owners of Whitman Communications." They clinked their glasses together and drained them. Erick refilled the champagne flutes. He stretched out so all but his head was immersed in the water. "I wonder what the poor people are doing tonight?" He grinned.

Erick's legs rubbed against Amy's, and that aroused him. He reached across the tub for her arm and floated Amy onto the love seat next to him. Submerged in the water, she weighed next to nothing. He had caught her by surprise. Her wet top fit loosely and slipped off her right shoulder. Erick's eyes were glued to the errant strap as she floated beside him.

"Wow, what the heck, mister!" She teased. Her expression was serious, but her mood playful.

Erick held up the bottle, "Easier for me to pour if you're over here." He refilled her glass and put his arm around her shoulders. She smiled and pressed the glass against her lips.

Pulling the loose strap gently off her arm, he whispered in her ear, "Oops, your strap's loose." Turning her toward him, he pulled the other strap off. Her top sunk into deeper water. He pressed her topless body against his and kissed her deep and wet.

CHAPTER 19

MONDAY MORNING AT 7:30 a.m., Erick breezed into the Whitman Communications warehouse for an all-employee meeting. Making his way to the center of the cavernous building, Erick jumped on top of a table to the roar of applause from the gathered employees.

"Thank you ... thank you," Erick smiled broadly and held the palms of his hands toward the crowd to calm them down. "Many of you know me. For those who don't, I'm Erick Olson, the new CEO of Whitman Communications." The crowd broke into applause again. Erick paused and surveyed the room. "Today is a remarkable day. This is the second time I've purchased Whitman Telephone Company. The first was over fifteen years ago for WesTel, and now a second time to free you from the corporate behemoth, LTE!" The crowd erupted in applause and hoots and hollers. For a moment, Erick locked eyes across the large room with Amy; the warmth of her gaze ran through him.

"We have a lot of work ahead, and I couldn't be more pleased with our team here at Whitman. Some of you remember me from our time with WesTel. For those who don't know me, we'll get acquainted over the next few months ... I'm sure rumors are flying, but let me be clear on one thing—my door is always open. If something's bothering you, please stop by and share it with me. Whitman's employees are our most valuable asset, our competitive advantage. Not only are we unable to provide quality service to our customers without you, we're unable to provide service at all. So, let's keep that line of communication open!

"Now, I recognize your time is valuable, and we have customers to serve, but before I let you get on with it, I want to introduce the senior management team. As I said earlier, I'm the CEO and will sit on top of operations." Pointing to Betty, Erick said, "This is Betty Olson, Vice President over HR and office administration. Betty will be meeting individually with each of you over the next several weeks." Now pointing to Amy, "And Amy Summers is our CFO, in charge of accounting and finance."

Preaching like a country evangelical minister, Erick mesmerized his audience. As his time ran thin, Erick looked from his perch to the hopeful faces of Whitman's employees like a hen watches over her chicks. In his most somber tone, he added one final note, "This is our opportunity to make Whitman Communications a great company for you and the community. Chances like this are rare, and when they occur, the moment must be seized." After a pause, he closed strong, "The time is now. This is our moment to write a new chapter in the Whitman story!"

The assembled employees clapped and hollered as though they were at a revival. They celebrated their new ownership with donuts and coffee. Employees left the rally pumped up and committed to following Erick into battle.

Erick took the corner office in the executive wing of the Whitman building. The office was large enough to hold a desk, two guest chairs, and a seating area with two leather club chairs and a matching sofa. The adjoining private conference room had an oval table with eight seats. It could be entered from the waiting area adjacent to his executive assistant's office space or directly from Erick's office.

"Mr. Olson, I have Mr. Britain on the line." It was Candice Wright, Erick's executive assistant, on the intercom. Candice had been hired from the university, where she had held a similar role in the English department. A prim and proper woman in her late twenties, she wore her long light-brown hair in a braided ponytail, equestrian style. It reached halfway down her back. Deeply religious, she had married at a young age and had a gaggle of children. Candice was the perfect fit to keep Erick out of trouble and run interference for him.

"Right, put him through, please … Skip?"

"Hi, Erick, settling in?"

"Yeah, we have a ton of stuff to do, but it's good to be back. What can I do for you?"

"I have some documents from Spokane Community Bank I'd like to drop off now that you're here. I thought I might come down tomorrow and deliver them personally. Give me a chance to see what you got yourself into. We can do it later if now's not a good time."

"No ... no, tomorrow's fine. What time were you thinking? I'd like for you to see the place."

"Late morning, let's say ten?"

"See you then." Erick bit his upper lip, wondering what Skip really wanted. Skip billed his time by the hour. Delivering papers in person made little sense. Erick couldn't think of a reason he would need to see the Company facilities unless, perhaps, the bank had concerns.

Looking out his office window at the Palouse wheat fields the following morning, Erick was startled by the sound of Candy breaking over the intercom, "Mr. Olson, Mr. Britain's here for your ten o'clock."

"Show him in, please."

"Hi Erick, good to see you back in the saddle."

"Thanks, it's good to be back." Erick looked into Skip's eyes and tried to read him. He stood and walked from behind his desk to shake hands with his lawyer. "Follow me. We can talk in my conference room." Erick led him into the room and motioned to a chair. "So what have you got for me today?"

"A handful of documents the bank signed but weren't included in the package we mailed last week. I could have mailed them, but I thought I'd take the opportunity to see what you bought out here firsthand."

"Well, thank you, Skip. You're always welcome here," Erick shrugged, unconvinced by Skip's explanation.

"On a related topic, Spokane Community Bank would like to meet you for lunch next week on Wednesday. I'll arrange it for noon at De Rosa's if you're free?"

"That seems odd. What does the bank want to meet about so soon?" Erick's brow furrowed.

"Sort of a meet and greet. Your loan is one of the largest in the bank's portfolio. They'd like to get to know you a bit and learn a little more about the phone business. Like I said, I'll set it up and plan to be there as well."

"Who from the bank?" Erick glanced at his calendar and noted he was open on that Wednesday. "Looks like I'm free Wednesday."

"Jason Rossi will be there for certain and I believe he may bring along someone else from the bank."

Erick watched Candy through the open door as he considered his lender's desire to have a lunch meeting so soon. She sat with perfect posture on a rolling chair, typing away on a three-part form. The clickety-clack of her IBM Selectric typewriter spilled into the conference room.

"What should I do to prepare?" Erick leaned back in his chair and crossed his legs.

"The meeting should be low-key. You'll be fine," Skip paused. "Buddy, I've got to run." Skip stood, snapped his leather briefcase shut, and moved toward the door. "I'll be in touch."

CHAPTER 20

MICHAEL ROMANO PICKED up the phone on the second ring, "Romano."

"This is Skip. We're on for De Rosa's with Olson next week, Wednesday at noon."

"Good, how'd it go with him?" Romano's pulse quickened.

"No problems. Erick's settling into his new role. Seemed surprised at the Bank's lunch request but didn't push back on it at all."

"Good. Anything else?" Romano made a note for lunch with Olson on Wednesday.

"I think you need to go easy on him at first. Erick doesn't know who you are or anything about you. This will be a big surprise for him."

"I'll let him educate me, but not for long. I need to see how my company can work with Whitman to get more of those government funds."

"Erick can be pushed into the gray area, but pushing him in too deep will be difficult."

"Yeah, Skip, that's what they all say. He ain't got no choice. If he don't play along, it won't end well for 'im."

"All I'm saying is, I can't control Erick. I plan to be at De Rosa's early. We can talk more then."

Romano laid the phone down and gazed out his office window, looking out over Spokane. He took a moment to consider how much trouble Olson might give him, if any. An evil grin spread across his face.

CHAPTER 21

THE FOLLOWING MONDAY, Romano sat fidgeting nervously in his oxblood leather chair, waiting for a call from Chicago. Acosta called over the weekend and told him Tony had something important to talk about this morning at ten. He hated conference calls and stiffened at the thought of one with Green Eyes.

Romano picked up his office furniture at a Spokane auction. The high-end pieces stood out in the well-worn nineteen-thirties former factory office. When he found the time, Romano wanted to complete the office transformation. He would add paneled walls, built-in bookcases, and new flooring. Meanwhile, business boomed, and Romano found himself short on time.

The phone on his desk rang. Michael snapped it up, "Romano."

"Michael, this is Joe. I've got Tony and Bobby in the office with me."

Romano's face flushed. He grew up with his cousin Bobby, and they were still close. Bobby ran the Family's adult film studio. They had never worked together, so having Bobby on the call puzzled Romano. He leaned back in his chair, anxiously waiting for someone in Chicago to start talking.

"We're looking to expand Bobby's filmmaking business," Tony said. "It may be wise to open a second studio away from Chicago. Since you've got vacant space in your Spokane building, that may be an option."

Romano leaned forward, listening intently. Though he was a part of the Family business, he valued the autonomy he enjoyed running the Spokane operation. His blood pressure shot up, sensing that freedom might be taken from him.

"I'm sending Bobby to Spokane to evaluate the vacant space in your building," Tony said, his tone sparking over the speaker. "He'll arrive early next week. We still need to finalize the travel arrangements."

"Bobby, you're welcome to stay with us at the house … We'll be offended if you don't," Romano said.

"Thanks, Michael. I look forward to it," Bobby said.

One week later, Michael Romano watched a cab roll into the litter-strewn parking lot below his office window in his rundown part of downtown Spokane. Dressed in a dark suit, Bobby Gallo climbed out of the back. He helped a skinny, platinum-blonde chick wearing a short, leopard-print skirt exit the cab.

Romano burst into his sixth-floor lobby as the elevator doors opened, "Bobby, welcome to Spokane!" Michael said.

"Thanks. I'm glad to be here." They embraced in a bear hug and parted as they continued to pat one another's shoulders. "Say hello to my girl, Misti."

"It's a pleasure, Misti." Michael admired her tight, round ass for a moment and then turned back to his cousin and winked.

"How's the little lady and kids?" Bobby asked.

"Everyone's fine. Jenny's lookin' forward to seein' youse guys later tonight. We'll have dinner at the house."

"Sounds great! I could use some home cooking."

Romano walked to his office door. "Let's go in my office and sit. We can talk business there."

"Sure." Bobby followed Michael into his office and turned toward Misti, "Why don't you stay out here and have some girl talk." He pointed toward Romano's secretary and pushed the door shut.

"This buildin' is our Spokane billin' operation, the 800 adult enter-tainment calls, the internet porn, and our call center—the whole thing." They moved to a sitting area with a small leather sofa and two club chairs. Romano motioned to one of the chairs. "Have a seat." Romano collapsed onto the small couch.

"Tony was talking about the phone sex last week. Ain't that the same as the internet porn subscriptions we sell?" Bobby leaned back and crossed his legs.

"They're similar, Bobby, but not the same." Michael leaned forward with his elbows planted on his knees. "We're what's called a billin' aggregator by the phone companies. Phone companies must charge their customers for services other companies sell over toll-free 800 numbers. It's somethin' the FCC makes 'em do. Our billin' company has contracts with the big phone companies. We collect thousands of phone numbers from people callin' our 800 services and funnel our charges to those numbers back to the caller's home phone company.

"But here's the truth, Bobby, it's not just phone sex. That's a big part of it, but there's astrology too. You call the 800 line and tell the girl your zodiac sign, and she tells ya what kind of day you're gonna have. And there's sports scores too. You want to see how the Cubbies did in an out-of-town game, so you call the 800 number."

"So you act like a middle-man?" Bobby's eyes seemed lost.

Romano looked his cousin over and thought about growing up as kids. Bobby was part of a new generation of wise guys who were more interested in making money than busting people up.

Romano's Spokane operation had sent nearly one hundred million dollars to Chicago in the most recent twelve months. To produce that level of cash through local loansharking, protection shakedowns, union rigging, and other old-school schemes in Chicago would take a large-scale effort. It would require a much larger endeavor than the scope of the current Chicago operation. Stealing on the internet was the future, and the Family had embraced it with open arms.

"Middle-man? Yeah, that's the crux of it. That's what it looks like to the phone company. Truth be told, we put a bunch of ads in mens and sports magazines advertising the toll-free numbers. When they call in, we grab their phone number and bill them. It's all done by the computer. The mark really gets nothing," Romano chuckled. "Then our charge appears on his phone bill under miscellaneous and other charges. Have you ever looked at your phone bill? Hell, it can go on for ten or fifteen pages. No one reads that crap. We show up on their bill as voice mail service, activation fee, service charge, or other services. There's a bunch of different terms we use to make it look legit. We bill 'em monthly, so on it goes."

"And they pay up?" Bobby shrugged his shoulders.

Romano spoke in a whisper, "Course they do, Bobby, it's their goddam phone bill. If they don't pay, they can get cut off." Romano leaned back and crossed his legs.

"Shit, don't they complain some?"

"Hell yeah, they squeal. Our contract with the Bell companies makes us have a complaint line right here in Spokane. We take their damn calls all day long. But here's the deal, a guy calls to complain, we tell him, 'Sure, maybe we can send you some billin' details, like the porn line you dialed in to. I don't know that might be embarrassin', don't you think?' Truth is most people don't look closely at their phone bills. With all the damn fees the phone company tacks on, a few bucks here, a couple bucks there, nobody notices."

"So you threaten them when they complain about the bill?"

"The girls have a script that breaks it to 'em gently. Most of 'em shut the hell up and let it go."

Bobby slumped in his chair, deep lines creased his forehead. "Billing aggregator, who would have thought. I never heard of such a thing," Bobby paused and rubbed his neck. "What about the porn sites? How do you sell subscriptions for the films I'm making."

"That's the best part, Bobby, where the big money is. We set up these free porn sites with a teaser. To watch a video, ya know, the ones you're makin', they gotta subscribe with a credit card. We tell 'em it's a thirty-day free trial, and the card won't be charged. Once they fall for it and give us the card number, we charge 'em! Thirty, sixty, ninety bucks a month, depending on the site."

"Who come up with that idea?"

"It was Acosta's idea. That there's one smart guy."

"And they give up their credit card like that, even though it's supposed to be free?" Bobby looked unconvinced.

"We tell 'em we need a valid card number to prove they're over eighteen," Romano chuckled. "Suckers."

"What happens when the guys watching porn complain?"

"Sometimes we have to refund, but first we have the talk. You know, 'Sir, your bill shows a charge for an internet subscription service.' We use fake names on the bill, stuff like Golf Review or Western Boating. That way, they ain't embarrassed if the wife sees it on the credit card statement. So they complain, and we say something like, would you like us to send a letter to your home listing the actual sites visited to jog your memory?' You know the girls break it to 'em softly. Sometimes they don't give a shit. I don't know. Maybe it's the single guys. If they don't back down after dealing with our customer service treatment, we refund the charges. Have to, or the credit card company might drop us. But hell, most people just pay their credit card bill, and we never hear from them. If they complain directly to Visa, the bank takes the charge off. Most are too embarrassed to fight it, though."

"Like their phone bills?"

"Pretty much the same business model, Bobby."

"How do you advertise our websites."

"We put ads for the free trials in girlie magazines. But the best way is using internet traffic brokers. I don't understand completely how it works. Somehow the brokers get our sites to pop up on top when people search for porn. Ain't cheap, but works like magic."

Bobby adjusted himself in the chair. 'What's Angela's part in all this?"

"She's down on the second floor. Her people design all the advertisin' for our porn sites and the 800 phone services. She lures the marks in so we can make the kill."

"How much cash is in this porn deal?"

"Grab your chair, Bobby. Our biggest day was six hundred large." He smiled wide with pride.

"Shit, six-hundred grand?" Bobby shook his head slowly from side to side. "That's huge."

"White-collar pays well, and we don't have to go around bustin' guys up."

"You done with the fightin', Mikie?"

"That's what Green Eyes wanted." Michael sighed. The truth was Romano missed the ways of the old days. He fought his way through high school and into his twenties. But the business was changing, and he accepted he needed to change, too.

"What are you doin' with all that cash?" Bobby's eyes were open wide.

"I produced over three hundred million dollars for the Family in Chicago over the past five years, a hundred million in the past year alone. It all comes from the credit card banks and phone companies so it's clean money and looks legit," Romano beamed.

Romano stood and walked over to a large interior window in his office. He looked out over the customer service department on the floor below. Dozens of women sat in tiny cubicles wearing headsets and answering phone calls from a lit-up switchboard.

"Come over here, Bobby. I want you to see this." Michael waited for his cousin to join him at the window. "This is the future of the Family business. We run two shifts because of the time zones. There are over a hundred girls in all. They're trained to handle the complaint calls with compassion and empathy. When it works, we don't have to issue a refund. The money is ours to keep."

Bobby stood at the window and faced the customer service agents sitting in their cubicles on the floor below. "You got some lookers down there, Mikie. Does the wife know about this?"

"Cut the crap, Bobby. You know I don't mix business and pleasure." Romano slid past his desk, dropping into his leather chair. "You wanna cigar?" He opened a box on his desk and offered it to his cousin.

"No thanks, but you go ahead. You got anything to drink?"

Romano grinned and reached into the bottom drawer of his desk. He pulled out a bottle of Tullamore whiskey and two glasses, clanging them together for impact, "Of course, cousin." He poured three fingers into the bottom of each glass and offered one to Bobby. "Raise your glass to Family!"

"Family," Bobby said.

They clinked their glasses together. Bobby slid into a guest chair in front of Romano's desk, the small whiskey glass held in his hand. "You miss the city much?"

Romano thought about the question for a moment. "The people, Bobby. I miss our people. Don't get me wrong, Spokane's an okay place. It's just our people ain't here. Ya know what I mean?"

"I think so, but hell, I never lived nowhere but Chicago. What the hell do I know?"

Romano flicked the long ash hanging precariously on the end of his cigar into the ashtray and spoke in a quiet tone. "You know, I want to get me a manager here so I can spend more time out of the office. Maybe expand on what I got going here. It needs to be a local guy that's smart, someone we can trust."

"Ya got anyone in mind?"

"Not yet. I still gotta run the idea by Acosta." Romano downed his drink and set the glass on his desk. "Enough business talk for now. Whaddya say we go to my place and get some noodles? I'll show you our vacant office space on the way out. It's two floors with no interior walls. You can make it into whatever finished space you need for your studio."

CHAPTER 22

RUBBING HIS TEMPLES, FBI Special Agent Richard Monroe stared at the Ferrari case file open on his desk. Visa's North America Fraud Division had provided thousands of complaints to his team. It appeared that Michael Romano's operation in Spokane ran dozens of porn sites. The sites required a valid credit card to activate free trial memberships. The hitch, Romano's company began charging monthly subscription fees immediately. A month ago, the complaints from customers handled by Visa's North American fraud group abruptly ended, leaving Monroe's investigation at a dead end.

"Agent Monroe, I have a fax for you from the San Francisco office," a young woman from the admin group stood in his doorway.

"Thank you." He reached out and took the twenty-page document from her.

Monroe leaned back in his chair and read the cover letter.

The Pacific Bell fraud prevention group in San Francisco had flagged suspect billing activity from a company in Spokane, Washington. There were excessive customer complaints regarding billing records submitted by Local Exchange Billing, LLC, a billing aggregator.

Agent Monroe pulled a yellow highlighter from his desk drawer and marked the company name. "Romano," he whispered.

An internal report illustrated an unusual trend in toll-free 800 number billing records. Reported calls had been increasing at a high growth rate, and customer complaints showed a similar pattern. The report eventually landed on the desk of Geoff Hunt—VP Controller. Hunt supervised the

Internal Audit function. The value of rejected calls had grown to over three million dollars a month.

Hunt sensed a fraudulent scheme and contacted the San Francisco FBI field office, which undertook a brief investigation. They identified Michael Romano as being involved with the business. Romano appeared in the FBI database as a suspected associate of the Chicago Ferrari crime family. The San Francisco field office director knew about Agent Monroe's task force and forwarded the file to him.

Monroe reached for the phone, heart racing. He dialed Hunt's number.

"Geoff Hunt, speaking,"

"Mr. Hunt, this is Special Agent Monroe with the FBI. Do you have time to speak with me now?" Monroe said authoritatively.

"Of course, what may I do for you."

"I'm in possession of a toll-free 800 number fraud report you sent to the San Francisco field office. I run a task force investigating organized crime. The company submitting suspect billing records, Local Exchange Billing, is on our radar.

"Great, I'm glad you're on it. What can I do to help?"

"Keep doing what you're doing for now while we investigate. And keep sending updates to the report you prepared if possible."

"I can certainly do that. At some point, our company may need to discontinue the billing arrangement with Local Exchange Billing, especially if we determine there is substantial fraudulent activity. We're not too far from that decision now."

"If you do cut them off, please let me know. I have your email on the report cover letter and will forward my contact information. We appreciate your help. I'll be in contact."

Monroe hung up the phone and drafted a short email to the Chicago Field Office Director requesting authority to shift resources from Chicago to Spokane and establish active surveillance on Romano and his company.

CHAPTER 23

ERICK LEFT THE office with plenty of time to arrive at De Rosa's Italian restaurant before noon. Not sure how long his lunch meeting with Spokane Community Bank would take, Candy, rescheduled his afternoon appointments for another day.

Driving through the Palouse, Erick noticed the pink and white flowers had fallen from the lentil plants, and preparations for harvest were underway. Now kissing the edge of age forty, the scent of crops and soil carried him back to childhood memories made on the family farm.

As the eldest son in a line of Swedish farmers going back six generations, Erick was raised to take over the family business when his dad retired. During his second year at WSU, he strayed from Ag Science to Finance courses. He discovered a world much larger than Whitman County. His dad was okay with this because his younger brother Alvin committed to carrying on the family tradition.

The phone call that altered his life forever came on a Saturday afternoon in October, his sophomore year. Most of his fraternity brothers were at an intramural football game. Erick used the opportunity to sneak off with Betty. They were holed up in the third-floor sleeping room he shared with five other guys. While Erick and Betty were lying in bed the phone rang.

"Hello," Erick said.

"Erick, there's been an accident," His dad said, his voice broken and weak.

"What happened? Is everyone all right?" Erick said, a knot turned in his gut.

"Alvin's … Alvin's in the hospital. The tractor rolled on him."

Erick gasped for a breath as though it were he who was trapped. The guilt of making love with Betty while his brother lay in a hospital gurney overwhelmed him. Erick swung his legs to the floor, slipped on his jeans, and walked to the window.

"How bad is it?" Erick asked and cradled his head in his hand.

"He's busted up pretty good. You need to come see him at Sacred Heart. We're there now."

Erick rushed to the Spokane hospital to be at his brother's side. Alvin passed the next day. Weeks later, during Thanksgiving dinner, Dad told Erick he expected him to redirect his studies toward Agriculture. For the remainder of the school year, Erick struggled to square his dream of pursuing a career in finance with his father's demands that he return to farming. His dad never forgave him for his decision to follow his passion for finance.

"Steering his Porsche off the interstate and into Spokane's downtown traffic, Erick pulled himself into the present. He parked in the lot across the street and entered De Rosa's restaurant, still burdened by the memory of his family.

Jimmy Delane greeted Erick at the front door. "Good morning, Erick."

"Morning, Jimmy, it's good to see you." Delane sat on Erick's board of directors. Erick spotted Skip Britain and two other men already seated at the table. "I see my lunch group in the back."

Erick headed toward the rear of the dining room. The group hadn't spotted him, and he tried to read their body language as he approached the booth. Skip seemed stressed—a small crack in his countenance gave him up. He picked up nothing from the others. Erick reached the table and made eye contact with Skip.

"Hey Erick, how are you?" Skip said, standing and reaching to shake Erick's hand. "You already know Jason from the loan process, at least from phone discussions," Skip waved his hand toward Jason, who smiled and lifted his hand in recognition.

Erick nodded politely to Jason.

"Let me introduce you to Michael Romano," Skip said.

Romano rose from his seat, reached across the table, and grasped Erick's hand with authority. "Good to meet you, Erick, especially seein' how we're in business together now." Romano gripped Erick's hand tightly and was slow to release.

Erick shot a puzzled look at Skip. He remembered Skip denied knowing Romano and felt caught in a trap. Romano's words 'in business together' struck a deep, ominous chord. Erick shuddered at the thought and felt himself withdraw from Romano.

The look Romano gave him left Erick uneasy. He searched deep into Romano's dark eyes for a hint of character and found nothing. Romano's eyes were hardened—cold and empty. Expensive clothing covered his body but did nothing to soften his image.

"Likewise," Erick said. He sat in the booth next to Skip.

"We were having a glass of wine. May I pour you one?" Skip asked.

Erick didn't usually drink during the workday but wanted to avoid offending Romano.

"Sure, that sounds good." Erick watched Skip pour the wine and then looked at Romano. "So, Michael, what's your relationship with Spokane Community Bank?"

"I own the bank. Well, at least most of it," Romano sipped his wine.

Shocked by the admission, Erick's pulse rate quickened. Alarm bells rang in his brain and he saw caution signs everywhere. He looked to Skip for help. Skip looked away.

"I had no idea, Michael," Erick paused. He took a deep breath to calm himself. "If you don't mind me asking, what's your primary business focus—finance?"

"Not at all. The bank is an investment. I own Romano Enterprises, it's where I spend the bulk of my time. Most of our business is creatin' data files from orders we take over toll-free 800 lines and then havin' phone companies bill the customer. You familiar with the service?"

"Certainly, it's the billing aggregator model," Erick said.

"Right. We own some payphones, too, mostly around Chicago."

"Chicago?" Erick repeated, surprised.

"Yeah, I'm part of a larger family business," Romano said.

"With cell phone technology advancing, what sort of future do you see in pay phones?" Erick asked.

"Right now, there's a lot of people can't afford a cell or a regular phone. Payphones work for them, and we can charge what the hell we want." Michael raised his hand and leaned over the table toward Erick.

Erick pushed back slightly from the table, the booth backrest pressing against his shoulders.

"I see your point," Erick said quietly. "Most new technologies don't immediately replace the current; it takes time. It can take a long time."

Thinking of what to say next, relief washed over Erick when Jimmy dropped two large pizzas on the table without saying a word. Romano peeled off a slice of sausage pizza and slapped it on a plate in front of him. He picked up a fork and then dropped it back on his napkin and gulped a mouthful of wine instead.

"Tell me how this FCC pool of money works," Romano said.

Hearing Romano's question, Erick's chest tightened. He grew uneasy with Romano's interest in the FCC subsidy program. He wondered how the guy even knew about the money pools. Erick had many tools in his toolbox that he could use to increase Whitman's take from the pools. To properly manage the risk, Erick needed to call the shots. There would be no role for Romano.

"We have CPAs prepare a study of our plant investment and expenses. Then we send the study to a group the government set up years ago. It's called NECA for short. They look at all the studies from over a thousand companies and determine how much each company receives from the money pools. In simple terms, the money pool reimburses us for handling long-distance calls for other companies, and it provides support so we can provide local phone service at a reasonable price in high-cost rural areas.

"It's a complicated process," Erick said cautiously and paused. "But, ultimately, our take from the pool is based on our costs."

"So more cost gets you more money, right?" Romano said almost casually while chewing a mouthful of pizza.

"That sums it up," Erick said, his neck muscles tightening. This discussion had gone too far. Erick didn't need Romano's help running Whitman. He lifted his glass and took a measured sip of wine.

"Whitman spends an extra hundred grand on, say … billin' services. How much cash will they get back from the money pool?" Romano's dark eyes locked on Erick.

"It depends. For example, if we spend an extra hundred thousand dollars on billing services, we might get thirty thousand dollars back from the pool. In some future year, when we file for a local rate increase with the state of Washington, we'll get the rest of it in our local customer rates."

"Shit. You hear that, Skip? Ya, spend a hundred grand and get it all back. It's like Christmas!" Romano pulled a cigar from his suit coat pocket and lit up, turned serious. "How do we get to them guys?"

"What do you mean?" Erick asked slowly in a soft tone.

"The guys decidin' how much cash we get from the money pool? How do we work with them to get more?"

A ripple of dread ran through Erick as he considered Romano's question. "If you're asking what I think you're asking, it's a horrible idea; they'd never go for it."

"Every guy's got his price," Romano sneered. "We just gotta find the right guy. Ain't that right, Jason?"

"That's right, Boss," Jason agreed.

"It's not a blank check. They've got internal controls to prevent fraud," Erick said. "Every extra dollar we pull from the pool means less for someone else. This whole process is watched very closely." Erick rubbed his temples.

"I wanna meet them guys."

"That probably wouldn't go over well. The NECA people are accustomed to meeting with telephone company employees and their cost consultants, not lenders," Erick said, feeling perspiration running down the back of his neck.

"Maybe, maybe not. We'll see." Romano laid his cigar in an ashtray and dug into his pizza.

Turning into the Whitman Communications parking lot a few minutes past two in the afternoon, Erick's head still pounded from his uncomfortable lunch conversation with Michael Romano. Erick couldn't wrap his mind around why the bank owner would take such an active interest in the telephone business. Romano asked about the mechanics of the FCC money pools Whitman received. It was apparent he read the loan proposal and did his homework. Romano acted more like an investor than a lender. Why?

Walking into the Whitman building, Erick pulled the cell phone from his pocket and dialed Skip.

"Skip here."

"Hey, Skip. Are you back in the office?" Erick felt rushed.

"I am. What can I do for you?"

"It's about Michael Romano. I thought you told me a while back that you didn't know him. The guy gives me an uneasy feeling." Passing Candy's desk, Erick forced a smile and pushed his office door closed behind him.

"My engagement agreement with Michael Romano prevents me from really discussing him or his business with anyone. Now that you're in a business arrangement with him and have met, I have more latitude."

"That sounds ominous. When did you start doing work for Romano?" Erick dropped into his office chair.

"It's not a long story. The founder of Spokane Community Bank passed away a while back. I helped the estate's executor find a buyer for their stock. I ran into Michael at a Chamber event, and he was interested in buying into the business. He had the cash. I've done some local legal work for him here in Spokane since that time."

"So Romano owns the bank?" Erick sat up straight.

"A controlling interest."

"And you knew this all along—what the hell, Skip?" Erick asked, anger eroding his composure.

"Look, Erick, after the Farmers Bank loan fell through, you were out of options. Either I let your deal die, along with your hopes and dreams, or I introduce you to Romano and all the baggage he brings with him. I chose the latter. Would you have wanted it any other way?"

"I'm not certain … I guess not." Erick accepted his ambition and myopic focus on closing the Whitman deal brought him to Romano's doorstep.

"I suppose I may have misled you a bit. As I said, omitting my relationship with Romano is driven by my engagement letter with him. My hands were tied. At the same time, I wanted to get you the financing you needed to close on the Whitman company."

"Look, I know how the business he's in works. I'm telling you, payphones and billing aggregation doesn't generate a ton of cash. Not the level where you would be buying banks anyway. How much did the bank stock cost him?"

"You know I'm bound by client confidentiality, so I can't discuss it directly. I can tell you the estate probate filing with Washington State indicated a fair market value of twenty million dollars, plus or minus. That much is public record."

"Where'd Romano get the money?" Erick's head pounded.

"I recall the funds were wired to my escrow account from a regional bank in Chicago."

"Chicago? Romano mentioned something about a family business in Chicago. What sort of business are they in?" Erick climbed from his chair and paced his office floor.

"I don't really know. My involvement with Romano has been local in nature, mostly employment issues and contract review matters for the bank."

"Look, cash the FCC distributes from the money pool is the golden goose for companies like Whitman. The system is easy to cheat, and it can be tempting to do so. There's lots of gray area, and I'm comfortable operating there, but I can't have someone like Romano weighing in." Erick massaged the knot in his neck.

"I don't believe Michael has any interest in managing a telephone company. He's a direct kind of guy, and sometimes his questions are unfiltered. I wouldn't read too much into it, though."

"Let's keep it that way," anger filtered through Erick's speech.

"Of course," Skip said, "but you need to accept Romano as a sort of silent partner, much as you would any significant creditor. He's a key stakeholder in your business."

"I can live with that," Erick dropped into his desk chair, exhaling deeply, and disconnected the call.

Taking a long draw from his water bottle, Erick considered Romano's Chicago ties. He wondered what type of business they were involved in.

CHAPTER 24

WHILE SURVEYING THE rooms of her new apartment, the sting of leaving her Grandmother's Seattle Queen Anne home hit Amy hard. Her new place in Pullman, located in a twelve-unit apartment building on the corner of Fir Street and 14th Avenue, was a comfortable walk from the WSU campus. The units were popular with graduate students and young professionals.

Amy's moving crew carefully maneuvered eclectic Japanese furnishings up the stairs and into apartment 22. The petite Amy sat in the corner in a velvet side chair, directing the burly, coverall-clad men to where she wanted each item placed. She had shipped the heirloom pieces from her grandmother's Seattle home to Pullman. Holding the furnishings close by eased the pain of relocating.

Amy closed her eyes for a moment and drifted back to her first night in Erick's rental house. The memory of being in the hot tub with Erick resurfaced. When his bare skin rubbed against hers, she shivered in delight. The passion rose until desire consumed the both of them. Remembering Erick's warm breath in her ear brought the moment back to life. The sound of furniture dropping to the floor slipped into her subconscious.

Amy's eyes shot open and cut across the room. "Careful," she chided the men, "that cabinet is eighteenth-century and irreplaceable."

Two weeks had passed since Amy and Erick arrived in Pullman. Each night, they made love with greater fervor than the night before. She had fallen hard but wasn't sure Erick felt the same. It was as though he hid his feelings behind that stoic Swedish façade.

Amy pulled her cell phone from her purse and called Alison. She craved the sound of Ali's voice.

"What's up, girlfriend?" Alison said.

"I'm moving into my apartment today, Ali. I miss you."

"What's wrong? Is everything still good with you and Erick? Now that you're officially an item!"

"I guess maybe I'm a little homesick. I was thinking about guys from my past. You know, looking for a pattern." Amy watched a worker carry her nightstand through the living room and disappear into the bedroom.

"You fall for older men. That's the pattern I see. You've been serious with three guys, and they were all older. And they were all risk takers, bordering on being bad boys."

"Stephan wasn't a bad boy," Amy pictured her high school tennis coach in her mind.

"Come on, Amy. The guy was in his mid-twenties and slept with you when you were still in high school. That's pretty bad and risky! And Zach was a bad boy through and through. He even corrupted you with that hacking group."

"You know, I wanted to move to China with him after he got his Ph.D.," Amy stared out the window, picturing the tall, muscular Chinese student, and remembered the stabbing pain she felt when he left for China. "And, if you remember, I started hacking in high school. It was my main hobby."

"I do remember, Amy, but Zach's hacking group at UW brought your skills to a whole new level."

"My pattern has been to get sucked in by an older guy and then dumped," Amy said in a defeated tone.

"Don't look at it that way. You didn't rush into things with Erick. He's different. You've known him a long time. You two seem good together. I feel upbeat about where you're headed together."

"I should leave the past alone," Amy said quietly. "I need to get back to my movers. Thanks for the pep talk."

"Love you. I'll try to come down and visit soon," Ali said, her tone soft and soothing.

Apartment 22, on Fir Street, would hold Amy's cherished possessions and provide cover from nosey Whitman Communications employees until she and Erick were ready to make their relationship public. The Company would mail routine HR documents to the apartment and assume that's where she lived. She needed an address for appearances. All of her free time would be spent with Erick.

CHAPTER 25

"**E**RICK, I'VE GOT Michael Romano on line two," Candy crackled through the speaker.

What the hell does he want? Erick hadn't left Romano any indication that he would have an active role in running Whitman Communications. Erick reached for the handset and punched line two. "Michael, what may I do for you?"

"I have an idea on how we can boost revenue at Whitman."

"What do you mean?" Erick twisted the phone cord around his index finger.

"I met some guys at a pay phone conference a while back. Turns out we have mutual acquaintances in New York. These guys at the conference bought a small phone company down in Louisiana a few years ago," Romano paused. "I asked them what we could do to get more from the FCC money pool, ya know, without standin' out like a sore thumb. They said my billin' company could bill Whitman for software consultin' services ... they thought two hundred grand a month wouldn't be outrageous given the size of Whitman."

"Michael, I can't pay an invoice when no work is done," Erick's chest tightened.

"Set it up so some of Whitman's monthly billin' changes run through my company. We can train my customer service girls to handle it. You need to set up the paperwork so it all looks legit."

Erick walked over and closed his office door, "The Feds will challenge us on this, even if the work is legitimate. They're all over these sorts of agreements." Erick's blood pressure rose, sensing Romano pushing him into a blatantly illegal arrangement.

"I'm tryin' to work with ya here. Chicago wants some return on their investment. This we gotta do to keep them happy."

"Who's in Chicago?" Erick asked. He looked to make sure his door remained closed. In the next instant, he regretted asking the question. No good could come of it.

"That ain't important. I told you before my business here in Spokane is part of a larger operation run out of Chicago. You and me need to make this work. We don't want them guys comin' out to help us."

"Look, I'm not going to pay two hundred grand a month for nothing," Erick said, anger flushing his face.

"It's your choice, play the game or walk away," Romano raised his voice.

"What the hell is that supposed to mean?" Erick barked.

"We own the bank, so we own your loan. You got covenants under the loan, and you already fuckin' broke 'em."

"I don't know what you're talking about. We're in full compliance with the loan requirements," Erick said, panic running through him.

"Really? Whitman's been around since the 1930s, are you sure you got up-to-date right-of-way agreements for all the telephone poles you got out in the farm fields? Cause the covenants say you got to have all the proper permits and agreements to operate. All of them."

"That's a technicality," Erick said in a defeated tone. Whitman had thousands of telephone poles spread throughout the county. Erick knew he couldn't produce a right-of-way agreement for every telephone pole in their plant records—no phone company could.

"Maybe so, but that's all I need to call the note due immediately or raise your interest rate a hundred-fifty points. Are you ready to deal with that?"

Perspiration ran down Erick's face, and his head pounded. He remained silent.

"That's what I thought," Romano said flatly. "I'll bill you two-hundred-large every month. We'll start this month—August. I'm gonna send half to Chicago. You and me split what's left, fifty grand each. I'll wire your cut to a bank in the Cayman Islands. Check with Skip Britain. He knows how to set up the account, so it's private."

"What's the split based on?" Erick asked.

"Does it matter?"

"I suppose not."

"It's how we do things. Pretty damn generous, don't you think? Twenty-five percent for doing fuckin' nothin'. Well, almost nothin'."

Erick bit his tongue until it stung.

"In the meantime, you work up an air tight agreement between our companies. Got it?"

"Alright," Erick said reluctantly. "Is that all?"

"One more thing," Romano's speech rang deep and clear. "I'll be taking Jason's seat on the board. He's busy with the bank and I need to keep close tabs on what's going on with Whitman."

Erick's chest tightened; there seemed no room for negotiation with Romano. "Okay, I'll take care of it," he caved.

CHAPTER 26

"**E**RICK, I HAVE Mr. Carlson from Cooperative Rural Bank for you when you're ready," Candy announced on the intercom.

"Yes, please show him in," Setting aside the fiber optic feasibility study he was reading, Erick stood from his desk and walked to the door to greet his guest. "Hi there, Dan, pleased to meet you," he extended his hand and shook Dan's.

"It's a pleasure to meet you, Erick. Thank you for taking a meeting with me. I'm out doing my quarterly visits with clients in our western region, so this works out well."

"My pleasure, Dan. I'm happy to visit with you." Erick returned to his desk and motioned for Dan to sit in a guest chair across from him.

"This is my first trip to Whitman County; the countryside out here is very scenic," Dan said.

"I'm fortunate to live in the Palouse. I grew up here on a wheat farm and went to WSU."

"Then buying Whitman is a homecoming of sorts for you."

"Indeed," Erick said and put on his most sincere smile. "So, what exactly is it you wanted to talk about?"

"Mostly, the products and services we offer the telecommunications industry and ways we may be of service to Whitman Communications."

The banker appeared to be in his late twenties and eager to please his prospective client.

"That sounds good, Dan. As you probably know, we recently closed on the company with LTE last month. Spokane Community Bank provided the needed loan to close the deal." Erick paused and glanced at the fiber optic study on his desk. "We have begun a project to take more of our plant underground and run fiber optic cable to our customers—a part of our broadband initiative. We'll be able to fund about a third of the cost through internally generated funds. We could use a line-of-credit facility to carry us through the construction phase."

"How much is the total project?" Dan asked, furiously jotting notes on a pad of paper.

"Around thirty million dollars, we're looking at a short-term line of credit of twenty million."

"Do you have a business plan with pro forma financial statements?"

He didn't even blink at the twenty million, Erick thought. "Absolutely … My accounting staff worked up a feasibility study." He slid the financial package across his desk toward Dan and smiled warmly.

Dan flipped through the package for a minute or so. "It looks like most of what we need is here. How soon would you like the line of credit established?"

"I think four to six weeks would be fine. Is that time frame something you can work with?"

"I can try to put it on the fast track; we normally take two to three months to get funded."

"I'd appreciate that."

"Let me review the package with our loan committee when I return to the Denver office, and I'll let you know. When we get approval, there are a few documents I'll need for you and certain officers on your board of directors to sign before we can fund. While I'm here, let me ask you some questions that will help me complete the application for you. There's a monthly fee on the balance available to draw. That can be managed by reducing the amount immediately available to Whitman. What do you think?"

"The project cost is a bit lumpy, so we should have the full twenty million available immediately."

"Alright, what about access? How do you want to request funds, by a phone call or direct wire?"

"Direct wire."

"Okay, the maximum per wire?"

"The balance available." Erick leaned back and sipped his coffee, took a deep breath.

"Will you provide us a list of approved accounts and routing numbers to which funds may be wired?"

"Is it necessary to restrict it to specific accounts?" Erick asked. Erick needed the flexibility to send money where it was needed.

"No, but the bank recommends that you do so."

"I'd rather not impede my flexibility to pay a vendor directly, so let's say no for now."

"The bank does require dual-control, with one employee to approve each wire and a second to initiate the transfer. You may have more than two employees on the list, but each transfer requires two separate individuals with bank credentials."

"Let's put me down as one and our CFO Amy Summers as the second."

"Anyone else?"

Erick paused for a moment, a plan still formulating in his mind.

"I think we should add a board member. Let's put down Michael Romano."

"Okay, anyone else?"

"That should do it. Candy can get you Amy's contact information on your way out. I'll get Michael's for you later." Erick grinned slyly. Having Romano on the account may prove helpful in the future.

Before leaving, Dan reviewed a slew of products offered by the bank. The bank had a business checking account available and a corporate Visa card program for telephone company employees traveling on business. As Dan spoke, Erick piled the brochures on the corner of his desk but paid little attention. The instant access to twenty million dollars in cash by electronic wire was the extent of his interest.

While Dan continued to drone on about the bank's products, Erick pulled a small journal from his desk drawer. He added the twenty million available from Cooperative Rural Bank under the column heading: *Alvin*.

CHAPTER 27

ERICK SHIFTED HIS gaze from the law office window facing Mt. Spokane back to Skip and then to the window again. Skip had lied about knowing Romano. The anger of betrayal burned within Erick.

"Seriously, Skip, how can you represent Spokane Community Bank *and* Whitman Communications in good conscience? That feels like a pretty big conflict of interest?"

"The bar might view it that way." Skip stroked his beard. "But in this case, the bank and Whitman are on the same team. More directly, you and Michael are on the same team. You may not like it, but that's the reality we find ourselves in."

"Romano threatened to call the loan due immediately if I didn't enter into a contract with his billing company, LEB. That sort of agreement is not inherently illegal, but the two hundred grand he wants to bill Whitman every month crosses the line. The fifty grand he says he'll kickback to me each month is way over the line." Anger sparked in Erick's tone.

"Look, Erick, this isn't how I wanted your deal to go down. I really do mean that." Skip paused, looking contrite. "Romano's got his hooks in me deep. I had no choice. You know him well enough now. There's no going against him. I can sit here and tell you how sorry I am all day long, but that changes nothing. The painful reality is, it's in your best interest to find a way to make this arrangement work."

"What's Romano got on you?" Erick asked, his forehead creased in worry. *Romano's got nothing on me for now.*

"Unfortunately, it's not one thing. I've stepped over the legal line any number of times for Romano. Each time I did it, he compensated me generously. After enough time went by, I was tangled in his net. For me, there's no turning back.

"There's still time for you, Erick. You can still walk away. If that's what you want, do it today. I'm certain Romano will buy your piece of Whitman at a discount. You haven't broken any laws yet. Once you cut that first check to LEB, you're screwed—stuck in a trap you can't escape. In all seriousness, today is the day to come to that decision."

Erick turned his gaze from the window back to Skip. "That's bullshit. I'm not willing to walk away from Whitman. I've got too much skin in the game. I need to somehow find a way to make this work, to control Romano's expectations ... I don't know how, but I'll find a way. What about his family connections in Chicago?" Beads of sweat formed and ran down Erick's neck.

"I've never met them. My business has always been local legal work, mostly employment law and filings for the bank."

"Do you know who they are?" Erick asked.

"I know a little about them. I'm not at liberty to discuss the matter. For now, you should assume the worst. If there comes a time when Romano believes you need to know more about his Chicago connections, he'll tell you."

"Not at liberty? What the hell, Skip." Erick leaned forward in anger.

"Sorry. When it comes to Romano, there are certain lines I simply cannot cross," Skip said and averted his eyes away from Erick.

"Do you have an account in the Caymans?" Erick asked cautiously.

"I do. It's in the name of a trust I formed domiciled there. Romano likes to run payments through shell companies on the Island," Skip paused. "Are you ready to start the process to open your account?"

"Sure," Erick said reluctantly. His heart beat quicker. Erick knew the IRS required US citizens to disclose foreign bank accounts when filing their income taxes. If Erick made such a disclosure, at some future point in time the IRS may ask where the funds arose from. If he didn't disclose the account, he would be in serious legal trouble should the IRS ever discover the funds. It was a catch-22. There were no easy answers.

"I have some forms for you to sign to open an account with the Bank of London in the Caymans." Skip handed Erick a pen.

Erick took the pen and carefully signed each page marked with a *sign here* yellow sticky note.

"Once I return these documents to the bank, the new account officer will call you. He'll walk you through some security access questions and assign you an account number. They'll email you the number as well."

Erick pushed the signed papers to Skip and slumped in his chair. "Where do you think we're headed with all of this?"

"As your attorney, I think you're in a pickle. Escape from guys like Romano and the organization he's a part of isn't possible. The best you can do is manage their demands on your business," Skip paused. "You need to recognize that those demands will increase over time. That's why mobsters get busted—they get greedy. They push for more and more, not fully realizing the risk, until one day, the house of cards collapses, and they find themselves behind bars.

"I'd advise you to look into the future. If you don't like what you see, devise a plan to disappear."

"Really? To where?"

"You're a smart guy, Erick. It'll be a one-way ticket, so pick a place you'll be happy to stay a long while."

"Do you have a plan?"

"Whoa there, buddy," Skip said, holding both arms out with his palms facing Erick. "Tell no one, leave no tracks. My destination must remain my most closely guarded secret. Same for you."

Erick nodded and let out a deep breath.

Back in his Whitman office, partially formed images swirled in Erick's head: Romano's dark, lifeless eyes, the double-crossing Skip, FCC auditors pouring over his books, FBI agents in the lobby, passport photos, and a look of grave disappointment on Amy's face. "Where to go? Where?" Erick whispered.

Erick tried to focus. His life could be on the line. Staring at his calculator, Erick wondered how long until Whitman Communications would crash. Of course, it couldn't be calculated.

CPA firms were well-equipped to detect unusual trends in expense levels. They would run fraud detection tests as a part of the annual financial audit. Undoubtedly, an auditor would catch Romano's LEB billing fraud at some point.

The Fed's monitor certain wire transfers to foreign banks. Recurring deposits from Romano into a Cayman account might garner unwanted attention fairly quickly—especially if Romano was under surveillance. An IRS investigation might follow. Erick would have no good answers to their questions.

Erick's escape plan needed to be pragmatic and as uncomplicated as feasible. Allowing him to disappear at a moment's notice. Extended family and friends would be left behind, unknowing and unaware of him alive and living well in a foreign land. He'd need travel documents under an assumed name and lots of money. And a place to hide locally while he waited for transportation out of the country. So many deceptions, so many lies.

What about Amy? *Will she come with me?* He wasn't sure. Her involvement in the Romano scam had been minimal, and she might not feel forced to run. As a CPA, she could be held culpable—a professional who should have detected the fraud. If she came clean, she might be let off the hook. *Especially if she turns on me.*

His personal bank account held nearly three hundred thousand dollars. He'd pick up six hundred thousand yearly for his share of Romano's billing fraud. If it continued for five years, he'd have another three million in the Caymans. *Will that do? Am I thinking big enough?*

"Erick, I have Richard Wolfe from the Bank of London on line two?" Candy announced over the intercom.

"Thanks, I'll pick it up," he sat up in his chair and stared at the blinking light, "This is Erick Olson."

"Mr. Olson, this is Richard Wolfe with the Bank of London in the Cayman Islands. How are you this afternoon?"

"Fine, thank you. I've been expecting your call."

"Very well then, I will send you a secure email with login instructions to our website. After you have logged on, there will be some security questions, and you will establish a password. I must warn you, the password must be sixteen characters, and the rules render the result quite nonsensical. I would recommend you commit both the account number and password to memory. And it's imperative that you place a written copy in an encrypted file or bank safe deposit box that the executor of your estate will have access to," he paused a moment. "Should the need arise. Otherwise, the funds might be inaccessible by you or your agent."

The word executor hung over Erick like a dark cloud. The banker's tone suggested he had dealt with executors in the past. He knew Cayman Island bankers dealt with a lot of dirty money brought to the islands by shady people. Many of those people died when they crossed the wrong person. That's what Romano was to him, the wrong person. Erick had no doubt Romano would kill him if he double-crossed their organization. This was a new paradigm for the *Financial Wunderkind*, being forced to sneak around the world to hide money in offshore accounts. It would take time to settle his nerves.

"Mr. Olson, are you still with me?"

"Yes … yes, I can do that," Erick said, coughing up the words.

"Champion. Now, there's the small matter of your initial deposit. How much will it be, and in what form? The minimum to open the account is one hundred thousand US dollars."

"I'll wire the hundred thousand to the account once my password is established. The wire will be initiated from my personal bank in Seattle. There will be monthly deposits thereafter."

"Very well, Mr. Olson. You should have the secure email soon. If I may be of service at any time, please call me personally, twenty-four-seven. It's my pleasure to serve you in any way I may."

Erick hung up the phone. Leaning back in his chair, he took in the view of the Palouse hills. Stalks of golden wheat waved to him in the gentle breeze. The money part of his plan began to form in his head. Leaving all his cash in the Cayman bank used by Romano seemed risky. Romano might have people on the payroll inside the Bank of London. Erick resolved to leave only the minimum required balance in the Cayman bank. Any cash above the required balance would be wired to an offshore bank in Hong Kong or Belize. Both countries offered privacy aspects similar to those of the Cayman Islands. The untraceable funds would remain parked safely until he disappeared. For the time being, Erick would keep Amy in the dark to protect her.

PART III

The Walls Closing In

Faster, faster, faster—
I spin.
Pulled away from—
all I know.

Spinning, spinning, spinning—
a centrifuge.
Extracting my soul
consuming it whole.

All that remains are bits
of bone and flesh. And greed,
the glue that bound us.

—Erick Olson

CHAPTER 28

August 2000

PUSHING HIS WORK aside, Erick answered the ringing phone. It was 6 p.m., and most employees had left for the day. "Whitman Communications, may I help you?"

"Is that you, Erick? It's me."

Erick recognized Sara's soft alto the instant it rolled into his ear. The sound soothed his nerves, as it always had.

"Sara, you're working late. What is it, after eight out there?" Erick said, glancing at his watch. He hadn't heard a word from Sara since closing the Whitman Communications deal. This didn't feel like a social call. He tapped his finger nervously on the desktop.

"Erick, if anyone ever asks," Sara whispered in a low tone, "this call never happened."

"That sounds ominous." Erick sat up straight. His heart beat quicker.

"Something's going on," Sara paused. "Something that has me frightened for you," the words seemed to catch in her throat.

"What is it?" His senses filled with panic. He recognized the serious lawyer tone. She had used it many times in their past.

"The FBI paid us a visit, Erick," she paused again. "Seriously, Erick, they asked about the Whitman Communications deal ... specifically, about you and the financing. They asked if there was any bad blood between you and the LightPoint people and wanted to know what we knew about a Farmers Bank loan falling through. They were guarded about details of their investigation and didn't share any useful information."

"Are you certain they aren't looking into something involving LTE, government contracts perhaps?" Erick felt his blood pressure rising.

"It's you they're interested in, Erick," Sara paused. "They knew about the Missouri motel propane tank explosion—that you and I were staying there on business. The agent asked about your relationship with the LightPoint group. I'm worried for you, Erick. It seems that they're trying to link the plane crash to the propane explosion. Crazy, right?"

"Where do you think they're headed with this," Erick said, anxiety breaking through his calm surface.

"I don't know. Something's caught their attention—something serious. Our executive team is pretty worked up about the visit. It's not every day the FBI shows up unannounced at our doorstep. Our General Counsel had me review the files related to the Whitman deal. I don't see anything out of the ordinary ... Do you have any idea why the FBI would show up here now?"

"Not a clue." Erick had a pretty clear idea but wasn't going to tell Sara. He wondered if the LTE execs insisted she call him to probe for information. Even recognizing the closeness of their past, Sara's loyalty would be with LTE now. Sadness gripped his heart.

"They asked about someone named Michael Romano." Sara sounded strong but hesitant. "We don't know him and told them as much ... Who is Romano?" she demanded.

"Romano has a billing company in Spokane. We have a consulting services contract with him," Erick said matter of factly. "What'd they ask about him?" If they were onto Romano's involvement, how long would it be until they discovered the billing scam?

"They wanted to know if we came in contact with him during the deal ... of course, we hadn't and told them so," Sara paused. "They wanted to know what we knew about Spokane Community Bank too. All we could tell them was that the bank financed your acquisition."

"Anything else?" Erick asked, wanting the conversation to end.

"I'll remind you, Erick. Don't lie to the FBI. It's a felony ... be careful."

"I will, and I appreciate you calling me with the heads-up."

"Of course, Erick. I don't want anything bad to happen to you."

Erick put the phone down. A tingle moved up his back, leaving a chill in its path. He needed to think and felt a headache coming on. Hell, he needed a drink.

Is it time for the escape plan, time to bail? Erick didn't think so. Besides, his plan was only now coming together. The need to disappear would appear when blood was on the floor, or at least the threat of blood. Then he would be willing to pull the ripcord on his life.

"Erick, everything alright?" Amy asked from Erick's open doorway.

Thinking he was alone, Erick was startled by the sound of another person. He looked up and met Amy's eyes. Concentrating on his conversation with Sara, he hadn't heard Amy at the door.

"Yeah, I was on a call with LTE. Anyone else still working in the building?"

"No. The two of us, that's it. The cleaning people show up in an hour or so."

Erick stood, walked over to Amy, placed his hands on her tiny waist, and brought her close to him. He needed Amy now more than ever and couldn't imagine pulling the ripcord without her. Erick kissed her long and sweet. Her moist lips were luxurious, like slipping into a warm bath. He held her tightly to his chest—too tight.

"Hey, I can't breathe," Amy whispered. "What did you want to do tonight?"

"Let's get something to eat."

Leaning against a stack of pillows, Erick set his laptop on the nightstand. Amy inched over and rested her head on his chest. The phone call from Sara had spooked him.

"What would you do if the FBI showed up unannounced with a list of questions?" Erick asked, his expression turned serious.

"Like in the movies?" Amy looked puzzled.

"Yeah."

"I don't know, probably be honest with them," she paused and pushed the hair away from her eyes, "It's about that call today, isn't it?"

"Amy, you need to keep this between the two of us. I haven't figured out what's going on, let alone how to plan for it."

"What happened?" She demanded and sat up in bed.

"The call was from Sara. She called to tell me the FBI showed up today on their campus asking questions."

Amy groaned at the sound of the other woman's name. "What were they looking for?" she asked, frowning.

"Mostly, they were interested in me and our financing for the purchase of Whitman ... It may have something to do with the lender. I don't know." Erick shrugged his shoulders.

"You're scaring me, Erick. Is there something you haven't told me?" She leaned back against her pillows and pulled the covers up to her neck as if to cloak her from whatever bad news he delivered.

Erick desperately wanted to confess to her all that he had done— the loan from the mob, the billing agreement with Romano—all of it. Her almond eyes pleaded for him to tell her everything. *If I tell her, she'll be complicit in the fraud.* Erick knew she took to heart the CPA ethics rules she swore to uphold. If he came clean, she might turn on him, stop loving him. As much as he needed her in his life, he wasn't confident she could be trusted to follow him down the unsavory path he traveled.

Erick looked into Amy's eyes, sensing her fear. "No. Of course not," he said quietly, trying to comfort her. "It's probably nothing."

CHAPTER 29

LEANING ON CANDY'S credenza while she typed a brief memo, Erick watched Amy working in her office across the hall. Her black hair tied in a ponytail painted a sharp contrast against the white blouse she wore. Amy looked up and caught him staring. A smile crossed her face and lit up Erick's morning–a warm tremor flooded his body.

Candy's phone rang with a call on Erick's line. "Erick Olson's office, Candy speaking. May I help you?" After a moment, she covered the mouthpiece, "It's Michael Romano on your line."

"Okay, I'll take it in my office." Erick hurried to his desk and picked up the handset. "Good morning, Michael." He braced himself for more unsolicited advice from Romano on how Erick should manage *his* company.

"I've been lookin' over this capital budget of yours. You got us spendin' ten million a year on new plant and equipment. That right?" Romano said.

"That's about it, Michael. We must upgrade our plant over the next ten years to provide faster and more reliable internet service." Erick pulled the capital budget folder from his file drawer and laid it on the desk.

"I've been talkin' to my pals in New York. They say there's a better way to handle buyin' that much equipment."

Erick's back tightened, "I don't follow."

"We're settin' up an equipment supply company based in Chicago— Telcom Equipment Supply. I got people there that will establish invoicin' arrangements with your vendors once you send me a list. Whitman will order all of its equipment through Telcom Equipment Supply."

"That's a bad idea, Michael. The regulators will expect cost savings if we use a captive supply company." Erick held up his mug and silently begged Candy to please bring him more coffee. His head throbbed. Michael had that effect on him.

"The guys back east are doin' it with that phone company they own in Louisiana. It won't stand out 'cause Whitman don't own the supply company. We'll keep the markup reasonable, say twenty percent. But hell, twenty points on ten million—that's two million a year. I'll kick back a quarter to you. That's half a mill."

"It's reckless, Michael." Candy handed him the mug of steaming coffee. He mouthed 'thank you' and walked to the window.

Erick looked out over his beloved Palouse hills and tried to think of a way to steer Romano in a different direction. But then again, an extra half-million dollars flowing into his Cayman account each year was an enticing offer. Suddenly embracing the supply company concept, Erick shuddered at his willingness to trade his reputation so easily for money. He had already stepped into deep water with Romano's billing company, so why not take one more step?

A fault deep within him shifted like a tectonic movement of the Earth's crust. In an instant, he felt himself slide away from the light toward Romano's dark eyes. He didn't know what would come next; each step he took would take him further from the man he once was. Working with Romano changed everything—there would be no returning to his old life. There would be no redemption. The days would be shorter and the nights darker as Romano's grip grew ever tighter.

"Ya still there?" Romano demanded.

Erick took a deep breath and exhaled slowly as he considered what he would say next. He needed to offer Romano something sweet enough to get him off his back and out of his business for a while.

"I can make this work," a nervous jitter ran through him. Erick paused, running numbers and complex financial calculations in his head. "Here's the deal, though, the supply company can't have one customer. I know two family-owned phone companies in the Midwest that will jump at the chance to participate in this supply deal. They'll want to see a financial benefit, though. We'll need a different split with them—one half for their companies.

"They buy about the same amount of equipment as Whitman?"

"Combined, I'd guess they're around ten million, so yes." Erick grimaced, still shocked by the sudden shift in his moral compass.

"See if they're interested, then get back to me. Meanwhile, send me the vendor list for Whitman."

"It won't be difficult to sell this to the two companies I'm considering. They're greedy as hell and already cheat the FCC money pool. Let me draft an agreement between Whitman and your supply company that'll pass muster. The other two companies can use the same template. I'll get something for you next week." Erick felt the walls close toward him ever so slightly and recognized he was the master of his own undoing. He accepted there was no one to blame but himself.

Undoubtedly, the independent auditors he engaged to review Whitman's annual financial statements would question the large software consulting services contract with Romano's company. The inflated equipment purchases would add to that pressure. Even in that unfavorable light, he did the mental math. The billing scheme dumped six hundred grand into his Cayman account each year, and the equipment kickback would bump that by another three-quarters of a million dollars. The downside would be an accelerated timeline when the scheme ultimately collapsed. But Romano wouldn't know that.

Erick's thoughts turned to his favorite accounting professor. When it came to grades, the professor had always joked that he had his price, but none of the students could meet it. Erick's price had been met, and it didn't feel good. In time, Romano's equipment supply company would draw unwanted attention from the Feds. In the same breath, he couldn't chase the image from his mind of the extra cash flowing into his Cayman account. The die had been cast. When the time came, all that remained was to collect the spoils and disappear into the darkness of night.

CHAPTER 30

HANGING UP THE phone after his call with Erick Olson, Michael Romano flipped open his Rolodex and dialed a number.

"Gino, I got a job for ya," Michael said, tapping his pinky ring on the desk.

Romano's business in Spokane was, by and large, white-collar. Still, from time to time, people needed encouragement to perform, and nothing got the job done better than a little intimidation. At six-foot-four and two-hundred-twenty pounds, Gino Russo filled that role nicely.

"What is it, Boss?"

"I need ya to go down by Pullman and keep an eye on Whitman Communications for me. It's in a podunk town called Colfax. Get a motel in town, then stake out the company parking lot. Keep tabs on who the hell's comin' and goin'. Take the camera and the long lens. Get some pictures."

"Whadaya looking for, Boss."

"Not sure, maybe people that look like they don't belong there, ya know? I got a feelin'. The company owner may not be tellin' me every-thin'," Romano said, massaging his bicep. "He's been pushing back on some changes I want to make. Now, all of a sudden, he's Mr. Cooperation. Makes me wonder what the hell he's up to."

"Like suits or the competition?"

"Yeah, anythin' that don't fit. Mostly, keep an eye on Olson. He's the owner. Tall blond guy. I'll send you a picture of him. Keep a log of when he leaves the buildin'. Take note of the time and when he gets back, too. Snap some pictures of anyone he's with."

"Do you want me to break in and set up some ears?"

"Not yet. That may be next, dependin' on what you find out."

"Got it, Boss."

"Good, call every day. And don't camp out in the parkin' lot. Keep your distance, and move around. I don't want to spook 'im."

After hanging up, Michael poured two fingers of whiskey over ice in a glass and wondered if someone had got to Olson.

CHAPTER 31

POKING HIS HEAD quietly into Amy's office at quitting time, Erick took a long look. He enjoyed watching her subtle movements. The way she rolled her wrist when writing and her chest lifting gently with each breath. He loved all of her. "Hey, ready to get something to eat?"

"Sure, I can wrap up now. Are you thinking Pedro's?"

"Of course," he chuckled. Erick knew nine of ten times she'd pick the family-owned Mexican restaurant. He watched her delicate hands close the laptop and store it in her backpack.

"Ready!" she said, joining him in the hall.

Erick set the building alarm and held the door for Amy as they left for his Porsche. Pulling from the parking lot, Erick noticed a dark sedan turning onto the road behind him. Its headlights were off.

Twenty minutes later, they were in Pullman with the sedan still following several car lengths behind them. Erick turned left onto Main Street and stopped at a red light with the sedan two cars back. He strained to make out the driver in his rearview mirror.

Nothing.

The phone call from Sara last Friday flooded Erick's mind. Could the FBI be following me? Romano? His chest tightened. He accelerated after making a sharp right on Hamilton. Then another right on Center Street—the sedan matched his turns and stayed one hundred feet behind.

"You missed the turn?" Amy said, a puzzled look on her face.

"I think someone's following us." Erick turned to make eye contact. Amy frowned.

The signal at Center and Washington turned yellow, and he stepped lightly on the brakes. Then, as the light turned red, he floored the accelerator, shooting through the intersection. His heart fluttered as anxiety spread through his body. *Who the hell is it?*

Amy turned and looked out the rear window. "Do you think it's the FBI?"

"I don't know." Erick paused, tapping his thumbs nervously on the steering wheel. "I guess it could be."

"Why would they be following us?"

"I seriously don't know, Amy. It may have something to do with the call I got from Sara. Who knows."

Amy bit her lower lip. "You're scaring me, Erick."

"He turned. He's gone, didn't make the light. It'll be okay, Amy." Erick checked the mirror again. The black sedan was gone, "Sorry if I frightened you." He relaxed his posture and took a deep breath. The danger had passed.

"How can we find out who that was?" Amy's brow furrowed in worry.

"Maybe I'll call the police in the morning ... see if they can help." Erick looked into Amy's frightened eyes. "It'll be okay, honey, I promise." Erick knew the police would be no help, and he wouldn't waste his time or theirs.

After they entered the restaurant lobby, Pedro showed them to a private table in the back away from the bar and several families having dinner. Erick ordered Margaritas for both of them. When their drinks arrived, he offered a toast.

"To old guys snagging young girls. Cheers."

"You're funny, Erick, and not old." She kissed him on the cheek.

The two sat silently, reading their menus for what seemed an eternity. Erick's stomach turned at the thought of the black sedan following them.

"Erick, do you think that car was really following us?" Amy laid her menu on the table.

"I'm not sure," Erick said and sipped his drink. In his mind, Erick replayed his conversation with Sara on Friday, searching for clues.

"I don't like it, not one bit," Amy said. She leaned back in her seat and crossed her arms over her chest.

"Sara thinks the FBI may believe the LightPoint plane crash and the propane explosion in Missouri are related. They know the LightPoint jet was headed to Dallas to meet with LTE. And they know I was staying at the motel in Missouri when it blew up."

"What? You didn't mention that last night," Amy said, surprised. "Why would they think you were involved in a bombing?" Amy's eyes narrowed.

"I don't know … There's no way to know where they're heading with their investigation." Erick shrugged his shoulders. "It may be a coincidence."

Amy crossed her legs. The long slit on her skirt opened up wide, exposing her tennis legs. "Well, I guess the link between you, LTE, and the motel explosion does look odd on the surface." She sounded unconvinced.

"I know … I know," Erick rubbed his cheek. "It may lead them out here at some point. Sara seems certain they'll be out to ask me questions. The stress of waiting is killing me."

"The whole thing is unsettling." Amy's smile turned down sadly.

"This is the FBI," Erick said, shaking his head, "The FBI."

A sense of loneliness filled him like a sailor alone at sea. He desperately wanted to share everything with Amy but didn't want to risk implicating her in the mess he'd made. Having someone to share the pain with would ease his mind. Keeping his misdeeds to himself would make it easier to disappear when the time came. And it would protect Amy, too. She couldn't disclose what she didn't know.

"You're not in this alone, Erick. You haven't done anything wrong." Amy paused and laid her hand on his, "I'm here for you."

Erick looked deep into her almond eyes, "Thanks, Amy. You don't know how much that means to me." Always stoic on the outside, the warmth of Amy's gentle touch tore him up on the inside. He knew he didn't deserve her.

CHAPTER 32

September 2000

SITTING AT HER desk, Amy scanned the list of accounts payable due the following week. She spotted an invoice from Local Exchange Billing for two hundred thousand dollars. "What the ...?" Amy groaned. The pressure on her temples increased. She massaged them with her index fingers to ward off the start of the recurring headache she'd developed since arriving in Pullman.

Amy's heart raced as she held the invoice in her hand, focused on the amount due. Erick had mentioned a billing arrangement with LEB. He had said it was for some minor billing and software support functions. Two hundred grand didn't feel minor.

Walking into Erick's office, Amy knocked on the open door. "Gotta second?"

Erick looked up and smiled, "Sure, what is it?"

"I received this invoice from LEB," she said, holding the sheet of paper in the air. "It's two hundred thousand dollars, way more than what we talked about."

"I don't think I mentioned a specific amount," Erick said, stiffening his posture.

"You said some minor billing support." Amy dropped into a guest chair across from Erick with a heavy sigh. "This seems way more than minor, Erick."

"Did you look at the agreement?" He looked back down at the papers on his desk. "It's all there. Two hundred grand a month."

"What work does it authorize? You do realize this will be flagged next year in the financial audit?" Amy massaged the back of her neck.

"They're providing support for monthly billing adjustments. Some cybersecurity and software testing as well."

"Cybersecurity? That's a highly specialized skill. Are they even qualified to do that? It never made sense to me to have this arrangement with them. Entering monthly billing adjustments into the system doesn't take that much time. I mean, seriously, it's a couple of hours a month, tops."

Erick remained focused on his work.

"Erick, are you listening to me? This is serious. What's going on here?" She squeezed the armrest, anger building inside her.

"There's a lot going on," Erick snapped. His eyes remained pointed toward the papers lying in front of him. "For now, I need you to pay the bill. It's a discussion we'll have another time." He tapped his pencil on a yellow pad—*tap, tap, tap.*

Staring at the amount due at the bottom of the invoice, Amy felt blood surging into her cheeks, flushing her face. "No," she demanded. "We need to discuss it now. I could lose my CPA license for paying unsupported invoices."

"Fine." Erick rose from his desk and stomped to the door. He poked his head into Candy's office and said, "Please hold my calls." Erick pushed the door closed, walked to the window, faced the Palouse, and tilted his head toward the floor.

He lowered his voice and shrugged his shoulders in submission, "We were going to have this discussion sooner than later." Erick turned slowly to face her. "There's a part of our financing you're not aware of. I sort of planned it that way."

"What the hell does that mean? What more is there?" She choked on the words, her heart sank.

"When Farmers Bank backed out, I was in a tough spot. Spokane Community Bank came forward in the final hour, offering to finance the deal. They were the last remaining solution to our financing problem." He looked away and bowed his head. Collapsing into a guest chair beside Amy, Erick leaned forward and placed his elbows on his knees. "Turns out the bank is controlled by associates of Michael Romano, the owner of LEB."

"I'm confused. Are you saying we have this billing contract because Romano owns the Bank and LEB—that he somehow forced us into this arrangement?" Amy's head pounded. This whole conversation made no sense to her.

"Romano's associates are based in Chicago and seem to be an unsavory group. They threatened to call the loan due if we didn't work with them," Erick's face had lost all color.

Shock ran through Amy. She had never seen Erick intimidated by anyone. She saw fear in his eyes. "How can they possibly do that—call the loan?"

"We have a long list of technical loan indenture covenants we must comply with," Erick said. He lowered his head. "They would argue that we don't have proper right-of-way agreements for all of our telephone poles. And they'd be right. No phone company does. Traditional lenders in our industry know this and let it slide. In most jurisdictions, after enough time goes by, a company is deemed to have a prescriptive easement if the land owner has never objected. It's a legal gray area. Spokane Community Bank would use it to force us out of the company."

"Romano's unsavory associates in Chicago… that sounds scary. What are you talking about exactly? The Mob?" Angry tears welled up in her eyes. She quivered and fought to hold them back.

"Mob, Mafia, organized crime, whatever you want to call them—"

"Erick, what have you done to us?" Amy pleaded. Panic overcame her. "How the hell would Romano even know about the right-of-way issue?"

"Romano knew a little bit about how our business works. He has some people in New York who own a small phone company down south. It seems they're advising him."

"What else does Romano want from us?"

"He's setting up an equipment supply company in Chicago. We'll purchase equipment through it." Erick cast his eyes toward the floor.

"With a markup, I presume," Amy said in a mocking tone.

"Twenty percent."

"Are you benefiting personally, Erick?" The moment the words rolled off her tongue, she reached to bring them back. It didn't matter whether he profited, only that he participated. Her face tightened, and her teeth clamped down firmly on her lower lip. Her eyes glazed over and were impenetrable—her whole face throbbed like the beat of a bass drum.

"Yes." Erick looked toward the window as though it might offer an escape. He looked back at Amy. She couldn't let him escape her probing eyes.

Amy sat speechless, her face frozen in anger and disbelief.

"There's a three-way split. Romano and I get twenty-five percent, and Chicago gets one-half. He deposits money in a Cayman account for me monthly."

"You have an offshore bank account?" She'd heard enough and stood to her feet. Reconsidering, she fell back into her seat and waited for the rest of the story.

"He required that I establish the account," Erick said, now calm and relaxed.

Amy sat quietly again, for a moment, and composed herself. She stared out the window. "Let me see if I understand what you're telling me. You agreed to all of this on your own and never thought to tell me what the hell we were getting into?" Her tenor was measured, steady. She returned her eyes to Erick. "How much of this does Betty know?"

"I kept the two of you out of it—to protect you." He reached for her hand, and she pulled away.

"What's the plan, Erick? Are you going to disappear to South America? Leave me to take the fall?" A concern passed quickly through her mind; *will I ever trust him again*? The thought passed, then returned, and couldn't escape, trapped in her stream of consciousness.

"Of course not. I've got a plan," Erick said softly, his face solemn. "It's better that you don't know until you decide—"

"Decide what?" she interrupted.

"If you're coming." He put his hand on her shoulder, and she stiffened. "I know this is a lot to absorb. Romano's greedy, and the scheme will fall apart at some point."

"I don't know if I'll ever trust you again, Erick." Bewildered, Amy stood and headed toward the door.

"Amy, wait," Erick cried out in desperation.

"No. Forget it. I need some air. Need to think." Amy pulled the office door open and threw it against the wall. She gasped for a breath and ran past Candy.

Erick jumped from his chair and followed her. He stood in the doorway to her office, blocking her path out. His face flushed and contorted.

"Don't do anything crazy. You're in this as deep as me," he growled. His conciliatory tone exhausted.

"Is that a threat, *Erick*?" Her voice now broken and weak. Tears streamed from her eyes, washing over her face, and falling onto her white blouse. She packed her laptop in its case and grabbed her purse. Turning toward the door, Amy snarled, "Get out of my way."

"Amy, that came out wrong. It's not what I meant." He reached for her shoulders with both hands, and she stepped back. "We can figure this out if we work together."

"I can't think. I'm leaving *now*." Her heart pumped madly. She considered running through the former collegiate football player.

Erick stepped to the side. Amy stormed down the hallway and burst into the company parking lot from the lobby like a thunderhead rolling across the Palouse.

CHAPTER 33

AMY WASN'T SURE she would ever enter the Whitman Communications building again. Nearly three weeks had passed since Erick confessed to betraying her. She had run from Erick, angry and hurt. She had no one to confide in. No one to turn to. Amy's career was invested in Whitman Communications, and her heart in Erick.

Wearing pajama bottoms, a hoodie, and sandals, Amy trekked on foot each morning to the local WSU Starbucks. The morning caffeine cleared her head and prepared her for work. She continued her role at Whitman, remotely from her apartment.

The morning after the blow-up with Erick, Amy dropped by his rental house while he was at work. Her intent was to gather her clothing and personal items. Searching desk drawers for her extra set of car keys, she stumbled on a handwritten note. Scribbled in Erick's hand, a poem filled the sheet of paper. It appeared incomplete, marked up in red pencil with doodles in the margin. The paper was stained in random places by drops of water. *Or tears,* she thought for a moment until the memory of his angry eyes overcame the thought. She leaned over and read the poem to herself.

Tiny Geisha

i have never seen such fury,
my tiny geisha turns on me.

fire lashes from her mouth,
almond eyes slice me like a blade.

i warn her: 'you're in as deep as me,'
her eyes fillet my chest—
expose a heart of ice.

ice she had once melted,
now she bears witness to the truth.

a man formed from greed,
with no soul. ice water flowing
through his veins.

she sees me clearly now,
destined to be alone—
a lone wolf raping and pilfering
corporations for pleasure.

she turns, flies from the building
into a brewing storm over the
palouse, black hair blowing wild,
breathing fire as if a dragon.

i feel the sadness of my dying
heart, as hope drips from my chest
like melted ice cream onto the floor.

She stumbled into the desk chair. *I'm no one's geisha*. Was there a hint of remorse in the poem or only self-awareness? If there was any contrition, she remained unpersuaded of its sincerity.

She read it again. In the margin, random words: redemption, apologized, sorrow, love. Words not yet in the poem, but emerging thoughts on the page. The poem was incomplete. It seemed Erick was trying to make things right between them. Focusing on the word 'love', she said softly, "I do still love you, Erick." Amy bit her lower lip until it hurt, climbed from the chair, and left the house.

Working from her apartment, Amy resisted the urge to call Erick. She let his dozens of calls go to voicemail, not at all certain she would ever trust him with her heart again. Erick hadn't told her about Romano and the fraudulent schemes to protect her. Amy accepted that, although it hurt her that Erick didn't feel he could confide in her.

Amy stayed with Whitman Communications partly for self-preservation. If she disappeared or ran back to Seattle, she knew any financial irregularities at the company could be pinned on her as its CFO. She didn't believe Erick would do that, but the FBI might still try.

Anxiously pacing the perimeter of her living room, Amy's heart overfilled with mixed emotions. She needed to be with Erick. To see him. To touch him. He had done wrong, but was it really any worse than her past? It's not like he murdered someone. Dropping into a chair, she sobbed, "Why did you do this to us?"

CHAPTER 34

ERICK SHOWERED AND dressed for work in an empty house. Without the sound of Amy padding barefoot across the hardwood floors, sadness filled the empty space she had left behind. The vacated closets, dresser drawers, and even her stall in the garage—left an open wound. A wound he struggled to recover from.

Erick called Amy countless times, and all his calls had gone to voicemail. He considered going to her apartment and begging for forgiveness, but his pride held him back. Work kept his mind busy, but his body only walked through the motions. After she had left him, Erick saw clearly how intertwined their lives had become. Without Amy, he was lost like a hiker without his compass.

Arriving at the office at 7 a.m. Monday, Erick spotted Amy's car in the parking lot. His heart exploded and flooded his brain with blood. Erick knew she had been working from home and in constant contact with Candy and other Whitman employees. She had avoided contact with him. No one had warned him she would be back this morning. The thought of seeing Amy again left Erick weak, like a teen asking a girl to the high school sock-hop. His knees nearly buckled when he stood from the car.

Erick rushed past his office toward Amy's and stopped at her door. She shuffled papers with her back to him and felt like a stranger. She wore jeans and a sheer white blouse. Her black hair pulled back in a ponytail, glistened in the morning sunlight. A wave of bitter regret flowed over him. Caressing every curve of her frame with his eyes, Erick longed to reach out and touch her again. Something in his heart twisted hard, and he wondered if he would ever hold her in his arms again.

He searched deep for the right words to start a conversation with the woman he loved, as though it was the first time they spoke. Erick knew he had to come clean now or lose her forever. He had no idea how she would react to the whole story.

Amy spun around in her chair and faced him as though she felt the weight of his stare. The anger from the last time he saw her no longer colored her face. She held a wary colleague's cool emotionally detached expression, not that of an adoring lover.

"Hey you," he said in his softest, most conciliatory tone, "can we talk?" He prayed she would say yes. Did he sense a nearly imperceptible wince of distaste when she first laid her eyes on him?

She nodded toward a chair without a smile. He longed for her smile.

Erick closed Amy's office door and sat in a guest chair. Amy walked from behind her desk and sat in the seat next to him. Her eyes met his, uncertain and tentative.

"I'm sorry." Erick reached across the open space between them and wrapped her delicate hand in his. "Let me tell you everything. Then you can decide if I'm worth forgiving and if you'll give me a second chance … If we can work through this together," Erick's demeanor cracked, and his eyes welled up. A single tear escaped, running down his cheek.

"Erick," she said it as though trying to comfort him, "I know this is hard for you."

He lowered his head and cast his eyes toward the floor. "I hurt the only person I care for. I'm so sorry." She ran the fingers of her free hand through his mop of wavy, blond hair. He had her other hand clasped tightly between both of his.

"Start at the beginning, Erick, and tell me everything," Amy whispered.

After a deep breath to organize his thoughts, he began. "It started with the Spokane Community Bank loan Skip brought us. Once Romano stepped in, it spun out of control ...."

For the next three hours, he shared everything he had done. Everything he had kept from her about the Whitman acquisition. When he got to the part about enticing two other small family-owned phone companies into the supply company scam, she bit her lower lip and shook her head from side to side, never taking her eyes off his.

Erick said, "Yeah, I guess they're as greedy as the rest of us. It's the glue that bound us." Toward the end, he laid out the details of the plan he had conceived for them to evade the mob and FBI and start a new life if they needed to run from the Palouse.

"I want you back, Amy, more than anything. I know you need time," Erick said, heart in his throat. Relaxing his posture, he let out a nervous laugh. "Take as much time as you need. I'll do whatever you want." Erick tried to read her expression.

A flat light filled her almond eyes and colored them with doubt. She stood and walked to the window, laid her palms on the sill, facing the Palouse. "The LightPoint plane and the barn explosion—that was the mob?" She turned and looked at him. He felt her eyes reach deep inside him, searching for the truth.

"It seems so."

"No more lies, Erick. Can you do that for *me*?"

He stood and joined her at the window. "Of course." Erick blew out an anxious breath and shrugged his shoulders, "I've given you a lot to think about."

Amy turned back to the window, her posture stiff. "It is a lot to process."

Erick felt her slipping away. He steeled his nerves and took a deep breath, "Can we talk about this further over dinner tonight?"

Amy turned to face him, her face washed stoic. "I'm way behind with work. How about Friday?"

CHAPTER 35

THE CUMULATIVE EFFECT of Erick's arrangement with Romano began percolating through the Whitman Communications organization. As if it weren't bad enough that Amy had learned what he had done. Now rank-and-file employees had started asking questions. Erick strode briskly into his conference room and dropped into a chair across the table from two quarreling managers.

"Look, you two, we're going to sit here until we get this figured out," Erick said, biting his upper lip. "Honestly, I don't understand the problem with putting refunds for product returns on the monthly customer billing statement."

"It complicates my billing process. How hard is it to simply take the product in return and issue cash back to the customer?" Leslie asked. She shot a sharp glance at the customer service manager.

"How does it complicate billing?" Erick asked.

"It's the billing vendor," Leslie said, with a hint of disdain in her eyes. "LEB seems to struggle with manual adjustments."

Romano. Leslie's sharp words stung. Romano's reach grew daily within Whitman, and his incompetence and greed began manifesting in routine business processes. The longer it continued, the worse it would become.

Erick sighed profoundly and looked Diane in the eye. "What challenges do your customer service reps have making cash refunds?" This has to end. If word of Romano's involvement spreads, it could bring down the whole business.

"The girls on cashier duty are busy. Processing a cash refund creates more out-of-balance events with the cash drawers, plus we need to keep more currency on hand. Every customer gets a monthly bill. It seems the billing system is the easiest way, and the process is in place. There's no reason a competent billing vendor can't handle it," Diane said firmly.

"What if we were to set a maximum cash refund amount—say fifty dollars?" Erick offered in a conciliatory tone. "Based on the list you sent me the other day, around ninety percent of the refunds are less than fifty dollars. We'll cash those out. The larger ones we, can run through billing, but it's only ten percent of return transactions. Can we try it for a few months? It feels like a win-win."

Both of the women nodded their heads in agreement.

Erick stood. "Good, then we're done here." He exhaled with relief. Erick knew this wouldn't solve his problem with Romano's billing company, but it would buy him time.

Erick left the office at 6 p.m. and drove to Amy's apartment. She met him at the curb as he pulled up in the Porsche. She wore crisp jeans and a crimson silk blouse unbuttoned to show a bit of cleavage. Her hair was down and caught the yellowish-light from the streetlamp, igniting a halo around her face. The smile he missed flashed on, and something inside him moved like butterfly wings grazing his cheek. He stopped short and jumped out to open the door for her.

"What a gentleman, mister."

"The least I can do for a beautiful woman." She shot him her blushing smile and cast her eyes downward as though embarrassed. Erick shivered, recalling the look she first gave him when returning to the office.

Amy's smile tonight seemed genuine. Still, it bothered him that she'd been holed up in her office for a week. She hardly spoke to anyone. Now that Amy had taken the time to process his misdeeds, Erick needed to know if she would stand with him.

"Where are we going?" Amy asked.

"I was thinking about the Pullman Steakhouse. Sound okay?"

"It's bound to get rowdy with the students back in town," Amy said with the slightest of frowns.

"Yeah, the place will be hopping later tonight, but it should be alright until after we finish eating."

"Any plans after dinner?" she asked.

"I have a copy of your favorite movie if you're game."

Erick had heard the story at least a dozen times, often enough that he understood why *Wargames* was Amy's favorite movie and how it influenced her life direction. Not only was it her all-time favorite film, but it also inspired her to minor in computer science.

The flick debuted in 1983. It starred an awkward Seattle high school computer geek named David, who hacked into the Department of Defense wargames computer. His escapades started a chain of events that might have resulted in a global thermonuclear war had he and his girlfriend not found a way to shut down the game.

"The popcorn's almost ready. What would you like to drink?" Erick asked. The room was filled with the sound of popping corn and the scent of melted butter.

"Maybe a glass of white wine," Amy said, a warmth radiating from her face. She dropped onto a small sofa facing the television screen.

Had she forgiven him? Erick hoped so.

Erick's thoughts returned to their conversation at dinner earlier in the evening. A rushing tide surged through him. Erick wasn't accustomed to sharing his feelings, but being with Amy at dinner tonight opened the floodgates.

"You know, I lost my kid brother in a farming accident," Erick said.

"That's awful, Erick," Amy furrowed her brow. "What happened?"

"Alvin was plowing a field on our family farm," Erick paused. "The tractor rolled on him. They got him to the hospital quickly, but he passed after two days."

"I'm so sorry," Amy said.

"After the accident, my folks insisted I change my major to Ag and return to the farm following graduation." Erick dropped his head into his hands. "I wouldn't do it. We stopped talking after a while and drifted apart. They ended up selling our family farm and moving south. I talk to Mom every once in a while. Dad has never forgiven me. All I have left of our farming heritage is the small farm in Grangeville my grandfather left me."

"I understand, Erick. You know I lost someone too," Amy's eyes filled with tears. "My parents were killed in a car wreck when I was seven. My grandma raised me."

"I'm sorry that happened to you," Erick said. Amy's hand was on the table, and Erick covered it with his.

Erick shared the pain he carried from his divorce from Betty, "A part of me will always love her, I suppose," he said.

Amy confided how her childhood friend, Alison, was really more of a sister to her. How they would do anything for each other.

Pulling himself back to the present, Erick focused on the glass of wine he poured for Amy. He grabbed a beer for himself and popped in the DVD. Reclining on the small sofa, the heat of her body stirred him.

"How many times have you seen this?" Erick asked.

"A bunch, but it never gets old. I love it. I identify with David. It's the hacker in me. You know, I got busted for hacking in high school—right? Some jerk cut me off in traffic and wrecked my car. It was road rage. I got his plate and tracked him down. Then I hacked his bank account and wired all his savings—twenty thousand dollars—to an orphanage in South Korea. It created a world of hurt for the jerk. Anyway, the FBI tracked me down. Given the circumstances and my being a minor at the time, I got supervised juvenile probation, and my file was sealed.

"My favorite scene is when they're on the island looking for the professor. The girlfriend suggests they swim across the sound to Seattle. He admits he can't swim, and she says, 'well, what kind of an asshole grows up in Seattle and doesn't even know how to swim.' Classic, he's an awkward computer geek like me."

"So you're a bit of a white-collar criminal, too," Erick said, eyebrows raised. He poked her lightly in the arm.

She shrugged off his comment and turned serious, "Erick, I've spent a lot of time considering everything you told me. I wasn't angry so much at what you've done with Romano. It's more that you didn't feel you could confide in me. I want to be with you more than anything, but I need to be able to trust you completely. Can I trust you to be honest with me?"

"Of course, Amy. It's what I want, too. I was trying to protect you. Now I see that keeping the truth from you was wrong." Erick laid his hand over hers.

"Erick, about your escape plan … If we have to leave the country, have you thought about how you're going to get travel documents for us," Amy looked him in the eyes.

"I have, but I haven't found a solution," Erick said, dropping his shoulders in defeat. He considered asking Skip for a contact but no longer trusted him. The attorney served two masters.

"Well, I was part of an unsanctioned hacking group at UW. The guy who ran the club is a Chinese national. He got me a fake driver's license so I could get into bars when I was underage. The ID looked real," Amy paused. "He may be able to help us now."

"Are you still in contact with him?" Erick's heart raced at the thought of getting a fake passport.

"He's in China, but I can reach him by email."

"Please do. Reach out to your contact and see if he knows someone." Erick squeezed her hand gently. Securing travel documents was the lynchpin of his escape plan.

Erick put his arm over her shoulder, and she leaned into him with her head on his chest. He listened to the pattern of her breathing, caressed the smooth skin of her arm, and inhaled her natural scent—closed his eyes and drank in the moment.

CHAPTER 36

October 2000

SITTING AT HER desk Monday morning, Amy struggled to compose an email to her former boyfriend. She dated Zach for three years during college. An impressionable undergraduate, Amy was smitten with the tall, muscular Ph.D. candidate. Zach lived in China, now working for the People's Liberation Army in their cyber-military unit. Amy had hoped he would stay in the States, but he couldn't resist the demands of the Communist Party, and off he went. She hadn't heard from him in years.

Pulling herself from the memory, she started typing.

> *Zach –*
>
> *How is everything in Beijing? I really hope you are doing well.*
>
> *Something has come up, and I could use your help. I need to get a passport and driver's license under an assumed name. It's a long story and best you don't know the details. Is there anyone you know in Seattle that could help me?*
>
> *Amy*

She hit send and walked to her office window overlooking the Palouse. A wave of apprehension ran through her. The hairs on her neck bristled. Thinking back to her college days, she wondered if Zach would judge her. He always had back then. Composing the email resurfaced old feelings. He was her first serious relationship, and the hurt of his leaving still smoldered within.

Amy thought about Erick. *He's my guy now.* Forgiving his arrangement with Romano is easy. It's not much worse than the hacking in my past. But not telling me really hurt. If he can be honest with me going forward, we'll be fine, she promised herself.

The tone coming from Amy's laptop indicated a new email. Heart pounding, she raced back to her desk. "Zach," she whispered as she opened the message.

> *Amy*
>
> *Nice to hear from you. Sorry, you're in trouble. My friend's family in Seattle has a print shop. I think they can help you. It's where I got the driver's license for you in college. I recall him saying his dad made near-perfect US passports. I'll get the owner's contact info and send it to you.*
> *Take care,*
> *Zach*

Amy read the email and sighed, disappointed the message wasn't more personal.

After lunch, Amy opened the second email from Zach containing the Seattle print shop owner's contact information. Jeff King owned the business. Amy placed an encrypted VoIP call from her laptop.

"Yes?" said the man on the other end.

"Jeff King?" she coughed to clear her throat as she said his name.

"Where you get number?"

"Zach Eng. We're on an encrypted call," she whispered quietly.

"What you want?"

"I need travel documents." Saying the words made her heart race. Amy knew that holding a fake passport would subject her to felony charges if she were caught.

"US passport?"

"Yes, and birth certificate, social security card, and driver's license, two sets, one for me, one for my husband." *Husband*, she thought, the sound of the word felt warm and familiar.

"Ten thousand dollars cash each, twenty total, you come Seattle," King said. "First, send picture way you want to look."

"When?"

"I mail form and instructions. You send picture. When ready, you bring money, twenty-thousand cash. Come alone."

They exchanged contact information, and the call ended in less than a minute. Amy slumped in her chair, exhausted.

CHAPTER 37

"**H**EY, I GOT back a few minutes ago. It's five-thirty. Are you about ready to leave," Amy said, walking into Erick's office. She took a guest chair across from him, kicked off her shoes, and rested her bare feet on top of his desk.

"Ha! It's Tuesday, and I'm already behind. Give me a minute to wrap up. How'd the hair appointment go?" Erick leaned back in his chair.

"Great, I love the new look," she fibbed. It was partly true. The problem is, she didn't *want* a new look.

"Platinum blonde?"

"No. I'd look like an Asian hooker. You'll have to go somewhere else for that, mister." She winked at Erick. "It's a dirty blonde color. The girl thought it matched my skin tone perfectly. Here's a picture." She handed him a small photo. "The stylist fitted me with a wig for the picture."

"Wow. It's hot."

Amy forced a smile.

"The stylist's camera had a setting for passport-size photos. She put the file on my thumb drive. If you get me your passport photo, I'll go to the post office and send all the forms to the guy in Seattle."

"Snail mail, really?" Erick asked, rubbing his cheek. "Old school."

"Yeah, someone could intercept an email. Snail mail is safer. That's the way he does business. He's super cautious, which I suppose is a good thing."

"Alright then, I'll get my picture taken tomorrow."

CHAPTER 38

"**H**EY, KNOCK KNOCK. Candy said you were looking for me," Amy said, tapping on Erick's door Thursday morning. She stood at the threshold of his office.

"Yeah." Erick leaned back in his chair, arms folded across his chest. "Please close the door and have a seat." He reached to the credenza and turned up the classic rock playing on the stereo.

"Worried about being listened to?" She pictured Romano in her mind's eye. An uneasy sensation swept through her.

"We need to be mindful of our conversations. What people may overhear," Erick paused. "I need to ask you something. How much access do you have to Whitman's servers?"

Amy sat in the guest chair across from him and crossed her legs. "During the transition, I have unrestricted administrator rights. Why do you ask?"

"Can you edit the server software and encrypt files?" He leaned forward on the desk, eyes narrowed.

Her eyes probed his. "Sure. The Microsoft overhead software keeps changing, but I can figure it out. Is there something you want to store in an encrypted format? There're easier ways to go about it." She tapped her fingers on the armrest nervously. *Why is he being so vague*?

Erick leaned back again, picked up his mug, and sipped coffee. "There may be some files I want encrypted. They would need to be on the server so I can access them remotely. Can you partition off an encrypted space on the company email server so that IT wouldn't have access? Set it up for you and me, and hide it so I could remotely originate emails from the Whitman domain?"

Amy's posture grew rigid. Her almond eyes narrowed and locked on his defiantly, "I can do all of that, but I need to know what you're planning first. I need you to trust me. No more secrets, *Erick*."

CHAPTER 39

STEPPING INTO THE elevator, Michael Romano pressed two for Angela's floor. He held a letter from Pacific Bell in his hand. Romano unlocked the door to Angela's office suite with his passkey and hurried down the hallway to her office.

"Angie." Romano grimaced.

"Uncle Mike, what's wrong ?" Angela furrowed her brow.

"We got a huge problem. Pacific Bell won't take our 800 billin' files anymore." Romano held the letter high and waved it around.

Angela frowned and rubbed her temple.

"Acosta has an idea on how to fix this. I need you to get a copy of a Pacific Bell phone bill from California. Have your people make an exact copy—the type of paper, font size, ink color, envelopes. Every detail. We'll use our P O Box here in Spokane for the payment address and our toll-free call center number. Instead of Pacific Bell, though, we'll call it Pacific Telephone Holding Company. Everything but the name, address, and phone number stays just like it's on the Bell bill."

Angela finished writing a note and laid her pen down. "One of my graphic artists used to work in Bell's billing department. I'm sure he can work up something."

"Great." Romano sat in a guest chair in front of Angela's desk. "This is gonna be a big project. Have one of your programmers figure out how to populate the new bills with call data from our billin' files. See if you can get the first batch ready to go out in the mail next month."

"Should I select the addresses randomly?" Angela leaned back and crossed her legs.

"Yeah, for the test run. Go back three billin' months and start there," Michael tapped his pinky ring on the arm of his chair.

"What kind of dollar volume are we aiming for when we go live?" Angela picked up her pen.

"Let's shoot for twelve million the first month," Romano grinned.

Romano watched Angela write $12 million on her pad and double underscore the figure.

"Thanks, honey. Let me know when you got a draft to look over." Michael stood and smiled. "Hopefully, this will fix it."

CHAPTER 40

November 2000

WORKING FROM THE Spokane FBI office now, the agents assigned to Special Agent Monroe gathered at a long table sipping coffee in the war room. Monroe stood between them, and a wall plastered with handwritten notes and photographs. Surveillance photos of Tony Ferrari, Joe Acosta, Michael Romano, Skip Britain, Jason Rossi, and Erick Olson hung on the wall. Post-it notes representing Local Exchange Billing, Chicago, Whitman Communications, De Rosa's, Spokane Community Bank, LightPoint Communications, Farmers Bank, and LTE were stuck to the wall as well.

Monroe turned to face the group and cleared his throat with a cough. The seasoned FBI agent studied the eager faces before him in an impossible effort to determine how his team might perform on the task before them. Staffed with young men and women full of energy, he felt that much older. Some were near the age of his children. His gaze moved slowly across the room, stopping briefly to greet the eyes of each agent sitting at the table. A skilled leader, he sensed the impatient enthusiasm of the youthful agents ready to get on with the job at hand.

"We've been at it a while now. I'd like to take a minute to recap where we are," Agent Monroe said, pausing. "We know Olson was in Peculiar, Missouri, working to buy a small phone company when the propane tank at the motel his team was staying in exploded. And we know he was negotiating to buy Whitman Communications when a competing bidder's jet blew up en route to Dallas. We also know that a board of directors member at Farmers Bank, the local bank Olson originally planned to use to finance the Whitman deal, had his barn blown up. It's not clear how these events are connected, but Olson's name coming up in all three seems more than a coincidence.

"As for Romano, we know his billing company, LEB, has sent millions of dollars of questionable invoices to Pacific Bell for 800 billing services. Romano's Spokane call center has been loosely tied to a credit card billing scam involving internet porn sites as well." Agent Monroe paced in front of his team. "We have active surveillance on Romano and his company, including phone taps. I'd like to get a warrant to tap his lawyer's phone—Skip Britain." Agent Monroe wasn't confident he had enough evidence to get a tap on Britain's phone.

"What do we know about Erick Olson?" Agent Monroe asked.

"We know he's divorced, and the ex-wife works at Whitman Communications with him," said one agent. "They apparently purchased the company together."

"And we know Romano owns a controlling interest in Spokane Community Bank, the bank that financed Olson's acquisition of Whitman Communications," said another.

"Our surveillance suggests there may be something going on between Olson and the company CFO," said Agent McCoy. "Her name is Amy Summers."

Monroe turned abruptly toward McCoy. "Tell me more about the CFO."

McCoy stood and brushed shoulder-length ash-blonde hair away from her eyes. "She's mixed-race, Asian-white, quite striking, in her late twenties. She was raised in Seattle by her grandmother. Her parents died in an auto accident when she was seven. Very smart, in the top five percent of her accounting program at the University of Washington, and picked up a minor in software engineering. She passed the CPA exam on her first attempt. She attended university on a tennis scholarship."

"Why do we suspect a relationship with Olson?"

"They appear to be living together. Summers has an apartment but seems to spend most nights at the house Olson rents."

"What's your gut tell you about this woman, Agent McCoy?"

"She's young and attractive. Olson's on the hard edge of forty, a failed marriage, good-looking guy, and rich. She's vulnerable because he's got all the power. It looks like a run-of-the-mill office romance to me." McCoy frowned and bit her lip.

"Has she traveled anywhere significant recently?"

"Lots of business trips to Dallas, Texas and Tampa, Florida, LTE has operations critical to Whitman Communications located in both cities."

"Add Summers to the board but off to the side until we have substantive evidence tying her to criminal activity. I will pay Olson a visit to ask about his relationship with Romano." Agent Monroe shuffled through a pile of paper on his desk. "We've got enough to get a warrant for a tap on Olson's office, home, and cell phones. We'll need more evidence to get taps on Betty Olson and the CFO. What's her name again?"

"Amy Summers." Agent McCoy handed him a picture of Amy for the storyboard.

"We need to talk to Ms. Summers as well. She may have useful information for our case even if she isn't involved. In the meantime, let's keep digging into the business dealings of Romano and his lawyer, Skip Britain."

Agent Monroe turned and walked to the window. It was 11:30. The sidewalk bustled with office workers headed to lunch. He dug his hands deep into the pockets of his suit pants and let his mind run. *How does the Whitman piece fit with Romano and Britain? Skip Britain seems more involved in Romano's business than Olson's.*

Dropping into his desk chair, Agent Monroe couldn't get Amy Summers out of his head. A father's concern for Summer's well-being overcame him. His daughter was about Amy's age, and he feared she may be getting herself into a deep mess.

CHAPTER 41

EAVING HIS OFFICE at 9:30 a.m., Erick walked the four blocks to Farmer's Grill. He'd arrived at the office this morning at 6 a.m. to listen in on an industry trade association meeting hosted in NYC. Now fighting with his umbrella against the wind-driven rain, Erick was starved for breakfast.

Farmer's Grill offered six booths covered in red vinyl-fabric from the seventies. The seats were cracked and faded from too many seasons like an old farmer's sun-damaged skin. US 195 ran past the building and on through town. Nestled against the windows, the booths offered a relaxed opportunity to watch the world pass by. Across from the booths, a long counter with a dozen round padded swivel stools covered in the same red fabric ran the length of the building. The air hung heavy with the smell of cooking grease and the sound of it sizzling against the stainless steel cooktop.

Escaping the rain into the restaurant, Erick greeted the owner with a smile. "Hey, Ray."

Raymond Anderson owned the place and served as the cook most days. Ray graduated from Colfax High School two years ahead of Erick, but he knew Ray well from their football days.

By this time of morning, the breakfast crowd had dissipated. The place was mostly deserted. Two elderly farmers nursing coffees at the counter rehashed their glory days. Erick nodded to the farmers and made his way to his usual booth at the end of the row, furthest from the door.

"What can I get you, buddy?" Ray asked, holding a pot of steaming coffee.

"I think I'll have the three-egg ham and cheese omelet, hashbrowns, and toast." Erick felt the pinch from his pants waistband. *I need to shake ten pounds.*

"Let me pour you some coffee," Ray flipped Erick's mug right side up, filled it to the top, and then turned toward the kitchen.

A few minutes later, sipping his coffee, Erick watched a middle-age man park his black SUV in front of the restaurant. The man and a woman with longish blonde hair exited the vehicle and entered the Grill.

Bells hung on the café door jingled as the stranger with a stocky build and gray hair and the woman entered the building. The woman looked to be thirty or so with a slender build. They were dressed for court. This wasn't unusual, given Colfax served as the county seat for Whitman County. They hung their coats on the rack near the door. The man looked over the farmers thoroughly and headed toward the last booth—Erick's booth—with the woman in tow.

"Erick Olson?" His voice was confident and deep. He held open a leather wallet revealing an FBI identification badge. "Special Agents Monroe and McCoy, FBI. May we join you?"

"Sure," Erick choked on the word, and his eyes shifted to the door, his only possible escape. He motioned to the bench across the table from him. "What can I do for you?" His heart raced. *Calm yourself. You knew they were coming sometime.* He wanted to stand and make a run for the door, but his feet were glued to the floor. His legs would have buckled had he attempted to get up. He sat still and waited like a kid in the principal's office.

"We'd like to ask you a few questions if that's okay?"

"Of course, but why not make an appointment?" Erick forced a calm, businesslike exterior. Inside, he trembled.

"Well, we didn't want to cause a big commotion. You can understand that—right?"

"Sure, makes sense, I suppose. Am I in some kind of trouble?" *What's he after? How did he know how to find me? Are they watching?*

Ray approached the booth in his white, grease-stained apron. "Trouble. What trouble? That was Erick's middle name in high school," Ray paused and surveyed the strangers. "May I get something for your friends, Erick?"

Erick nodded to Monroe.

"Sure, coffee, please. Black."

"I'll take the same, please," said McCoy.

"Thanks, Ray," Erick said.

Ray made his way back to the kitchen.

"Everyone on a first-name basis around here?" Monroe asked.

"Pretty much," Erick said with a casual shrug of his shoulders.

"Quaint," Monroe said.

"Dressed in that suit, they know right off you're not local. What's this about? I'm fairly certain you didn't come all this way for Ray's coffee." Erick bit his lip. His initial uneasiness turned to mild annoyance.

Ray sat full cups of black, steaming coffee in front of Agents Monroe and McCoy and dropped a large plate with an omelet in front of Erick. He placed his hand on Erick's shoulder and squeezed. "You know damn well my coffee's the finest in all of Whitman County." The two shared a laugh that went back twenty years. Agent Monroe sat stone-faced as Ray returned to the grill, still chuckling.

"It seems that you have business relationships with some people we're interested in learning more about," Monroe said.

Agent McCoy pulled a small notepad from her suit coat pocket and made a note.

Erick thought back to his call with Sara and reminded himself not to lie to the FBI. Pulling a napkin from the dispenser, he blotted the perspiration from his forehead.

"How well do you know Angela Michieli?" Monroe asked.

"She's on my Company's board of directors."

"How did she get on your board?"

"I invited her. As a part of buying the company, LTE wanted a group of women and minority small business owners to have a role. I put a group together and let them buy into the company and have a role in governance. Her name came up through the Chamber of Commerce." *This isn't so bad.*

"Do you do business with Michael Romano?"

"Yes, some." Panicked, Erick lifted a fork full of omelet to his mouth with a shaking hand.

"What type of business?" Monroe asked.

"Michael has a billing software company and a call center in Spokane. We contract with him for some of those types of services," Erick focused on his steaming cup of coffee to avoid Monroe's eyes.

"How much do you spend on his services?"

"It's not huge. I don't have that figure in memory." Erick shifted in his seat and looked out the window.

"Would you say it's more than one-hundred-thousand dollars per year?"

"I believe so," Erick's heart pounded. He glanced at McCoy as she jotted a note and then reluctantly looked back into Monroe's intense stare.

"How did you finance the acquisition of Whitman Communications?" Monroe's steely eyes burned into Erick.

"Spokane Community Bank provided the loan."

"Are you aware Romano owns a controlling interest in the Bank?"

Erick shifted uncomfortably in the booth. "I don't know much about the bank. Our lawyer identified them as a possible lender, and ultimately, they came through for us."

"What's your lawyers name?"

"Skip Britain. His office is in Spokane."

"Are you involved in 800 billing services or payphones?"

"We don't do anything directly with the 800 toll-free segment, though I'm sure we have customers who are dialing those services over our lines, and of course, we have agreements with billing aggregators to bill those services. Whitman does have some payphones, mostly on the WSU campus and in bars and restaurants throughout Pullman. It's not a profitable business. We offer it as a public service to the community."

"Do you have any plans to leave the country, Mr. Olson?"

Erick struggled to maintain a calm exterior. *Be cool, calm ... steady, even breaths.* He had watched himself in video recordings during regulatory witness training sessions in the past. Erick was confident he appeared calm to Agent Monroe. Emotions raged inside him like a hurricane making landfall.

"No, I've got a company to run. I do plan to take a short trip to Idaho to celebrate Thanksgiving."

Agent Monroe offered a half-smile and reached into his coat pocket, "That won't be a problem. Here's my card. If you think of anything else, please call me. It would be best if you kept our meeting to yourself."

"Alright. Let me ask you something, am I a suspect in your investigation?"

"Not at this time. There are some things we're looking into with Romano and Michieli. Did you know Angela Michieli is Romano's niece?"

"Really? They never mentioned it." *Skip, you son-of-a-bitch.*

"That's it for now, Mr. Olson," he slid out of the booth and locked eyes with Erick. Pulling a money clip from his pants pocket, Monroe peeled off a ten-dollar bill and laid it on the table.

Erick watched as the agents made their way to the coat rack and out the door. He wondered what Monroe was onto. His interest seemed greater in Romano than in Whitman Communications, which was reassuring.

Erick held the business card and read it aloud, "Special Agent Richard Monroe, Chicago Field Office." His half-eaten greasy omelet rested on a plate on the table. The other half was stuck in a knot in his stomach. He couldn't bear another bite. Gulping the last of his tepid coffee, Erick waved goodbye to Ray and left the café.

CHAPTER 42

AMY WALKED SPECIAL Agents Polak and Greenfield back to the Whitman Communications' building entrance at 10 a.m. Her heart still raced from the unexpected visit.

"Ms. Summers, thank you for answering our questions," Agent Polak held out his hand. "Here's my card. If you think of anything else, please call."

"Of course." Amy stood at the door momentarily and watched the agents walk across the parking lot.

Rattled by the FBI interview, Amy stopped by the breakroom to make a cup of tea before heading back to her office. Her hand trembled while holding the mug under the hot water dispenser. Boiling water splashed from the shaking mug onto her wrist.

"Ouch!"

"What's wrong, Amy." Erick's voice pierced the quiet.

"Nothing, I spilled some hot water on my hand." Amy dabbed a damp paper towel against her wrist.

"Have you got a minute? Something important has come up," Erick's brow furrowed.

Amy sat down at the breakroom table, "Sure."

Erick glanced around the room. "Not here. My office."

They had been together long enough for Amy to sense Erick's uneasiness. She stood and followed him down the hall to his office. He led her in and pushed the door closed. Erick dropped onto the small sofa in his office and motioned for Amy to sit in one of the club chairs.

"I don't want to frighten you, Amy. But—"

"It's too late for that. What the hell's going on," Amy scowled.

Erick narrowed his eyes. "I had visitors this morning at the café. Two FBI agents approached me and wanted to ask questions."

"Me too. Two agents left not ten minutes ago," Amy's chest tightened.

"Well, they obviously planned it that way, to question us separately." Erick leaned back and crossed his legs. "They were mostly interested in Romano. About the agreements we have with LEB. The agent asked me how much we pay Romano's billing company annually. I told him it was over one-hundred thousand but didn't have the actual number off the top of my head."

"Erick, a hundred thousand a year—really?"

"What did he ask you?" Erick rubbed the back of his head.

"Same. They asked about Romano and any business we did with his companies. I gave him the amount in the agreement. Two-hundred thousand a month. Nearly two and one-half million a year!" Amy's heart sank.

"Crap," Erick frowned.

Amy watched Erick's hands trembling.

"Do you think that's going to come back on us?" Amy sipped her tea.

"It may. There're lots of numbers in our accounting books, it really only makes it look like we're not on top of things."

"Do you think they'll be back?" Amy bit her lip.

"Maybe. Probably. Who knows. I want to talk with Skip about this." Erick stood and walked to his desk. "There's something I need you to look into about the guy running the FBI investigation—Special Agent Monroe. I'll catch you up later."

CHAPTER 43

LEANING BACK IN his desk chair, Erick gazed out his office window to the Palouse. The rain had turned to snow, and a light dusting covered the recently planted winter wheat crop.

It seemed to Erick that Agent Monroe lacked any concrete evidence. If Sara was right, they'd keep digging until they found something solid. Something tangible.

An official investigation into Whitman Communications' records would quickly uncover the billing contract with Romano. It would take longer for the fraud on the FCC subsidy pool to surface—that would buy them some time. If indicted, though, NECA analysts working with the subsidy funding mechanism would be quickly deployed to Whitman's offices; the Washington State Commission would jump on the bandwagon soon after. The house of cards they built would tumble down upon them in a few short weeks.

Erick's mind ran wild. He gasped and struggled to catch his breath. "Be calm," he told himself, but the words had no effect.

Erick picked up the office phone on his desk to call Skip's cell number. *Agent Monroe seems to know a lot about my business.* He replaced the handset in the cradle and reached into his briefcase. Fishing out his cell phone, he placed the call.

"Skip Britain here."

"Skip, I had a visitor today." Keenly aware Skip was no longer a trusted confidant, Erick chose his words carefully.

"Who was it?"

"Special Agents Monroe and McCoy from the Chicago FBI came to speak with me."

"Did they come to your office?" Skip sounded stressed.

"No, they hit me up at the café during breakfast. They've been watching me." Erick took a deep breath and tried to calm himself.

"This is not good, Erick."

"No kidding. What should I do?" Anger colored Erick's voice.

"Look, they probably want to get you to work with them, try to tie you to something illegal first. You know, set you up and then make a deal. Try to stay cool for now."

"That's easy for you to say. If they offer me a deal, won't I have to testify?"

"That's usually a part of it."

"No way." Erick's heart skipped a beat. "I've looked into Romano's eyes. He would kill me in a heartbeat." Erick's chest seized with terror as visions of sitting in a courtroom witness box facing Romano rushed through his mind. "I could never testify against him."

"Keep your options open. At some point, testifying against Romano and his associates may be your one way to avoid prison."

"Do you think they'd give Amy and me witness protection?" Erick's head pounded.

"They might, but let's not get too deep into hypotheticals for now ... What exactly did Monroe ask about?"

"Mostly if I knew Romano and did business with him. He asked about Angela Michieli, too. And they seemed to know a lot about Spokane Community Bank. Why would they have a Chicago guy on this?"

"Someone's following the money trail between Chicago and Spokane. You got sucked into it because of your business ties to Romano."

"I'm worried about the billing contracts I have with Romano. Those agreements could sink me. My signature is on that contract."

"Is there any way to redirect it onto someone else?" Skip asked.

Erick wracked his brain. The one person he could implicate was the CFO, and he would never do that to Amy. As a company officer, she might already be tainted by contracts she should have reviewed for propriety. "None that I know of ... I'd like to keep Romano out of this."

"I don't think we need to bring him in yet. Let's wait and see what the FBI's next step is first. I need for you to keep a level head, Erick."

"Something else came up." Erick inhaled deeply.

"What?"

"Monroe said that Angelia Michieli is Romano's niece. Did you know that?"

"No," Skip paused, "but he told me to put her on the director list."

"What the hell, Skip, will this information keep dribbling out over time? Are there others?"

"He knew you asked me for a list of minority and women-owned small businesses for consideration on your board of directors. He sent me a list of names."

"Romano picked my directors?" The blood rushed to Erick's head. *Can I trust any of them?*

"No," Skip paused, "but I did add a few of the people he suggested to the list I provided you. Angela was one of them. I think some of the names he provided may be customers of Spokane Community Bank."

Erick leaned back in his seat and cupped his chin in the palm of his hand. "Who else from Romano's list is on my board?" Erick spit.

"Jimmy Delane. Romano loaned Jimmy the money to refurbish De Rosa's a few years back. And, of course, Jason Rossi from the bank."

"Great. Fucking wonderful. Do you even recognize how bad this is?"

"It's bad, I get it, but the directors aren't really your big problem. Your future rides on keeping Romano happy. If you find a way to accomplish that, it'll buy you some time."

"Skip, we go back a long time, and I know you're up to your neck in this shit too, but can you promise me one thing?" Erick paused, searching for the right words. "Promise me you'll give me some warning before you tell Romano the FBI came by. I haven't done anything to implicate him, and I won't, but it looks bad on the surface. I don't trust that asshole."

"You have my word. I know that may not mean much to you any-more. But believe me, when I tell you, yes, I'll give you a heads up. As I said, though, let's give it a little time. The FBI will be back and either ask more questions or have enough to try and force you into a deal helping them." Skip's tone turned soft. "Even if you lead them on, saying you'll help out, you'll have time to disappear. But they'll be watching. You'll need to do it quietly. And they'll try to follow you too, but only to a point. You're not the prize here, and neither is Michael Romano. They want the Chicago boss. They'll give you time and freedom to move around while they wait."

"Are we talking months? A year?"

"I'm afraid there's really no way to know."

Erick disconnected the call and prayed Skip valued their past relationship enough to ward off Romano for the time being.

CHAPTER 44

ERICK FINISHED STUFFING documents into his briefcase and stood from behind his desk. "That should do it," he said quietly. It was the day before Thanksgiving. Erick and Amy planned to leave the office early to spend the long weekend at the Grangeville farm he inherited from his grandfather.

Erick cherished the farm. It was a part of his family heritage. Erick's grandparents, Lars and Ada Karlson, immigrated to America from Sweden in 1901. They traveled west along the Oregon Trail, eventually finding central Idaho. The family homesteaded one-hundred-sixty acres of farmland in Idaho County near Grangeville, working that acreage until Grandfather died in 1980.

Grabbing his briefcase, Erick walked across the hall to Amy's office.

"Knock, Knock. Are you ready to go? It's almost three." Erick tapped lightly on her office door frame. Butterflies tickled his insides at the thought of spending the holiday alone with Amy.

"Almost. Let me grab my laptop." Amy stood and slipped the computer into her messenger bag.

They walked across the parking lot to Amy's car. "Do you want me to drive?"

"Sure." Amy handed him her keys.

Erick started the car and jumped on the highway, heading south. He reached over the console, taking her hand in his. "It's going to be a great weekend, Amy." He relished the opportunity to spend some downtime with her.

Erick awoke early the following morning and headed for the kitchen. After downing a cup of coffee and a bowl of oatmeal, he turned the television to the Macy's Thanksgiving Day Parade, a family tradition.

"Good morning." Amy stretched her arms behind her back. "You're up early."

"Morning," Erick said. Walking to her, he pulled Amy in close and kissed her. Holding her in his arms, Erick savored the warmth of her skin.

"I smelled the coffee." Amy yawned deeply.

"Here, let me pour you a cup." Erick filled a mug and sat it on the counter. "I was getting things ready for an early dinner." It was customary in Erick's family for the men to cook Thanksgiving dinner.

"Kind of early, isn't it?"

"I need to finish thawing the hens," Erick said. He filled a large bowl with water and ice cubes. Next, he reached into the refrigerator, pulled out two Cornish game hens, and dropped them in the bowl. "That should do it. A few hours and they'll be thawed."

"So, what's on the menu," Amy asked and sipped her coffee.

"You're going to love it," Erick said. He laid the dishtowel over his forearm and posed like a waiter. "We'll start this evening with a jumbo shrimp cocktail, then move on to a fresh spinach salad with a raspberry vinaigrette dressing. Our main entrée will be Cornish game hens stuffed with long-grain wild rice, mashed potatoes, and green beans with almonds. I also have a fine Chardonnay from a renowned California winery and, of course, pumpkin pie with whipped cream for dessert." When finished, he bowed.

"Excellent, excellent. It all sounds delicious," Amy said, applauding.

"My pleasure, Mademoiselle." Erick grinned broadly. "Would you like breakfast? I already had a bowl of oatmeal, but I can whip you up an egg while I'm in the cooking mood." Taking care of Amy made him feel warm to his core.

"Thanks, but I'm good with coffee."

"Then let's sit at the kitchen table and have our coffee. I want to review the list for our escape plan." Erick's tone turned serious.

"Okay." Amy moved to the well-loved oak table and sat down.

Erick took the chair next to her. "I don't want to get down in the details right now. Let's stay at the ten-thousand-foot view," he paused and pulled a notepad and pencil from his briefcase. "Alright. What's the status of our passports and other travel documents?" Erick put the eraser end of the pencil in his mouth.

"Jeff King has them ready. I'm planning to fly to Seattle next weekend to visit my Grandma. I'll pick them up then." Amy sipped her coffee.

"How's your grandma doing?" Erick could see the pull of Seattle in her eyes.

"Same. Her dementia is getting worse. I hope she recognizes me." Amy shrugged her shoulders.

"I'm so sorry to hear this, Amy. Take as much time as you need to be with her."

"Thanks, Erick. The weekend should be enough for this trip."

"Are we still good with using Brian and Honey Sanderson for our new names?" Erick grinned at the thought of them being Mr. and Mrs. Sanderson.

"Yep, that's who we'll be." Amy winked.

"And you're okay picking them up on your own?" Erick's eyes narrowed in worry.

"It's my hometown, Erick. I'll be fine." Amy twisted to look out the window. "Besides, he said to come alone."

"Okay," Erick said, looking over the list. "I spoke with our pilot, Wilford. He's on board. I picked up two burner cell phones. They're in the guest bedroom charging."

"What about the bank credentials for Romano," Amy asked. She frowned when she said Romano.

"Right, that's my last item for this morning. I have the paperwork to add Romano to the Cooperative Rural Bank line of credit account. Since you and I are employees and officers, the bank used the Whitman Communications building address for our credentials. Because Romano is a director and not an employee, they insist on using his home address."

"How will that work? Won't they mail the token device to him directly," Amy said, her brow furrowed in concern.

"I want to fill out the bank's form using your apartment address. That way, they'll mail his token to your apartment."

"Okay, that should work. What about Romano's phone number?"

"I'll give the bank the number for my burner phone. I'll need to disguise my voice, I've been practicing." Erick's chest puffed out with pride. It was a workable scheme.

"And his signature?" Amy's eyes narrowed.

"I've been practicing signing his name using tracing paper. I think I have it down well enough. The bank needs it on their signature card to put him on the account. After that, everything should work electronically." Erick picked up a spoon, and absent-mindedly stirred his tepid coffee.

"Is that it for the list? I'd like to watch some of the parade on TV." Amy pushed her chair away from the table.

"Sure, I think that covers everything. I want to go out to the barn and make sure the tractor starts up. Tomorrow morning, I need to spend some time filling holes and smoothing that old dirt road behind the barn." Erick's heart tightened with apprehension. Memories of his brother's tractor accident fogged his mind.

"Right, and I need to install security cameras in the house and barn tomorrow." Amy stood and walked toward the living room television.

CHAPTER 45

AT 8 P.M., the Monday after Thanksgiving, Amy and Alison sat across a small table from one another in a downtown Spokane coffee shop. Both leaned on their elbows, sipping hot coffee, their faces inches apart. Two weeks had passed since Erick and Amy's interviews with the FBI. The two women whispered in hushed tones.

"You're scaring me, Amy. Why do we need to switch cars?" Ali's brow narrowed, carving deep crevices across her forehead. "Have you been hacking again?" she sounded worried.

Amy's eyes darted around the room, from table to table, unsure what she was looking for. Her heart thumped in her chest. It could be the FBI, mob, or nobody—she really didn't know.

Amy looked deep into Alison's eyes. "It's more serious than that, Ali." She felt the panic in her heart push tears to her eyes. "Something went bad with the Whitman deal," she cried out softly.

"What do you mean?"

"Erick got involved with the wrong people. We have a plan to fix it. I'll tell you everything, but not now. You won't be in any trouble—I promise." She pulled a tissue from her pocket and dabbed her moist eyes.

"Are you both in trouble or is it *him*?" Anger sparked in Ali's voice.

"It's all on Erick, but I'm implicated in much of it. You know how these things can blow up on the CFO." Amy paused and took a deep breath. "I need to follow this through to the end."

"Oh no, Amy. You know I'll do anything for you."

"I know, you're my best friend. The closest friend I've ever had." Amy looked around the room again.

"We *are* best friends ... Do you love him, Amy?" A concern beyond Alison's years washed across her face.

Amy paused, caught off guard. The two women locked eyes again, "Yes. Well, I think I do. But now, with all the trouble he's brought down on us, I'm conflicted. I'm confused."

"Damn it, Amy! He's your boyfriend. It's not like you're married. You need to think of yourself, your future." Ali said loudly.

"Ali, quietly." Amy hushed. She glanced around the coffee shop. People were staring. "I feel like he needs a second chance. I can't walk away from him now." Amy dabbed fresh tears from her eyes.

They sat for a quiet minute, sipping their coffees and searching each other's faces. Amy wanted to tell Ali everything. Spill her guts right out on the table but couldn't. They were both bound by the CPA ethics statutes. If Ali knew the truth, she would be obligated to report them to the authorities. Amy reached across the table and laid her hand on Ali's for comfort. More than anything, she wanted to be held and soothed by someone who loved her—she was poised on the edge of a breakdown and craved the human touch.

"You know you can't change who he is—*right*?" Ali whispered.

Amy looked at her hand resting on her friend's and sobbed.

"Are you okay," Ali asked.

"No ... I don't know. I think so." Amy pulled back her hand reluctantly and sat straight in the chair—steeled herself. "It's time, Ali." She surveyed the people in the coffee shop a final time, her eyes darting from face to face.

Amy passed her coat under the table and took Alison's in return. They stood and embraced, then walked out together, switching places several times. Amy slid into Alison's car and drove off into the dark.

Amy arrived at the Sunset Hill Motel ten minutes later and camped in the parking lot. She pulled the hood of her sweatshirt tightly over her head and slouched deep in her seat. The only light escaping the vehicle was the soft glow of her laptop. She scanned the motel's Wi-Fi service from her computer, searching IP addresses on the motel's frequency. There were many guests watching porn sites, but no sign of her target.

Amy tapped her fingers nervously on the laptop case. "I haven't got all night, come on," she whispered.

"Yes! Finally!" Sitting up straight, Amy danced her fingers across her keyboard once he logged onto the Wi-Fi signal at 10:30 p.m.

Amy used a specialized software patch she wrote to briefly seize control of Special Agent Monroe's laptop. She loaded a program onto his computer that would broadcast his GPS location and allow her to track his movements. Using a fictitious name, she added herself as an administrator on the laptop. She created a password that permitted her to log in whenever he was connected to the internet. She exited and rebooted his machine remotely. She seized his computer for less than a minute and left no footprints.

CHAPTER 46

December 2000

E RICK HURRIED FROM his office and headed toward Amy's, carrying a file folder. As Erick rushed by Candy's desk, she glanced up, puzzled. "Hold all my calls," he said. A few quick steps later, he knocked on Amy's open office door, "Got a minute?"

"Sure, what's up?" She closed the binder open on her desk and slid it to the side.

Erick pushed the door shut and sat in her guest chair. "We've got NECA problems," he spit out the words and then took a deep breath. Erick laid the file on her desk. "Read this letter from Virginia Knox. She's an analyst with NECA." His expression was stilted and formal.

Amy opened the file folder and read the letter. Erick watched her intently, searching her face for a reaction.

The NECA analyst had compared Whitman's estimated costs for the coming year to those submitted by LTE the previous year and questioned two categories that had increased by thirty to fifty percent. Estimated billing costs were greatly inflated due to the consulting contract with Romano's company. Equipment procurement costs were higher as influenced by the supply contract with Telcom Equipment Supply in Chicago.

Lips pursed, Amy looked up to Erick. "We knew this would happen at some point. This is all driven by Romano. Honestly, I thought NECA would wait until we file the final cost study next year in June."

"We need to respond in ten days," Erick bit his lip and exhaled deeply. "They could suspend our subsidy payments. I'd like you to draft our response."

"I can do that. Any guidance?"

"On the billing cost, send them the consulting services contract with Romano's company and explain it's an interim solution to help us get off the LTE billing platform. NECA should buy that explanation. For the equipment cost questions, let's tell them we're still working to establish favorable vendor arrangements. Be general. Let's leave Telcom Equipment Supply out of this for now."

"I can do that. But why not send the support documents for the supply company?" Amy's brow furrowed.

"It's my 'layers of sand theory.' Once we submit answers to their questions, they will likely send a follow-up seeking support documents and more information. I want to leave a layer of sand covering the support documents. We'll brush it away to expose the docs once an adversarial party digs deeper." He paused and straightened his posture. "For now, we provide what they specifically asked for."

Amy leaned over her desk, a worried look held fast in her eyes, "Are you asking me to deceive them?"

"It's not deception, nor is it full disclosure. More like something in the middle," Erick said softly. He averted his eyes from Amy to the window.

"Yes, but—"

"Look," Erick interrupted, reestablishing eye contact, "we need to get them off our back for a few months." He stood and moved toward the door, then stopped and faced her in frustration. "Hey, sorry for being short with you. Romano's getting under my skin," he waited for her to accept his apology.

Nothing.

"If NECA withholds the subsidy funding for a few months, we're sunk. We'll miss loan payments and violate our loan covenants. I'd like a draft by Friday morning, if possible." Erick pulled the office door open and turned back to Amy, "Thanks."

She didn't respond, but the sharp light in her eyes spoke volumes.

"Don't be so glum. It'll work out, I promise." Erick forced a smile.

CHAPTER 47

SITTING IN THE Felts Field airport terminal, Romano watched the Cessna Citation roll up and park. The flight crew lowered the door with its integrated steps. Tony Ferrari appeared in the opening, his obese body filling the space. A gust of wind blew a few strands of grey hair into his eyes. Patting them back with his hand, he climbed down the steps to the tarmac. Joe Acosta followed close behind. There would be no record of the passengers arriving in town. The manifest was wiped clean.

Michael Romano rushed through the glass door to greet his guests. "Uncle Tony, good to see ya." He extended his arm and shook hands with both men. Tony pulled Romano in and hugged him.

"Everything arranged?" Tony asked.

"Yea, it's all set. You're stayin' in the Davenport–top drawer. The car's waitin' out front." Romano reached into his coat pocket and pulled out two hotel card keys. "Here ya go, Boss, the rooms have already been paid for."

Pulling up in front of the hotel a few minutes later, Tony latched his green eyes onto Romano, "Why don't you hang out in the lobby? We'll drop our bags in the rooms and come down for a drink in a few minutes."

Romano watched as the two passed through the revolving door and entered the elevator. "Gino, stay with the car. We'll head to the restaurant when they're ready." Romano entered the lobby bar and found a small table with three leather club chairs adjacent to a fireplace. He made himself comfortable and waited.

Acosta had visited before, but to Michael's knowledge, this was Tony's first trip to Spokane. He crossed his legs and tapped his pinky ring on the chair's armrest. Tony seemed pleased with the billing arrangement between LEB and Whitman. And equally so with the operations of Telcom Equipment Supply. Still, something bothered Tony, or he wouldn't be here two weeks before Christmas.

At 5 p.m., the elevator pinged, pulling Michael away from his thoughts. He waved his thick arm at Tony and Joe. They took seats at his small table, and a cocktail waitress requested their drink orders—three whiskeys and some crackers to snack on.

They sat in awkward silence in front of the fireplace. The mobsters sipped their drinks and watched well-heeled guests pass by. Michael was apprehensive, unsure if the meeting would begin now or during dinner. Would he be congratulated on doing a great job in Spokane or reprimanded for some failing—he had no idea. He sat fidgeting like a child at the adult's Christmas dinner table.

After staring blankly across the lobby for a few minutes, Joe said, "Not a bad place, Boss."

The noise from two dozen people flitting in and out of the lobby filled the space with indiscernible chatter. A layer above the background noise, cheery holiday tunes spilled from an antique player piano. The hotel common areas had been formally dressed for Christmas, creating a bright and festive atmosphere. The two men from the windy city looked out of place wearing custom-tailored, dark suits and silk shirts from Chicago's garment district. It wasn't so much their clothing as it was their reclusive and sullen dispositions as though they were attending a funeral.

After what seemed a long minute, Tony responded, "It's a historic building. Reminds me of the old downtown hotels back home." He stuffed a handful of fish-shaped crackers into his mouth.

Romano sat pensively, planning to speak only when spoken to and then with the word economy of a poet. He knew his superiors were not conversationalists. It was his place to listen and learn; he accepted he had little wisdom to offer in return. They spoke with their eyes and posture, subtle body movements. Michael learned to read the unspoken language by growing up among them. The weight of their presence pressed on his chest like meat in a pressure cooker.

"Do you want to deal with the lawyer while we're out here this trip?" Acosta sipped his drink.

Tony sighed deeply, "No. We'll handle that separately."

Michael's heart raced. Were they talking about Britain? There was no way to know.

At 6 p.m., Tony stood from his chair and tossed down his throat what remained of his drink, "Gino out front? We're ready."

Romano led his visitors through De Rosa's lobby to his reserved table at the rear of the restaurant. They had barely settled in the booth when Jimmy Delane arrived with menus.

"Good evening, Mr. Romano. It's so nice to see you," Jimmy said. His eyes sparkled. He was at his best serving guests.

Michael looked up and smiled broadly, "Jimmy, say hello to my colleagues from Chicago, Tony and Joe."

"Pleased to meet you. Welcome to Spokane," Jimmy said with an engaging smile. "I have menus here for each of you; may I get you started with something to drink?"

Tony looked toward the empty bottle of wine on the red and white checkered tablecloth with a candle stuck in its mouth. "We'll have a bottle of wine." He turned his green eyes toward Jimmy and motioned toward the bottle.

"Jimmy, why don't you pick out a nice red," Romano said softly.

Jimmy returned in less than a minute with the wine and poured a glass for each of his guests.

Tony offered a toast, "To Family." He raised his glass.

Michael and Joe responded in unison, "To Family," and raised their glasses to meet Tony's.

Michael shifted nervously in his seat. "How was the flight?"

Stonefaced, Tony turned his head toward Michael. "Flight was okay. I'm not a fan of small jets, but they're convenient as hell."

A half-smile broke on Acosta's face, "Yeah, a little bumpy for my taste."

Straightening his posture, Romano took a sip of wine. "Is there something in particular you want to see while you're out here?"

Tony and Acosta exchanged glances.

Tony sipped his wine slowly, sat the glass on the table, and sighed deeply. "Erick Olson. Does he know about our bid on Whitman?"

"No. He knows there was a bidder from Chicago, that's it." Startled, Michael coughed. He hadn't thought about the other group in the Whitman auction for months.

Tony lit a cigarette and took a long pull. "Olson coming through for us?"

"He pushed back a little at first, but I laid it out for him." Romano felt beads of perspiration collect on his neck, then slowly run down his back.

Joe leaned forward, "We received word from an informant the Feds have been asking questions. Sounds like they might have hit on Olson."

"Whadaya want me to do?" Nervous and heart beating faster, Michael rubbed his thumb on the wine glass. He looked at Joe first and then reluctantly shifted his eyes to Tony.

"You need to educate him on being an associate," Tony said. He flicked the ash from his cigarette. "Let Olson know he can be replaced. He needs to understand there's no graceful way to part—"

"There's no way out. He's one with us now," Joe interrupted sharply.

Tony shot a disapproving look at Joe; he didn't usually take kindly to interruptions. "Joe's right. He's either with us or against us. There ain't no middle ground."

"I had a talk with him. I'll do it again and make it stick this time." Michael took a sip of wine. "What'd Olson tell the Feds?"

"Our informant didn't know. Only that they interviewed him," Acosta said. "They talked to the people at LTE too. It may be a fishing expedition. Hard to tell, but we need to get in front of it."

Tony blew a lung full of smoke to the side. "I want you to keep the phone company clean, as clean as possible. Don't be calling attention to it. The LEB billing arrangement and Telcom Equipment Supply are fine for now. Just maintain the status quo until this blows over. Don't get any side deals started. We've got big plans for Whitman down the road."

"Once we blend the internet porn into the phone company, the payoff will be *huge*," Joe said with a broken smile.

Romano relaxed back in his seat, confident the worst of the evening had passed. "I'll set him straight, Boss."

"You do that," Tony said. "Now, let's get something to eat."

CHAPTER 48

ERICK WASN'T PLEASED with the thought of spending the afternoon with Michael Romano in Spokane. Romano's secretary called Candy to schedule a face-to-face meeting with Erick. She called this morning and provided no agenda. Romano demanded Erick be in his office at 3 p.m.

Arriving early, Erick watched Romano's office building from his Porsche for several minutes. Running fingers through his hair, he wondered what Romano wanted. Each contact with the mobster grew more intense. Chills ran through Erick at the thought of a ruthless Chicago crime family pulling Romano's strings and, in turn, his own strings. A headache grew behind his temple.

So far, Erick had done everything asked of him. He feared Romano was setting the stage for even more fraud. His heart raced with the thought of further ramping up the fraudulent schemes. The cash they were extracting from the federal subsidy pool was not sustainable. Any further increase would surely be detected.

Erick stepped from his car, strode purposely through the parking lot, and entered the building, determined to talk sense into his unwanted partner. Romano's office was on the sixth floor. Stepping off the elevator, Erick greeted Romano's secretary. She walked him back to Michael's office.

Romano stood at the window behind his desk, "take a seat, Erick," he said curtly. Romano motioned with his left hand to an empty chair in front of the desk. "This won't take much time."

Head pounding, Erick sat in the chair, "The purpose of this meeting wasn't clear, Michael," he coughed up the words unevenly.

"It's about how the Family business operates," Romano sighed and dropped into his chair. "You worked for a big company before. You know about all that bureaucratic crap. It's different here. That big company way means nothin' to us."

Erick's heart beat quicker. He didn't appreciate Romano's ominous tone. "Different in what way?"

"Every way," Romano boomed. "Ya, see, we don't have the government regulatory agencies pokin' around so much. It's more the FBI and cops that gives us headaches. We got a certain way of doin' business. Back in Chicago, Tony's the boss. Then there are guys like me—capos who run divisions," Romano paused and smiled with his mouth closed. "I run the Spokane division. You run Whitman for me. You're not Italian, so you can never be in the Family," Romano took a deep breath and looked Erick in the eye. "You can do good as an associate, though. But associates gotta play by the rules."

"Rules, what rules?" Erick's chest tightened.

"That's where you and me got a problem," Romano frowned.

"You lost me, Michael, what problem?" Perspiration beaded on Erick's forehead.

"You broke the cardinal rule. Never talk about Family business with outsiders. Never!"

Erick's chest tightened, "I wouldn't do—"

"Enough! Don't fuck with me," Romano interrupted. "We got people planted everywhere. We know the FBI was down in Texas askin' questions at LTE, and we know they tracked you down at Whitman."

"Are you following me?" Erick asked. Filled with panic, he wanted to bolt for the door, but his feet wouldn't budge.

"Ain't like that, but we keep tabs on associates. That's the way it is."

Erick threw up his hands in surrender. "Okay, alright. Two FBI agents cornered me a while back at breakfast and asked some questions, but I didn't tell them anything … it didn't seem important."

"I'll be the judge of that," Romano picked up a pencil. "You get their names?"

"The guy is Special Agent Monroe. The woman's name is McCoy, I think," the words spilled unevenly from Erick's mouth.

"What'd they want?" Romano jotted the names on a scrap of paper.

"They asked if I do business with you," Erick said quickly. "I told them about the consulting services contract with LEB." Sweat soaked through the armpits of his shirt.

"Anything else?" Romano's eyes narrowed and turned darker.

"No. No. He seemed mostly interested in my business with you." Erick wondered if he should tell Romano that Special Agent Monroe knew about Angela being his niece.

Romano leaned forward with fire in his eyes, "Somethin' like this happens again, you come to me! Pronto! Anybody asks about the business, you tell me! Keep your mouth shut. Got it?"

Erick straightened in his seat, "Yeah."

Romano leaned back, crossed his legs, and lowered his speech to a whisper, "One last thing. You need to make this work, or you lose. You can be replaced," he paused. "Now get the hell outta here."

Erick's legs trembled, barely holding his weight on the elevator ride down to the street level. He stumbled through the lobby and out the door to the safety of his car. Wild thoughts spun in his head. *Are they watching me? Following me? What about Amy? What do they know about her? Is she in danger?* His heart twisted like a pipe in a vice.

A sudden, sharp need to be with Amy overwhelmed his senses, leaving him with myopic tunnel vision focused on returning to her side. Jumping into the Porsche, Erick ripped through downtown and turned onto the highway headed to Colfax.

CHAPTER 49

ERICK HAD BEEN unusually attentive following his Spokane meeting with Michael Romano earlier in the day. He clung to Amy all afternoon in the office like a lost puppy. Now, at eight in the evening, they were lying naked in bed. Something in him had turned, but Amy wasn't sure what.

"We've got to make some changes," Erick said.

Amy ran the tips of her fingers softly against his lower back. "It wasn't good for you?" she cooed with a coy smile. *It's always good for the guy.* It was too for her, this time.

"No, no. It's not that," Erick said, pulling her closer until her skin pressed against his.

"What then?"

He reached over to the nightstand and turned the stereo up.

"I think the FBI might be watching us. Maybe Romano, too."

"In here? In our home?" She felt safe in Erick's embrace but still worried about Romano. She'd never met the man, but her impression from the stories Erick told painted a picture of pure evil.

"I doubt it," Erick said.

"You seemed different after your meeting with Romano today—nervous or anxious, maybe even frightened. What happened?" She thought back to the panicked look on Erick's face when he arrived back in the office after his meeting with Romano.

"The guy is scary evil. He said if I don't do as instructed, he'll get rid of me," the color left Erick's face.

"Get rid of you? He threatened you?" Amy said, her heart racing.

"He was vague, but it was definitely a threat," Erick rubbed his forehead. "Did he scare me? Yes. I have no choice but to play along with Romano until I find a way out."

"*We*, Erick. *We'll* find a way out," Amy said, snuggling up against him.

"Can you get your hands on a bug sniffer?"

"I think so. If not, I can build one. I can build a jammer to disrupt their transmission signal, too."

"The sniffer would be better. If there's a signal and we jam it, they'll know we're on to them. That might not be good," Erick paused and rubbed his chin. "I think we should assume the FBI is recording our telephone conversations and have access to emails and phone records. Romano may be listening too. We should only use the phone and email to purposely send them in the wrong direction."

"For the escape plan?" She thought for a moment about her backup plan, woven into his like a secret code on a treasure map. Amy wasn't convinced her plan would ever be activated, but if necessary, it might be her one path to freedom. The small deception made her feel a little dirty, like a double agent in a James Bond film.

"Right." He pulled an extra pillow behind his back and propped himself up. "I think we should have a code word for the escape plan. I've been using Alvin, after my brother. How does that sound to you?"

"I like that. Alvin, it is," Amy smiled.

"The stuff we want to keep hidden, we discuss face-to-face outdoors or with loud background noise," Erick adjusted his pillow.

"That should work. Current surveillance technology won't pick up our voices mixed with the music," Amy said.

"Good."

"We should avoid cell texts." Amy's brow furrowed in thought.

"Right, they can get those."

"What about our internal messaging service in the office?" Amy sat up halfway, leaning on an elbow.

"Good point. How secure is it?"

"Messages stay on the server for a while—maybe a month—and then IT deletes them. There's no permanent record. With my admin access, I can write a patch to erase ours after an hour or a day, whatever you want."

"Let's go with two hours. That should leave enough time for us to pull up messages before they disappear."

"I'll take care of it tomorrow." Amy rested her head on Erick's chest. She could hear his heartbeat, slow and steady.

"The Porsche is too visible as an escape car. I'm going to rent a non-descript vehicle through the company and stash it nearby. Will Alison switch cars with you again?"

"I think so, but she was pretty nervous last time. I feel like I should tell her something about what's going on." Amy's heart sunk at the thought of implicating Ali.

"The best way to protect Alison is to keep her in the dark, Amy."

"Will you be sad to leave the Porsche behind?" Amy said, frowning.

"It's leased."

"And I thought I snagged a rich guy." She smiled and wondered where they'd be in a year.

CHAPTER 50

ERICK'S EYES BLINKED open from a bad dream. He climbed from bed and shuffled into the kitchen quietly so as to not wake Amy. Like most of his recent dreams, Michael Romano played a prominent role. Two weeks had passed since Erick's come to Jesus meeting with Romano. Not only had Erick's distaste for Romano grown, but he was now genuinely terrified of the mobster. Romano's angry words kept resurfacing in Erick's mind, 'You need to make this work, or you lose. You can be replaced'.

Erick and Amy were staying at his Idaho farm, celebrating their first Christmas together. They arrived the Friday before and planned to stay through New Year's Day. Erick started the coffee pot and sat at the kitchen table, looking out over the snow-covered Palouse hills. Five months had passed since he first met Romano. Erick struggled to find a path forward for Whitman Communications. With Romano's ever-rising demands on the business, Erick seriously doubted he could steer the company away from trouble for another six months. *The wheels will surely fall off the bus by summer.* "Shit."

"Did you say something, Erick?" Amy stood by the doorway to the kitchen.

"No, I was thinking. Good morning ... rather, Merry Christmas." Erick stood and walked to Amy, placing his hands on her hips.

"Merry Chrismas, Erick." Amy rose to her tip-toes and kissed him.

"Did you sleep well, honey?"

"I did. It's so quiet out here in the country, I always do." Amy dropped into a kitchen chair. "Coffee ready?"

"I think so. Let me pour you a cup."

Erick filled two mugs with steaming coffee and joined her at the table. "Here you go. I'll rustle up some breakfast in a bit."

"Thanks," Amy smiled.

Erick glanced into the living room to his Grandfather's artificial tree with twinkling mini-lights sparkling like a beacon. Saturday, they had reclaimed the tree from the barn along with a box of ancient decorations. They spent the afternoon decorating the tree and the rest of the house. Several gift boxes were spread out beneath the tree.

Walking into the living room, Erick picked up a small wrapped box from under the tree. Returning to the kitchen, he sat beside Amy and laid the box on the table. "This is for you, Merry Christmas.

Amy looked down upon the box with longing eyes.

"Go ahead, Amy. Open it."

Amy carefully peeled the wrapping paper from the box and lifted the lid. She reached in, pulled out a gold heart-shaped locket on a gold chain, and held it up in front of her.

"It was my Grandmothers. She brought it over from Sweden in the eighteen-hundreds," Erick said.

"It's beautiful, Erick. I love it. Thank you so much." Amy leaned toward Erick and kissed him.

"There's a clasp on the side that opens the locket. You can put a picture of someone important to you inside."

"I'll use a picture of you and me, of course. You're so thoughtful." She stood and headed toward the tree. "Give me a second, I have something for you."

Amy grabbed a box from under the tree and rushed back to the kitchen. "Merry Christmas, Erick." She laid the box on the table.

Erick picked up the box and shook it against his ear.

"What are you doing?"

"Trying to guess what's inside. It's something my family always did."

"Any guesses," Amy asked.

"Nope, you've fooled me." Erick pulled the wrapping paper off and opened the box. The scent of fresh leather hit him before he pulled back the tissue paper, revealing the messenger bag inside. "Coach. This is really nice and definitely something I can use. Thank you, Amy."

"I wanted to update your look. Messenger bags are all the rage."

Erick leaned over the table and kissed her. "Thank you."

Eating leftover ham and cheese sandwiches the day after Christmas, Erick dropped another gift-wrapped box on the kitchen table in front of Amy. He had held it back an extra day because he didn't really view it as a Christmas gift. It was more utilitarian, and he wasn't entirely sure how Amy would react to it.

"For me, Erick? Amy smiled.

"It is, but I wanted to keep it separate from Christmas. Go ahead and open it."

Amy tore off the wrapping paper, and her mouth fell agape.

"It's a revolver, Amy. A Smith and Wesson 38 Special," Eric said in a serious tone.

"I ... I see that. What am I supposed to do with it, Erick? Don't I need a license or something to even have it?"

"It's for our Alvin plan. You'll probably never use it beyond the practice range. But if something unexpected comes up, I want you to know how to use it. How to use it safely. We can take it out behind the barn after lunch, and I'll give you your first lesson."

"Erick, I don't think I could ever shoot someone ... kill someone. That's way past my comfort zone, way past any distinction between right or wrong." Amy said weakly.

"Not to worry, Amy. We'll be shooting at targets: Cans, bottles, paper silhouettes of bad guys, and a variety of other things. I want you to try it and maybe start to get used to the idea of using a weapon if the time ever arises." Erick slid his chair beside Amy and laid his arm over her shoulder. "It'll be fine, honey. We'll take it slow. As slow as you want."

"I don't' understand why I would ever need to use a gun, Erick." Amy's brow furrowed deeply.

"Self-defense, Amy. That's the only reason, and it's unlikely to happen. But if it does happen while we're on the run, and it's a case of him or us, I want you to know what to do. The way that happens is with practice and being comfortable with your weapon." Erick looked into her eyes. "Do you trust me?"

"Of course, I trust you."

Erick took her hand in his. "Let's work with the revolver a little each day while we're here the rest of the week and see how you feel about it by the time we leave for home." Erick leaned over and kissed her on the cheek. "Deal?"

"Deal," Amy whispered in a defeated tone.

CHAPTER 51

January 2001

SPECIAL AGENTS MONROE and McCoy appeared, unannounced, at 10 a.m. in the Britain & Son law offices requesting Skip Britain. Asked by the receptionist if they had an appointment, Monroe pulled a badge from his suit coat pocket and asked her to get him promptly. *She knows damn well there's no appointment.* The receptionist left in haste and returned a minute later with Skip in tow.

"Skip Britain. May I help you?" Skip said without emotion.

Agent Monroe stepped closer to Skip. Close enough to smell his cologne and feel the warmth of his breath. Monroe read his eyes. The lawyer wore a composed, professional facade on the outside. On the inside, Monroe sensed Britain was riled by the uninvited intrusion.

"Special Agents Monroe and McCoy with the FBI," he reached to shake hands. Monroe flipped his badge open with his free hand, but Skip didn't seem interested in their credentials.

Skip politely shook hands with the two agents.

"We'd like to ask you a few questions. Is there somewhere we may speak privately?"

Skip motioned toward the hallway. "We can use my conference room. Come this way, please."

They entered the conference room, and Skip shut the door. Monroe and McCoy took seats on one side of the long mahogany conference table. Skip sat directly across from them.

"What is it I can do for you, Agent Monroe?"

"I'd like to ask you a few questions related to an ongoing investigation," Agent Monroe said, pulling a small steno pad containing his notes from his suit coat pocket.

"It's my pleasure, go ahead." Skip smiled and stroked his beard.

"How well do you know Michael Romano?" Monroe nodded to McCoy, and she pulled a yellow legal pad from her messenger bag.

"He's a client." Skip crossed his legs and averted his eyes.

Agent McCoy scribbled a note on her pad.

"What's the nature of your business with Romano?"

Skip turned his eyes back to Agent Monroe. "I do occasional legal work for him. Mostly employment matters for his billing company."

"Anything else?" Agent Monroe said without looking up from his notes.

"Odds and ends. It's all protected by attorney-client privilege," Skip said in a smug tone.

"Do you know Erick Olson?" Agent Monroe asked.

"I do. He's a client and a friend. We were in the same fraternity at WSU."

"Do you know of any business relationship between Olson and Romano?"

"I can't help you with that. If there was a relationship, it would be protected attorney-client communication." Skip looked away and tapped his fingers on the table top.

"I see," Monroe said, annoyed. He'd anticipated Britain would hide behind client confidentiality. "Have you traveled to the Cayman Islands in the past?"

"I have."

"For what purpose?"

"Vacation, it's an island in the Caribbean."

"I know where it is," Monroe smiled and let out a subdued laugh, accepting Britain would be hard to rattle. "Have you dealt with any Cayman-domiciled banks?"

"Not for me personally, but I have assisted clients in the past with establishing offshore bank accounts and transferring funds."

"I suppose you won't say which clients?"

"Sorry, that's protected," Skip shot Monroe the smug smile again.

"Of course, it is." Monroe pushed back from the conference table and stood. "I think that's it for now, Mr. Britain."

Agent McCoy dropped her yellow pad into her leather messenger bag and stood next to Monroe.

"I'll walk you out," Skip said. He stood and pulled the door open.

Stepping into the elevator behind Agent McCoy, Monroe sighed and pushed the lobby button hard. Letting out a quiet laugh, he turned to McCoy. "That went about how I anticipated."

McCoy smiled, "Well, you didn't expect a confession, did you?"

"Ha! I wish." Monroe turned cautious. "I think I got under his skin a bit. He's a pretty cool customer, but we rattled him a little. Our surveillance will pick up his next move. Hell, he's probably on the phone with Romano this very minute, and we're taping the whole conversation." Agent Monroe mimicked Britain's smug smile.

CHAPTER 52

MICHAEL ROMANO AND Gino huddled over surveillance pictures laid randomly across a small conference table in Romano's office. "Nothin' else, Gino? This is everything you found?" Romano asked, irritation cutting his voice harsh.

"Yeah, Boss," Gino repositioned some of the photos on the table.

"Any trouble getting' in?" Romano asked.

"Nah, Olson and the girl are both in Tampa on business. I bugged the phones in both their places and planted some ears, too," Gino grinned. "I spent half-an-hour in the girl's apartment, not much stuff there at all. Don't look like she spends much time at the place."

"She's probably over at Olson's gettin' pounded every night," Romano said with a guttural laugh.

"You want some of that action, Boss?"

"Nah, too skinny for me. I'd be afraid of breakin' her in half." They both laughed.

"You went through everythin' at Olson's?" Romano shuffled the papers on the table.

"They must keep personal papers at the office. This is all I found," Gino said. "I hear lots of guys keepin' everything on computers now."

"Yeah, the paperless office shit. That's gonna change the way we do things someday." Romano picked up a picture of a banker's business card and a Caribbean travel brochure. "This Cayman bank's the one we sent him to, so it's nothin'. The Caribbean crap might be for a vacation—who knows. What about the rental car contract?"

"I found the contract in a desk drawer along with the keys?"

"Have we seen him drive it?"

"Never seen it. It's for a Ford Explorer. Wasn't in the garage either."

"It could be for bad weather when he don't want to drive his Porsche. Still, somethin's not right. Keep an eye out for the car," Romano slapped the papers on the table, "I don't buy it. No one lives this way, with no personal papers in their house. And who the hell rents a vehicle and doesn't drive it?"

"Seems kinda strange, Boss."

Walking to his desk, Romano dropped into his chair. "Gino, I got a job for ya tomorrow. Give ya a short break from watchin' the Whitman building."

"What is it, Boss," Gino said, lowering himself into a guest seat.

"Guy's flyin' in from Chicago at 9 a.m. I need you to pick 'im up."

"Okay. Where do I take him?"

"Bring 'im here. Tony called. We gotta take care of somethin' important. This guy will do the deed."

"Someone gettin' whacked, Boss?"

"Yeah. Some cash went missing from one of the Cayman accounts," Romano paused and bit his upper lip hard. "Our banker says they can't pull the money back. We'll work the guy over until he transfers it to us. Then, we end him. Tony wants to send a message."

"One of us or an associate," Gino asked.

"Fortunately, it ain't family." Deep worry furrows formed on Romano's forehead. "About tomorrow, this guy you're pickin' up's not much on small talk. Just get 'im and bring 'im to me. Don't be tryin' to talk 'im up."

"How do I find him?"

"I got the flight information. His name's Gerald Carter. He's six foot, blond hair, and got a slim build. Oh yeah, walks with a limp and has a long scar on his face—some kind of war hero. You can't miss 'im."

CHAPTER 53

SITTING BY THE fireplace, Erick nursed a gin and tonic after arriving home from the airport. The glowing fire and flickering television, tuned to CNBC, provided the only light in the room. He had the sound muted. Erick glanced at his 45 caliber pistol on the end table. His chest tightened. Papers had been rearranged on his desk in the other room. Someone had been in the house while he and Amy were in Tampa on business.

Erick recalled his conversation with Special Agent Monroe. He wondered if the FBI would have broken in without a search warrant. Was Agent Monroe after him or was it Romano? There was no way to know. Erick took a sip of his drink and savored the tangy flavor of the gin.

The image of Romano's dark eyes filled Erick's mind. He gasped for a breath. Could Romano have broken in? He picked up the pistol, the cold metal chilling his hand. Pulling back the slide, Erick listened to the comforting metallic sound of a round dropping into the chamber. He returned the weapon to the table.

Deep in thought, the sound of the front door opening brought Erick back to the surface. He laid his hand on the pistol.

"Amy?" he called out, "I'm in the den."

She found Erick and sat in the club chair next to him. "Why are you sitting in the dark, Erick?"

"It's mood lighting," he deadpanned.

"What's your mood?" She smiled, reached out, and touched his shoulder.

He picked up the remote and turned the sound on the television volume up high.

"Concerned. Something doesn't feel right."

"What is it?" She leaned toward him, her brow furrowed.

"Someone's been here ... been in the house," He leaned closer to her.

"Do you think the FBI would break in?" Amy asked.

"I don't know ... I had some papers on the desk. Someone moved them while we were in Florida. I'm certain of it." Erick's heart dropped at the sight of her frightened expression—eyes narrowed, mouth agape. He wrapped his hand around hers to calm her fear. "It's probably nothing, Amy."

"Yeah, but you're not sure," she leaned toward him and whispered into his ear.

"No. I'm not." Erick had promised not to keep secrets from her. He wouldn't lie, even if the truth frightened her. "If they're looking for something on Romano, they won't find it here," he said confidently. Erick's hands trembled with the realization that someone broke into their home and rifled through their personal belongings.

Amy sat up straight in the chair. "What if it *was* Romano?" Amy's speech was broken and weak, her face colored in terror.

"He'd have no reason to break in," Erick said unconvinced. He accepted it was more likely Romano than the FBI.

"It's the mob. How much reason do they need?" Amy said, clear and strong.

"I've done everything he's asked." Erick's heart pounded as he recalled the meeting in Romano's office. Romano had said there was no way out. He knew about the visit Agent Monroe paid Erick. They seemed to have eyes and ears everywhere.

"I don't like it, not at all," Amy said, crossing her arms tightly over her chest. "This is harder than I thought it would be."

"We need to be cool and act normal." Erick looked deep into Amy's worried eyes. "We're safe for now; they're only watching and listening," he said, trying to comfort her. Erick squeezed her hand firmly to reassure himself.

PART IV

Alvin

One door closes, another opens—
so they say. What if that door
leads to a darker place?

The night opens a passage
in what was a wall. I take her
hand, we step through into the
Palouse.

We run through
        golden fields of wheat,
We run through
        moonlit nights,
We run through
        our greatest fear.

The mob searches.
The feds follow.

When the land ends,
we slip into the sea.
Emerge in a new world.

—Erick Olson

CHAPTER 54

February 2001

THURSDAY AFTER LUNCH, Amy sat in a conference room with several other managers. They listened to changes Betty proposed to Whitman's medical insurance in the coming year. The cell phone in Amy's suit coat pocket vibrated, nearly startling her to her feet. She carried two cell phones, a Nokia for business and personal use and the burner pre-paid flip phone Erick got her months earlier for their escape plan. Erick paid cash for the burner, which could not be traced to them. Only the burner phone was set to vibrate.

Pulling the cell phone from her pocket, Amy flipped it open. A text message appeared: *Alvin*. Her heart raced; it was time.

Excusing herself from the meeting, Amy left for the restroom. Anxious tremors ran through her limbs. Leaving the conference room in a hurry, she tripped and nearly fell.

Erick and Amy rehearsed the first part of their escape plan a dozen times—there was little margin for error. Amy's car was ready, with the fuel level never below one-half. She had fifty-thousand dollars in cash and a 38 caliber revolver, with extra ammo, hidden from view in a safe welded in the trunk compartment of her Mazda. There were two packed bags containing clothing and critical papers. Among the essential papers were her new passport and other forged identity documents. If this was it, she knew exactly what she had to do. There wasn't much time.

Amy locked the bathroom stall. Her heart pounded, and her fingers fumbled with the keypad as she punched the last number redial button.

"Amy," Erick said, eerily calm.

"What happened, Erick?" She whispered the words so softly she could barely hear herself speak.

"You need to wire the money and leave now." Erick's tone was confident.

Amy's heart skipped a beat, and her hands shook. "Erick, I'm scared. I'm sorry, I didn't think I would be, but I am." Amy's heart raced.

"It'll be okay. You've got this. Follow the plan—the clock's running. You need to be gone in fifteen minutes. Complete the wire and leave. I'll see you at the farm tonight." The call disconnected.

Amy sat on the commode for a minute and took deep, cleansing breaths to collect her resolve.

Returning to the meeting, Betty's eyes met Amy as she entered the room.

"Everything alright," Betty asked.

"Yeah. I'm really sorry. I forgot about a dental appointment I had scheduled a while back for today," Amy lied. The blood drained from her face. "I'll be out the rest of the day. I'm so sorry."

"That's okay, we can finish this tomorrow," Betty said, smiling.

Amy turned and rushed to her office. She glanced at the clock hanging on the wall behind her desk. Flashing 1:10 p.m., her chest tightened. She needed to be on the road in ten minutes.

Amy's fingers trembled on the keyboard when logging into the company's Cooperative Rural Bank account. She initiated a wire transfer of twenty million dollars from Whitman's line of credit to a numbered account at the Hong Kong National Bank in Hong Kong. "I can't believe I'm doing this," she whispered. Emailing the bank vice president, Amy assured him that while a wire to Hong Kong was unusual, it was necessary to pay a vendor from the Asian region for equipment Whitman Communications had purchased for its fiber optic cable project. He should call Erick immediately on his cell for confirmation if necessary. The smell of her half-eaten lunch lying on the desk caused her stomach to cramp in pain.

After initiating the wire, Amy logged into the account a second time, this session using Michael Romano's bank login credentials to approve the wires. In under five minutes, she completed the wire and printed the confirmation.

Amy placed her laptop and a portable disk drive in her computer case, grabbed her coat and headed for the parking lot. Legs trembling as she walked toward her car, she struggled to put on a pair of oversized sunglasses. Amy moved deliberately, trying not to look guilty, but thought that might make her look even more suspicious. Sitting in her car, she took a deep breath and pulled down the visor mirror to study herself. Seeing the terror in her own eyes, she shuddered in fear. Amy started the car and shifted into gear. She turned north from the Whitman parking lot onto US 195 and drove toward Spokane.

CHAPTER 55

ERICK ARRIVED AT Skip Britain's law office in Spokane at 12:50 for their lunch meeting. Sitting in his car in the parking garage across the street from Skip's office, Erick recalled their conversation from this morning.

"Erick, it's urgent we meet today. Can you come to my office around lunchtime? Say one o'clock?" Skip rushed his words.

"What's happening? Why the urgency?" Erick asked, brow furrowed in worry.

"I don't want to discuss it on the phone ... It's serious."

"Okay, okay. I'll be there."

Erick climbed from his car now and crossed the street to the office building. Entering Skip's reception area through the unlocked door, he called out, "Hello, anyone here?" Erick shut the door and locked it, as it usually would be during the lunch hour.

There were no sounds in the office suite, and that was unusual. Erick headed for the hallway leading to Skip's office. From the corner of his eye, he caught the image of Skip's receptionist lying on the floor. Blood covered her face.

"Oh no," Erick gasped. He rushed to her side and knelt down, feeling her neck for a pulse.

Nothing.

Erick's heart raced. He stood next to the reception desk for a moment, panicked. Taking a breath to compose himself, Erick stumbled down the hall to Skip's office. The office door was ajar. He saw Skip's blood-soaked head before entering the room. Erick stood frozen. Skip's pants were pulled down to his ankles. Taser probes remained embedded in his genitals. Three severed fingers covered in blood lay in a neat row on the desk.

Wild thoughts rushed through his mind. Who did this? Romano? Am I next?

Erick left the office in hurried terror. Pulling out his burner cell, he typed a one-word text to Amy: *Alvin*. Erick hoped she had the strength to carry out their plan.

Eyes glistening with tears, Erick rushed down the stairwell, two steps at a time. He didn't know if the tears were for Skip or himself. Safely in his vehicle now, Erick checked for emails on his Whitman cell phone. The screen indicated one unopened email with *wire confirmation* in the subject line. He pulled out the burner cell phone and called Amy.

"Erick, is it you?" Amy asked, softly.

"Yes, are you on the road?" Erick scanned the cars around him to ensure he was alone.

"I'm driving to Spokane now to swap cars with Ali ... I'm scared, Erick. What happened?"

"We'll talk tonight. You know what to do when you get to the farm?" He ignored her question. The truth would panic her further.

"Yeah, like we practiced ... Have you left?"

"I'm getting ready to leave now. I need to get the Explorer ... I got the wire confirmation. Good work. We're golden."

"Be careful, Erick. I need you."

"We need each other. I'll see you in a few hours," Erick said as he started the car.

CHAPTER 56

MICHAEL ROMANO NURSED a whiskey alone in his office, waiting for a call. The Family used dozens of shell LLC companies to carry out its business endeavors and clean the proceeds. Each company had multiple bank accounts, and money flowed freely between the LLCs and domestic and foreign banks, resulting in an original customer transaction being lost in a sea of flowing money.

"Fuck, Britain," Romano spit in anger.

Romano's phone rang.

"Yeah?"

"It's done."

"Good. Did he transfer the money back?" Romano stared out the window into the gray afternoon.

"It took some effort, but he did."

"Tony will be pleased." Romano grinned.

"I hung around the area briefly, and someone showed up. Tall, well-built blond guy. He saw the bodies. Looked pretty shaken. I thought you should know."

"Bodies?" Romano asked, caught off guard.

"Yeah, the secretary got in the way."

"Too bad," a hint of sadness from Romano.

"Couldn't be helped."

"Okay, thanks. I'll deal with the visitor." Romano squeezed his whiskey glass firmly, and the blood flushed his face. "Olson," he said quietly.

Romano hung up the phone and called Erick Olson. "Whitman Communications, Mr. Olson's office, this is Candy. May I help you?"

"Yeah, Candy, Michael Romano, do you know where Erick is?"

"He had a lunch meeting in Spokane today. May I take a message?"

"Tell him we need to talk. What about the accountin' lady? Is she in?"

"If you mean Amy Summers, no, she had a dentist appointment this afternoon. Would you like to leave a message for her?"

"No, just Erick, thanks." Romano slammed the phone down. Something about Olson lodged in his mind as an incomplete thought. The thought had weight, though, and dragged down Michael's mood. *Trust, it's about trust. Can I trust the son of a bitch?*

Romano reached into his desk drawer and pulled out the bottle of whiskey. He poured another drink, walked over to his office window, and looked out over the dreary Spokane winter cityscape. He missed Chicago. His little corner of Spokane reminded him of home, but it wasn't the same.

"Hey, Boss," Gino said, walking into Michael's office. "Did Gerald get things taken care of?"

"It's done." Michael reached for the whiskey bottle and poured Gino a drink. "To family," Michael toasted. He reclaimed his desk chair.

"To family," Gino replied and took a sip. He dropped into a guest chair facing Romano's desk. "What about Olson, Boss? Is he gonna work out?"

"That's the question of the day, Gino. He ain't proven himself yet," Michael sighed.

"Seems like a smart guy."

"No doubt. Britain was smart too. Too damn smart for his own good," Michael took a sip of whiskey, its burning warmth a welcome relief. "If Olson runs, we'll track 'im down. Put out a hit on 'im and the girl."

Michael took another sip and closed his eyes. What the hell? If Olson's like most bean counters, he'll send some cash offshore to the Caribbean and plan to lead a life of leisure on the damn beach. The problem is, we got men over there and find guys like Olson all the time. It may take a while, but sooner or later, they surface, and then—game over!

CHAPTER 57

"**L**ISTEN UP, PEOPLE. We have a situation," Agent Monroe said, walking briskly into the war room to brief his task force. "We received word from the local police that Michael Romano's lawyer, Skip Britain, was found dead in his Spokane office. Shot twice in the head. Appears as though he was tortured too ... They killed his receptionist as well," Monroe paused. He looked out the window to the Spokane afternoon traffic and inhaled a deep breath. "Spokane police detectives will take the lead in investigating these two murders. We'll assist in case the trail spills over into our investigation.

"Do we know where our persons of interest are right now—Michael Romano, Erick Olson, Betty Olson, and Amy Summers?" Monroe asked, spitting out the names. "It's possible one of them is involved in this."

"We have an agent with eyes on Michael Romano. He's in his office building. Hasn't left all day," an agent said.

"I spoke with Agent McCoy. Betty Olson's vehicle has been in the Whitman parking lot since this morning. She hasn't been observed leaving the building," another agent offered. "Erick Olson's vehicle is not in the company lot. The CFO, Ms. Summers, was seen leaving around 1:15 p.m. We don't know why."

"Do you think Summers is involved?" asked another agent.

"I don't know. Could be any one of them or none of them," Monroe frowned and bit his lip. "Put out a BOLO for Erick Olson and Amy Summers with the local police in Spokane and Pullman and the Sheriff's departments for Spokane, Whitman, and the surrounding counties.

Send them descriptions of the persons, vehicles, and plate numbers. If apprehended, have them held for questioning."

"What if we don't make contact soon?" asked an agent.

"Then we visit Ms. Olson and see if she knows where Erick Olson and Summers are," Monroe said.

"What about Romano, Boss?" asked another agent.

"We'll let the Spokane police question him if any evidence from the Britain Law office crime scene leads them in that direction."

"Boss, what about mass transit?"

"Let's check airline passenger manifests, train depots, and bus stations—see if they've purchased tickets to leave town. Our best bet for now is someone spotting one of their vehicles," Monroe walked back to his desk. "Alright, back to work, people!"

It was game on for Agent Monroe. A dead lawyer and two missing telephone executives, all persons of interest. Whatever happened at Romano Enterprises and Whitman Communications today, all of a sudden, there were a lot of moving parts.

CHAPTER 58

THE EVENING AIR held a stiff chill. The early February night sky had darkened, cloaking the small Idaho farmhouse from any vehicle passing by. A passerby was unlikely. Situated behind a knoll, the house hid a quarter-mile off a lightly traveled county road.

Sitting alone in the dimly lit living room with a 38 revolver on her lap, Amy didn't believe she could actually shoot anyone. She wanted badly to call Erick but knew not to—*have to follow the plan*. Her mind ran wild with broken thoughts. Was Erick really on his way? Would Romano find her? What about the FBI? Amy felt like an actress in a romantic tragedy where the married boyfriend disappears with the money and the wife. The girl left to take the fall. *Calm yourself. He'll be here soon.*

Amy had eaten only half her lunch and was starved for dinner. She laid the weapon on the cushion beside her and opened her laptop to book their flight to Cancun tomorrow.

Drifting in and out of sleep, Amy awoke to the sound of car tires rolling on gravel. A pair of headlights swung across the front of the little farmhouse, and the living room illuminated for a brief moment. She grabbed the revolver and pointed it at the door.

Three knocks on the door. Amy trembled and squeezed the gun tightly.

"Amy, are you there?"

"Erick!" Amy dropped her gun on the coffee table, ran to the door, fumbled with the latch, and threw it open. She collapsed into his arms.

"Thank God you're here." She buried her head in his chest.

"Why are the lights turned down?" He reached for the light switch and flicked it on. A burst of bright light filled the room.

"I was afraid someone would see. I just turned on the one table lamp," Amy reached up and kissed Erick.

"We're hundreds of yards off a secondary road. We'll be fine." Erick smiled with confidence.

Amy returned to the old, faded, floral sofa in the living room and sat with her hands on her knees. Erick opened two beers from the fridge and sat next to her. She scooted up against him and rested her head on his shoulder; she felt safe again. Still, she wondered silently about their future. Would their relationship thrive with increased time spent together, or would they find new faults in one another? All that she knew for certain was they were leaving the country. There was no turning back.

"Did you call Wenatchee?" Erick asked.

"Yeah, were in luck. Wilford's available tomorrow. It's all set."

"Good. I need to unload the Explorer and put it in the barn. Did you unpack your car?"

"It's all in the bedroom."

"Were you able to switch with Ali?"

"Yeah."

He set his beer on the coffee table and swallowed her in his arms. She could feel the strength of his upper body through his shirt. He kissed her for a long while, and she cherished every second. When he released his grip on her and began to stand, she pulled him back onto the couch.

"Don't you leave me again, mister."

"I need to unload the car. I promise I won't go anywhere without you."

CHAPTER 59

THE NEXT MORNING, the sun worked its way through ancient, yellowed bedroom curtains and awakened Erick. He slipped quietly out of bed to make a pot of coffee and started breakfast. Amy groaned and rolled over without opening her eyes.

Half-an-hour later, Amy walked into the kitchen wearing blue pajama bottoms and a spaghetti-strap, loose-fitting white top. Erick loved the look of the fabric against her warm skin tone. Her face looked rested and fresh.

"The smell of coffee woke me up," she said, smiling and stretching her arms toward the ceiling. "What are you cooking for breakfast?"

"Fried eggs, bacon, and toast," Erick smiled broadly.

"That sounds good, I'm starved."

"Looking like you do, I could skip breakfast and take you right here in the farmhouse kitchen." Erick flirted to ease the tension from the ordeal they faced ahead.

"You expect to get laid when you didn't even buy me dinner last night, mister?"

"Good point, my bad."

She put her hands on his hips and rolled up on her toes for a morning kiss. "I missed you. Promise you won't leave me again."

"Missed you too, and now that I know the rules of the game, I'll certainly be buying you dinner tonight and tomorrow and the next."

She reached out and gently pushed his shoulder, "Stop, you're being crazy."

Erick turned to the stove and flipped the eggs. "Did you get us tickets to Cancun?" His expression had turned serious.

"Yeah, last night. We're all set. What about the last leg of the trip?"

"I've got Wilford working on that. We can't make reservations until we get a firm date from his guy in Mexico." Erick focused on the eggs. Bacon sizzled in a second skillet.

Erick tried to exude confidence. In reality, he recognized their escape plan held unknown danger and a high risk of being apprehended.

After breakfast, Erick stood on the front porch with his ear to the wind—listening. He looked toward the Nez Perce Tribal Reservation and trained his ear to the sound of a turboprop engine.

Amy stepped onto the porch and handed Erick a mug of hot coffee.

"Thanks." He put his arm around her shoulder and turned his ear back toward the reservation. "Do you hear that?"

"Yeah." She looked to the horizon and pointed, "I think I see him."

"Yep, that's the plane. Let's grab our bags," Erick said. They stepped back into the farmhouse.

Erick smiled at the sight of Amy emerging from the bedroom dragging her two rolling suitcases with her computer bag strapped over her shoulder.

"You think this is funny? What's left of my life is in these bags." Amy frowned.

"Here, let me take the large one, and you grab my small bag."

They switched bags and walked around to the backside of the barn. Wilford waited in the idling plane.

"Good morning, Erick, a fine morning to be flying, don't you think?" Wilford said as he stepped from the plane onto the gravel landing strip.

"It's a gorgeous day. Here's the cash. Count it if you like. We'll load our gear."

"We've done business before, I trust you." Wilford smiled.

Wilford held up the thick manila envelope as if to weight its contents. He dropped the envelope onto the copilot airplane seat and climbed back into the plane.

"Buckle up!" Wilford called out over the roar of the engine. He taxied the plane to the far end of the runway Erick had repaired over Thanksgiving, turned, and took off into the wind.

After they reached cruising altitude, Wilford turned his head toward Erick. He said, "It's about an hour-and-half to the Vancouver airport. I've already filed my flight plan with Canada, so we're good to go."

"Okay." Erick wasn't concerned. They'd be long gone by the time the FBI figured out they flew to Vancouver. "Did you find us a guy in Cancun?"

"It took a while, but I found a guy I served with. You can trust him. I've got it all written down for you. Six grand for him to take care of you and two grand to fix the passport issue. All cash."

"Two thousand of bribe money for the passport stamp?" Erick asked. His heart sank with the thought of letting a stranger in on his plan.

"Yeah, that's the way it works down there. People getting paid off all the time." Wilford smiled. It was apparent he felt comfortable operating in this clandestine world.

Erick relaxed in his seat. The pieces of his escape plan were coming together. Wilford was a solid guy, and Erick believed he could place his trust in him.

Erick thought back to the bar in Dallas when he first brought Wilford into his plan.

"So you're thinking wheels up around 4 p.m. tomorrow," Wilford asked.

"That should work," Erick said. He took a sip of his gin and tonic. After a long minute, Erick looked up from his drink to Wilford. "I need to ask you something."

"Shoot," Wilford said with eyes narrowed. "Anything."

Erick fiddled with his drink for a second or two. "Do you ever fly out of the country?"

"Occasionally, I get clients heading for Canada or Mexico, which I'm fine with. I got into a bit of a scrape a while back flying mercenaries around Central America, so that's definitely out." Wilford held out his palms in mock protest. "Is there somewhere you need to go?"

"There may be. We're having some legal problems with the phone company. Amy and I may need to bail on short notice," Erick said. Sweat beaded on his forehead. "I need you to keep this to yourself."

"Of course, Erick. Sorry to hear this. Where were you thinking of heading to?"

"First stop would be Vancouver, BC. That's where I could use you. To get us there."

"That's doable," Wilford said, picking up his beer and taking a sip.

"Then I'll need someone in Cancun to get entry stamps on our new passports. Once that's fixed, Amy and I will fly to South America. It's best you not know where," Erick said. He looked around the restaurant to make sure no one was listening.

"I have contacts down in Mexico from my navy days, mostly retired pilots. I'll ask around if you'd like."

"Please do. And mums the word." Erick ran his finger across his lips.

Air turbulence startled Erick back to the present. He watched the gentle Palouse hills reveal their majesty from ten thousand feet. Heartstrings anchored deep in the land pulled back hard as the plane carried him away from his home for the final time.

It had taken Erick fifteen years to find his way home after moving to Seattle. Once again, he found himself leaving the Palouse behind, this time on a one-way ticket. He knew he could never return. His heart sank, and his chest tightened. The sadness of those thoughts were offset by having Amy at his side. Erick's face flushed, realizing they would be together from this moment forward. He would be happy anywhere, so long as he had her to share it with. And with the twenty million dollars, they could settle comfortably anywhere in the world. Erick turned his head from the window and smiled at Amy. He reached across the aisle and took her hand in his, squeezing it gently. She smiled back.

CHAPTER 60

STANDING IN FRONT of his team in the war room at 7 a.m., Agent Monroe scanned the sea of exhausted faces. He sipped his cup of coffee and began speaking in a measured tone. "As you know, we lost contact with Erick Olson and Amy Summers yesterday afternoon. We had hoped we would pick them up again this morning, but it looks like they're in the wind. The BOLO we issued yesterday has come up empty. Our mission now is to find them. I'm heading out shortly to meet with Agent McCoy at the Whitman Communications building in Colfax. We'll interview Betty Olson to find out what she knows if anything." Agent Monroe frowned and rubbed his temple.

"I need the rest of you to get pictures of Erick Olson and Amy Summers to the security officer at every airport within three hundred miles of here. Find out if Olson has ever charted a private aircraft and, if he has, who the pilot was, where they went, and the type of plane. Let's get local law enforcement to check bus stations and the Amtrak station to see if anyone matching their description purchased tickets. Review the security camera footage at every public transportation hub. Expand the BOLO to the ten state western region and get pictures, vehicle descriptions, and plates to every law enforcement office in the area," Monroe paused and looked into the faces of his team. "Any questions?"

"Boss, are we assuming Olson and the girl are together?" asked an agent.

"Let's not assume anything. They may have split up to travel separately to a predetermined location and time." He rubbed his stomach, acid burning through its lining. "Anything else?" the room went quiet. "Okay, good. Let's get on it!"

A dejected Monroe fell into his chair. "Where the hell are you, Olson?" he mumbled to himself. Monroe could understand if Michael Romano disappeared suddenly without a trace. Tony Ferrari had the resources and experience to pull that off. Not Olson, though.

Monroe held his head in his hands, trying to think of an escape method that would appeal to Olson. He was too smart to use the airlines, and he couldn't drive his Porsche fast enough to outrun their phone calls. Buses were a possibility, but to where? He picked up the phone to make the call he dreaded: the Chicago field office director.

CHAPTER 61

SPECIAL AGENT MONROE eased his Tahoe into the Whitman Communications parking lot and stopped beside Agent McCoy's vehicle. He stepped out and motioned for her to follow him. They entered the building through the customer entrance and approached the receptionist.

"May I help you?" the young woman asked.

"Special Agents Monroe and McCoy with the FBI, would you please have Betty Olson step out here?" They flashed their badges at her.

"Of course. Is this about Erick and Amy? Neither one showed up for work today," she said in a worried tone.

They ignored her question, "It would be best if you get her now," Monroe said.

The receptionist left her desk and returned a minute later with Betty.

"Betty Olson? Special Agents Monroe and McCoy with the FBI," Agent Monroe flipped open his ID for Betty's inspection.

She looked at the ID, and her jaw dropped in disbelief. "Yes, I'm Betty. May I help you?"

"Is there somewhere we may speak privately?"

"We can use my office," Betty said, still appearing puzzled.

The agents followed Betty down a long hallway. Monroe picked up a definite vibe from Betty. She seemed bewildered at their presence. Monroe wondered if she knew what her ex-husband and Amy Summers had been up to. The agents followed Betty into her office and sat in guest chairs across the desk from her.

Monroe began, "Ms. Olson, when was the last time you saw your ex-husband, Erick Olson?"

"Erick?" Betty's brow furrowed in worry. "I suppose it would have been yesterday morning here at work. Erick left for a meeting with our company lawyer in Spokane around 11:30. Why do you ask?"

"We want to question him about his relationship with Michael Romano. Do you know Mr. Romano?" Monroe looked directly into Betty's eyes as McCoy took notes.

"Erick put him on our board of directors. I don't really know him well. We met once at one of our board meetings. I do know we have a contract with his company for some sort of billing support services. Erick worked on the details for that arrangement. I'm focused almost exclusively on HR matters." Betty adjusted herself in the chair.

"When was the last time you saw Amy Summers?"

"I was in a meeting with her yesterday shortly after lunch. She got a call from her dentist's office reminding her of an appointment she had forgotten. She left in a hurry and didn't return ... Which was odd for her. I'm—" She focused on her desktop in concentration.

"Odd in what way?" Monroe interrupted.

"She's super organized. Forgetting an appointment is highly out of character for her," Betty said with a distant look in her eyes.

"I suppose not calling in this morning is out of character as well?" Monroe asked deliberately.

"Yes, definitely. I'm concerned for her. She didn't answer her cell phone when I called. I planned to send someone by her apartment at lunch to check on her." Betty's eyes narrowed in concern.

Agent Monroe turned toward McCoy and nodded. Monroe had instructed McCoy to address the possible affair between Erick Olson and Amy Summers.

"Betty, how closely does Ms. Summers work with Erick Olson?" McCoy asked.

"She's our CFO and has an ownership interest in the company. They work together almost daily."

"Do you believe she may be with Erick?" McCoy locked eyes with Betty.

"I don't think so. If there is a business reason for them being out of the office today, it would be on our corporate calendar," Betty crossed her arms over her chest and leaned back in her chair.

She's uncomfortable with the implication, Monroe thought.

"Are Summers and Olson romantically involved," McCoy asked as gently as she could.

"No ... Maybe," Betty stumbled over the words, and her face blushed. "I think there's something going on between them. They've been discreet and haven't made anything public."

"Have you noticed any unusual activity in your bank accounts over the past few days?" McCoy continued.

"I did get a call from a concerned bank vice president at Cooperative Rural Bank in Denver. We have a line of credit with them. He said Erick drew down twenty million of the line yesterday afternoon, which seemed unusual. He's a financial wizard. I'm certain he has a good reason," Betty said as she nervously tapped a pencil on her desk.

"Do you have online access to your bank accounts?" McCoy stood and moved to the side of the desk, where she could see Betty's computer monitor.

"Of course."

"Would you mind logging on to see if there are any transactions out of the ordinary?"

"Sure thing," Betty said. She pulled up the Cooperative Rural Bank website on her computer, entered her ID and password, and hit enter.

Not a valid password or ID flashed on the screen.

"Strange. The system didn't accept my credentials." Her panicked fingers raced across the keyboard a second time.

Not a valid password or ID flashed on the screen.

"Let's try our local bank," Betty said, her hands shaking. After two attempts to log onto the company's Farmers Bank account, she raised her hands in defeat. "I'll have IT look into it."

Monroe asked, "Do you know anyone who may have wanted to harm Skip Britain?"

"What? Of course not. He's a sweet guy. Erick and I have known him since back in our college days. Is there something wrong with Skip?" She sat rigid in her chair. Worry lines creased her forehead.

"Ma'am, he was murdered yesterday in his office, along with his receptionist," McCoy said softly.

"Oh my God. No." She slumped in her chair and held her head in her hands.

Agent Monroe felt his heart sink. *It's the hardest damn part of the job, telling someone a person close to them has died.*

"Who would do that?" Tears filled her eyes.

The two agents exchanged glances. "That's what we're trying to figure out," Monroe said.

A worried expression filled Betty's face. "You don't think they're after Erick, do you ... Or me?"

"No, this seems to have more to do with another of Britain's clients," McCoy said.

Betty lowered her head and shook it slowly from side to side in disbelief.

"I think we're through here for now. Before we leave, I'd like to have Agent McCoy take a look at a few of your employee personnel files. Here's my card. Call me if you think of anything else or if you find something odd in the company books. And call me if either Erick or Ms. Summers contacts you. I'll show myself out." Monroe dropped a business card on Betty's desk and walked toward the door.

"I'll have Candy help you with our personnel files." Betty looked at Agent McCoy and wiped her eyes with a tissue.

"Agent McCoy, I'll see you back at the war room after you finish up here," Monroe said from the doorway.

CHAPTER 62

TURNING HALFWAY IN his pilot's seat, Wilford smiled at Erick. "We're crossing the Canadian border now. We'll begin our approach soon."

"Tell me about the guy you found for us in Cancun?" Erick asked, filled with apprehension.

"Martin Owens, good man. Former Naval Aviator, like me. We served together years ago. You'll be in good hands with him. He runs a charter service out of Cancun."

"Are you good to stay here in Canada for a week?" Erick bit his lip. Adding Martin to the plan worried him, but so did having Wilford left as a loose end.

"Yep. Got my skis in the back. I'm going up to Whistler for a week.

"What about your plane?"

"I made arrangements to have it stored at the airport." Wilford smiled and turned back toward the steering column. "Buckle up. We're ready to begin our descent."

Rolling up on the tarmac near a gate with several other small aircraft parked nearby, Wilford turned in his seat again. "Even though you're connecting to a flight to Mexico, you'll have to go through customs. Shouldn't be too bad, though."

"Yeah, we should be good. I stashed our weapons back in the farmhouse, and we have ten grand cash each." Erick's heart beat faster. Both Canada and Mexico have strict gun control, and they couldn't risk bringing their weapons across the border.

"Martin will have a gun and ammo for you in Mexico. Be careful, though. It's illegal as hell to carry there," Wilford let out a chuckle. "Which is kinda strange given all the drug cartel action down that way. Seems like everyone is armed!"

"We'll be fine," Erick said and looked at Amy. She faced the window and couldn't see him. Costa Rica's strict laws wouldn't permit Erick to carry a gun there, either. He took a measured breath and exhaled. Doesn't matter, he thought, once we leave Cancun, we won't need weapons.

Leaving customs with Amy two hours later, Erick glanced at his watch—1:30 p.m.

"There's the check-in for Aeromexico." Erick pointed to a long counter with lines of travelers.

"Great. Let's get rid of these bags and get our boarding passes," Amy said.

Waiting in the boarding area half an hour later, Erick turned to Amy. She was typing something on her laptop. "Hey, is there a Wi-Fi signal here," he asked.

"There is," she said smiling.

"Can you take a minute and see if anyone has tripped the surveillance cameras at the farm?" Erick asked softly.

"I already did. Nothing yet."

"Good," Erick breathed a sigh of relief. He accepted once the FBI found the farm, they would discover Wilford next and then figure out Erick and Amy were heading to Cancun.

CHAPTER 63

THE FBI TASK force war room buzzed with activity in the late afternoon. The original eight-member task force had doubled in size. At Special Agent Monroe's request, detectives from Spokane and Whitman counties and the Spokane PD had been temporarily assigned to support the team.

"Boss, a Sheriff in Idaho, received several calls from tribal members complaining about a plane flying low over an Indian reservation this morning a little before 9 a.m. They're used to seeing small crop dusters and larger planes during fire season, but reports suggest it was a passenger aircraft which would be unusual," agent Polak said.

"Where?" Agent Monroe stood from behind his desk.

"Near Grangeville, Idaho. It's about a three-hour drive from here."

"Call the sheriff and see if there are any airstrips in the immediate area capable of handling a small passenger plane. Tell him you're headed that way. See if he can get you with the people sighting the plane. Show the witnesses our aircraft file pictures and try to determine the aircraft make and model."

Monroe devoured a stale jelly donut in three bites. He licked his fingers. His call with the Chicago Field office director hadn't gone well. The director wanted Olson found quickly so as not to jeopardize the broader Ferrari investigation.

"People, talk to me. What else do we have?" Monroe asked.

Agent McCoy looked up and said, "I followed up with Betty Olson after lunch. She still hasn't been able to get online access to the company accounts, but she has spoken with their banks. Yesterday afternoon, a wire transfer for twenty million dollars was sent from Cooperative Rural Bank. The funds were wired to a numbered bank account in Hong Kong. The wire was approved by Michael Romano and initiated by Amy Summers."

"Romano! Why the hell would Romano be authorized to access Whitman's bank accounts?" Monroe barked in disbelief.

"Apparently, Romano's on the Whitman board of directors. Betty Olson wasn't aware he had access to company bank accounts. His involvement seemed to take her by surprise."

"Could Summers and Romano be working together?" Monroe asked.

"I'm fairly certain Ms. Summers is romantically involved with Erick Olson, Sir," McCoy said. "Our surveillance hasn't picked up any contact between Summers and Romano."

"Run the traps. We can't rule out a Summers and Romano tryst. People will do strange things for that much cash. Can we follow the money?" The donut turned in his stomach.

"Yes and no. There's no fiscal treaty with the US, so Hong Kong won't tell us anything about the account or its owner. They did confirm it was a valid account and received a twenty million dollar wire transfer this morning."

"Speak with the lending officer at Cooperative Rural Bank. Let's see what they know about this transaction."

"Yes, Sir," McCoy said.

"Get me the documents supporting the wire from Cooperative Rural Bank. We have enough to get an arrest warrant on Amy Summers for wire fraud," Monroe sighed deeply.

"What about Olson," McCoy asked.

"We don't have enough on him yet." Monroe frowned. He couldn't help but wonder if the crime would fall on Summers as CFO, which was a regular occurrence with white-collar schemes.

"I'll get those documents for you."

"Anything else, McCoy?" Agent Monroe asked.

"There may be, but I don't have all the pieces yet."

"Spit it out. Tell us what you do have," Monroe scowled.

"The wire transfer email authorization and confirmation disappeared from the company's servers." Agent McCoy paused. "Fortunately, the bank was able to provide them.

"Remember how we never overheard incriminating conversations over the taps we placed on their phones? All of their computers are linked by instant messaging software. They may have planned this whole thing by typing messages back and forth. Funny thing, though, Betty Olson said the entire company file history of instant messages vanished last night. It's viewed as an informal means of communication. The files are never backed up. The only people who can delete messages are the IT group, and they say they didn't do it.

"I asked to look at the employee personnel files for the IT group, and while we were there, I had them pull Amy Summers' file. Because she had worked with Erick Olson to purchase the company, her file had no resume or employment application. I checked with the UW records department, and it turns out she was an accounting major with top grades and a minor in software engineering, which we knew. What we didn't know was that she was a handful of classes short of a second BS degree in software engineering—"

"I don't like where this is headed," Monroe interrupted. The rest of the team had stopped their work and listened closely to McCoy.

"Oh, it gets better. When Summers was an undergraduate, the university participated in a hacking challenge. Participants from around the country attempted to hack into a secure system established by NSA. Nearly two dozen groups signed up to play, including our Summers and several Ph.D. candidates from software engineering programs around the country. Three successfully hacked the system: Summers and two other groups from MIT. It took the other two groups nearly two weeks to get in. Summers teamed up with a UW software engineering Ph.D. candidate named Zack Eng. They hacked it in less than a week. This was her minor, for God's sake."

"So we've got a couple of damn geniuses on our hands, a financial wizard and a software phenom. She's probably encrypting everything they touch electronically." Monroe pounded his fist on the conference table.

"Sir, I think we have to assume she left a virus of some sort in the Whitman computer system and may still have access and control to delete or encrypt files."

"Get with our cyber experts and establish a list of actions Summers could take to disguise their movements, given her level of skill. Can she access and change an airline passenger manifest or tickets purchased on Amtrak or at the bus station? What could she do with credit card point-of-purchase location information? Have we put any of their files on our system yet?

"Not from my visit."

"Let's make certain we don't." Monroe turned and walked to the window, hands thrust deep into his pants pockets. "I wonder ... will Summers take a deal?" Monroe whispered to himself.

CHAPTER 64

A LATE WINTER SQUALL rolled in from the northeast. The storm obscured the view of Lake Michigan from Michael Romano's vantage point in Tony Ferrari's Chicago office. Tony sat at his conference table across from Joe Acosta. Romano sat nervously next to Joe.

"What are you thinking, Boss?" Joe asked

Tony turned to Romano and latched his angry green eyes on him. "This fucking mess happened on your watch, Michael," Tony paused and leaned forward over the table. "What the hell's going on with Whitman?"

Romano shifted uncomfortably in his chair, "I don't know, Boss. He saw Britain's body, maybe that spooked 'im, and he ran ... I don't know." Romano bit down on his upper lip and averted his eyes.

"Twenty million gone missing ... Tell him what you found, Joe," Tony shifted his stare to Acosta.

"It doesn't look good, Michael," Acosta crossed his legs and faced Romano. "I spoke with our informant. The Whitman CFO, Amy Summers, initiated the twenty million dollar wire from Cooperative Rural Bank to a numbered account in Hong Kong. The bank records show that you approved the wire."

"Me? I don't have access to Whitman's bank accounts. They must have put me on the account because I'm on Whitman's board. I swear, I got nothin' to do with this. They're trying to pin it on me," Romano said panicked. Beads of sweat broke out on his forehead. He pulled the pocket square from his suit coat and swiped at his face.

Acosta leaned toward Romano. "We know you didn't do it, Michael. They must have been planning this for some time now," Acosta paused.

"Think back, Michael, were there any clues? Did you ever get a feeling they were working on a plan?"

"No. Never. Olson's been doing what we ask him to do," Michael said, his words trailing into silence.

Tony leaned back in his chair and took a deep breath, his eyes closed as though weighing a life-or-death decision. "We gave the asshole every chance—had the talk with him. Maybe it *was* seeing his lawyer's body."

Joe frowned. "You think that would have scared him enough to do this? Son of a bitch can't believe it will end well for him."

Tony pulled a cigarette from the pack on the table and lit it, holding the match until it burned his thumb. He dropped the match, inhaled deeply, and held the smoke in his lungs. When he exhaled, the dirty-white smoke curled on its way to the ceiling. "What the hell else could it be? They were pals."

"Probably thinks he's next," Romano said.

"He is, now." The green eyes darted back to Romano. "We need to find him—and end it for good."

"What about the girl?" Acosta asked.

"Get rid of her too. First, work them over and find the missing money. Make certain they wire it back before we finish them." Tony stood and walked to the window, faced the Chicago gloom. "What about Olson's wife?"

From his seat, Romano could hear cabs on the street below, honking their horns as they vied for fares and a place on the road. He relaxed a bit and took a deep breath. *I'll be in a taxi to the airport soon enough.*

Joe rubbed the back of his neck. "Ex-wife, Betty. She's still working at the Whitman office."

"Good. She's got a lot of phone company experience. We'll let her run things for now." Tony reclaimed his seat.

"Should Michael talk with her?"

"She needs to know the score."

"I'll take care of it, Boss." Romano shifted in his seat.

"For the hit, are you thinking Gerald?" Joe asked. A sinister smile broke across his face.

"He's the best we've got. Check with our informants first to see if we can find where Olson's hiding. At least narrow it down to a town." Tony leaned over the conference table and crushed his cigarette into the ashtray.

CHAPTER 65

WATCHING LUGGAGE TUMBLE onto the Cancun carousel at 10:30 p.m., Erick didn't pay much attention to the people crowed around him. Erick reached to grab one of Amy's bags and set it on the floor next to her, grunted, and dropped his shoulders. Twelve hours had ticked off since leaving the farm this morning, and he was exhausted.

"Erick Olson?"

Startled, Erick's heart skipped a beat. He turned to face the voice.

"Martin Owens, I'm your ride." The athletic-looking man around Wilford's age stroked his close-cut beard.

"You caught me by surprise," Erick said, heart pounding. "How did you know which flight we were on?" Erick reached to grab the last of their checked luggage.

"It was easy. When we get your passport issue fixed, it will be much harder for people to track you," Martin said with a tight, closed-lip smile. "Let me help you with those bags."

"Thanks." Erick dropped the last bag and stepped to the side, exposing Amy. "This is Amy," he said quietly, still unsure about his new friend.

"I'm parked out front," Martin grabbed Amy's two large bags effortlessly, one in each hand, and headed toward the exit.

Climbing into Martin's SUV, Erick sat up front. Amy took a seat in the back behind Martin.

Martin started the vehicle and drove toward the parking toll gate. "I got you an ambassador suite at the Tipton Resort. It's a bit off the main drag and quiet. Sort of an upscale family resort. You'll be safe there for a few days."

"What about registration?" Erick asked with consternation.

"Not to worry. I married a local gal and have dual citizenship. The room's registered to a friend of my wife on the friend's credit card. Avoid the front desk, and you'll go unnoticed." Martin reached out and patted Erick on the shoulder. "I've got your back."

Twenty minutes later, they pulled up in front of the Tipton Hotel. Erick looked toward the hotel buildings but could make out few details. The night sky was pitch-black. Sidewalks on the grounds leading to the lobby were lit by low pedestal light standards, casting a soft glow on the walkways.

"Here are your key cards," Martin said, holding two festively colored cards. "Like I said, the room is under a family friend's name. It's probably best that you pay cash for meals and whatever else you need during your stay."

"That won't be a problem." Reaching into the side pocket of his carry-on bag, Erick pulled out a thick envelope. "Here's the cash for taking care of us and getting our passports stamped," Erick paused and scanned the area surrounding the SUV, searching for prying eyes. He saw no one. Relieved, he took a deep breath. "Our new passports are in here, too."

Martin took the package and peeked inside, "Alright then. Let's get you up to your room. You're on the fifth floor with a balcony."

Stepping into their room, Erick exchanged phone numbers with Martin.

"Thanks, Martin. When will I hear from you?" Erick said forcefully, wanting to leave Cancun as soon as possible.

Martin shrugged, "It'll be two or three days until I can get the passports stamped. Then you're free to go. With the weekend, we're probably looking at getting you out of here Monday."

"So, Monday morning?" Erick's pulse rose. He wanted out of here fast.

"Monday morning at the earliest. I need to check my Mexico customs guy's work schedule," Martin said. "Before I forget, I need to give you this. Wilford said you may need it," he pulled a holstered 45 caliber pistol from his belt. "Take care with this. There's no legal way for you to have a handgun on your person under Mexican law." Martin's eyes narrowed.

"Thanks, let's hope I don't need this," Erick shrugged. "Get us out of here Sunday, and I'll bump your fee by three grand." Erick leaned forward aggressively.

"I'll let you know tomorrow morning. No promises," Martin said. Unfazed, he turned and stepped into the hall, closing the door behind him.

Leaving their suitcases on the floor, Amy and Erick stripped to their underwear and fell into the bed, exhausted.

Erick's sleep was fitful, interrupted by a stream of dreams resonating deep in his subconscious.

Amy, wake up. We need to go. Erick and Amy hurried from the bed and escaped their hotel room down a darkened stairwell and into the streets of Chicago. They ran through alleyways in the dark. Panicked, they fought their way through thick fog. Erick's vision was cloudy as though he had been drugged. Street signs shifted in and out of focus, never clear enough to surface a memory of place.

Dressed in nightclothes—shirtless and pajama bottoms for him and a pink negligee for her—they ran barefoot as fast as they could. They tripped over the sleeping homeless and trudged through garbage-strewn streets in their desperate dash toward freedom.

FBI agents followed close behind—men who were young, fit, and determined to catch their prey. The sound of their footsteps grew closer. Erick watched the light reflected off Amy's silky-black hair disappear as she rounded the corner of an abandoned, red-brick tenement building. He followed her around the corner and froze. A Ferrari goon held her tight against his body with a ten-inch tactical knife pressed firmly against her neck.

"Tony wants his money back, asshole," the man growled.

Amy's eyes were open wide in terror. Her expression pleaded for help. Erick stood on the sidewalk at the apex of the building, in full view of the FBI and Ferrari's goon. *I have to save her.*

Erick raised his pistol toward the goon. *It's a twenty-foot shot. What if I miss? What if I hit Amy?* A drop of blood trickled from Amy's neck onto the shimmering blade and spilled onto her pink nightie. Light from the corner streetlamp reflected off an object held in her hand. Erick tried to focus. *What is it? Her gun! She remembered the revolver.* His eyes locked on hers. He watched as she turned the nickel-plated weapon toward the goon's groin. Erick mouthed to her, *flip off the safety.* She always forgot the safety.

"FBI, drop your weapon!" The agents crouched with guns drawn, twenty feet behind Erick.

Feet glued to the concrete, Erick stood like a statue with his pistol sighted on the goon. His rapidly beating heart was the only sound he heard, and it was deafening. Erick's life with Amy rushed through his mind's eye, frame-by-frame. His heart pounded for her.

"Erick Olson, drop your weapon now!"

The crack of gunfire echoed through the canyon of tall buildings.

Erick shot up in bed and gasped for air. Sweat covered his body, and his breathing was labored and uneven. He looked at Amy. She slept peacefully like a child. He stroked the small of her back, relieved it was a bad dream.

The nightstand clock read 3:00 a.m. Erick gave up on sleep and sat on the balcony in the early morning darkness. He looked across the sea toward their new life together. His mind took them to a place their bodies wouldn't arrive for days.

CHAPTER 66

SLEEPING IN THE balcony lounge chair since 3 a.m., Erick felt the rising sun burn through his eyelids, awakening him. Erick snuck quietly back into the room so as not to wake Amy. He stood for a moment and watched her sleep. She was so peaceful and lovely. A warm sensation surged through him like sunshine on a spring day. In two days, they would start life over—together.

After a long, hot shower, Erick slipped into the terrycloth bathrobe provided by the hotel. He knelt by the bed and gently kissed Amy on the cheek. She stretched her arms, and her almond eyes blinked open.

"That's a nice way to wake up," she said.

"You should get dressed. I'll order breakfast."

"Just get a pot of coffee. I want to go down to the beach to eat. A breakfast burrito sounds wonderful!" Amy climbed out of the bed.

"We should eat in the room. The fewer people that see us, the better," Erick said, his brow furrowed deeply.

"Erick, I'm not sitting in this room for two or three days. I'll go stir crazy." Amy insisted.

"Okay, I'll compromise. There's a pool side café. We can eat there." Erick smiled. "But look, we need to spend most of our time up here until we can change our appearance. Maybe you can make us a hair color appointment after breakfast?"

"Sure," Amy said.

While Amy showered, Erick stashed most of their cash and Martin's gun in a wall safe mounted in the closet.

Erick and Amy sat on the balcony for half an hour, enjoying their coffee and gazing at the ocean. After Amy finished her second cup, Erick stood. "Let's get something to eat. Are you ready?"

"Yeah, I'm starved."

"Are you bringing your laptop along?" Erick asked.

"Of course." Amy slipped the messenger bag strap over her shoulder and was ready to go.

Walking into the poolside café, Erick headed for a table with a view of the pool and ocean beyond.

"How's this table," Erick said to Amy, smiling.

"Perfect." Amy nodded toward the water. "What a view!"

Once their server appeared, Erick ordered breakfast burritos and orange juice for both of them.

"When do you realistically think we'll fly out of here?" Amy leaned back and crossed her legs.

"Tomorrow or the next day. I'm expecting a text from Martin anytime now." He took a bite of his burrito. "Can I get you to check again and see if the FBI found the farmhouse yet?"

"I can do it now on the hotel Wi-Fi signal." She slid the laptop onto the table, and her fingers danced around the keyboard. "Okay, I'm connected to the farm security system … shit!" she gasped and looked at Erick.

"What is it," Erick's eyes narrowed.

"Look here," she spun the laptop screen toward him. "They were there last night at nine."

Erick studied the video playing on the screen. "It looks like several sheriff's deputies, and maybe the guy in the suit is FBI—hard to know for sure. I don't recognize him." Erick spun the laptop back to Amy. Tried to appear calm.

"What now?" Amy asked, distressed.

"We need to transition into our new identities. If we're stopped by the local police, we need to be Brian and Honey Sanderson. We haven't much time." Erick already had a good start on his beard. "You know, it's just you and me now … together."

Amy pulled off her sunglasses and looked at Erick. "I'm sad to leave grandma and Ali behind, but I'm happy I'm with you," Amy said with melancholy.

Erick draped his arm over her shoulder and hugged her. "Thanks, me too."

Erick's burner phone vibrated with a text. He glanced at the screen, *I'll pick you up at noon Monday and drive you to the airport. I'll be in touch.*

"Who was it," Amy asked.

"Martin, we're on for Monday at noon. I hoped the extra cash I offered him would get us out of here tomorrow. The customs guy must be slowing us down."

"I've got good news," Amy said, looking at her laptop screen. "I made appointments for us online for this afternoon at three with Dani at The Hair Emporium."

"Great. Go ahead and make our flight reservations for late Monday afternoon," Erick said.

CHAPTER 67

AMY TYPED ON the keyboard and pulled up a list of scheduled flights from Cancun to Panama City. She could feel Erick watching her. "Okay, looks like there's one at 4 p.m." Amy looked up at Erick. We'll need to stay two nights in Panama City and then fly on to San Jose."

"Really? Two nights? Erick said.

He seemed frustrated. "Yeah, everything is booked up. Must be tourist season or something."

"That's fine. The airport's about twenty minutes from here, so a 4 p.m. flight should work. That gives us over three and a half hours to clear customs and make it to the gate. Go ahead and book it."

Amy laid her new credit card with the name Honey Sanderson on the table. Her fingers ran across the keyboard, responding to prompts, "Okay, we're all set," she said.

"Can you get us a furnished condo in Playa Langosta? Something nice on the beach," Erick said with a faraway look in his eyes.

"Sure. Let's see, there's a lot to choose from."

After scrolling through property listings for a few minutes, Amy pulled up pictures of an available unit. "This one looks nice. Three thousand a month," She spun her laptop around to show Erick.

He scrolled through the pictures and announced, "Perfect, go ahead and set it up,"

"Okay, It won't take much time," Amy said.

Amy typed while Erick sipped his coffee.

"Alright, we're booked for the rest of February and then through the end of June. That should give us enough time to find something permanent."

"Great, can you see where Agent Monroe is?"

She opened a new window, pulled up a GPS application program, and typed 'Monroe.' A map appeared on the screen. "Looks like he's in Spokane," she said without looking up.

"Good. I figured sending Wilford to Whistler would slow the FBI down a bit."

Amy relaxed in her seat and opened the email application on her laptop. Turning slightly so Erick couldn't see the screen, she discreetly opened an unread email from Special Agent Richard Monroe from yesterday evening.

> *Ms. Summers –*
>
> *The DOJ is prepared to offer you a deal. Return the twenty million dollars and lead us to Erick Olson's location, and we'll recommend leniency to the court. It appears you are in a good deal more trouble than you bargained for. At a minimum, you're looking at wire fraud. If they decide to make an example out of this case, you could be facing federal racketeering charges as well. Think of yourself and your future. You need to act quickly.*
>
> *Special Agent Richard Monroe*

Amy closed the email and dropped it into an encrypted folder. Her chest tightened, and she bit down on her lower lip until it stung.

"What are you reading?" Erick asked. You looked puzzled.

She smiled and slipped her laptop into its case, "Puzzled? Really? I was checking my spam folder. Are you ready to head back?" Amy smiled.

CHAPTER 68

AT 8 A.M., Saturday morning, Agent Monroe burst into the war room. "Okay, listen up, people. Agent Polak interviewed two witnesses yesterday evening who saw what they identified as a Cessna 208 flying low near Grangeville, Idaho. One of them thought he saw the plane land at a nearby farm. Agent McCoy has confirmed, with Betty Olson, that the company has chartered that type of plane several times for business trips to Dallas and Tampa. We obtained a search warrant for the farm last night. At around 9 p.m., Agent Polak and several sheriff's deputies entered the farm house. It appears Olson and Summers have been there recently. Two vehicles were in the barn. A rental in Olson's name, the second owned by a close friend of Summers.

"The owner-pilot is one Wilford Johnson. He's a retired naval aviator based in Wenatchee, Washington. His wife says he's on a job. Johnson didn't say where he was headed. We don't have much on him. The tail number on his aircraft is N3794N.

"Let's get on this now! I want to know every place that plane's been for the past three days. Contact the FAA with the tail number. Get out a map and draw a circle two thousand miles from Grangeville. They had to refuel within that distance. And get me a complete profile on the pilot."

"What if he goes international, Boss?" an agent called out.

"He'd have to identify himself by tail number when he leaves US airspace. I suppose he could fly low and try to sneak into Canada or Mexico." Monroe stood quiet for a moment, considering the steps Olson might take. "Contact border patrol. See if any low-flying aircraft have been reported near the borders of either Canada or Mexico. You never know. And check with the air traffic controllers in both countries. See if Wilford filed a flight plan to enter their air space."

Monroe retook his chair and spun around to study the wall collage. A much-relished euphoria ran through him. *Olson is making this too easy,* he thought. *Flying a Cessna puddle-jumper, we may greet him at his destination.*

"Boss, I got a hit," an agent called out a few minutes later. "Wilford filed an inflight flight plan yesterday morning to enter Canada and land at Vancouver, BC International Airport."

Monroe rushed to the agent's desk. "Did he indicate a round trip?"

"No. He intends to stay for a week."

"Call the consulate office in Canada and get one of our agents over there to inspect the plane. See if the local police will assist." Monroe's heart beat wildly. He loved the chase. It was like playing chess with a worthy opponent.

"Boss, Agent Polak's on the line."

"Put him on speaker," Monroe said, "Polak, what do you have?"

"This morning in the daylight, we searched the farmhouse for evidence and found something odd. There are active surveillance cameras in the house and the barn. We searched the attic and uncovered a high-speed data router. They may have been watching us search the damn house."

"Okay, leave the cameras and router alone," Monroe exhaled deeply. "I'll send a cyber-team to check it out. Good work. Did everyone hear that? I don't think they're playing games. They set the cameras so they'd know when we found the farm."

"I accessed Wilford Johnson's credit card file. Looks like he re-fueled in Vancouver, BC," an agent said, looking up to Agent Monroe.

"What other charges are on the card?" asked Monroe. He found it odd that Wilford used his credit card.

"It looks like a hotel at Whistler Ski Resort has placed a hold on his card for eighteen-hundred dollars. It's a couple of hours drive from Vancouver."

"Do we have a picture of the pilot yet?" Monroe asked, thumping his finger on the table.

"We have an old one from his pilot license twenty years ago." An agent turned his monitor toward Agent Monroe so he could see the picture.

"Go with that for now, but check with the Washington State DMV and see what they have on file. See if we can get a current photo from his wife … Get the picture and Whistler hotel information to our agent assigned to Vancouver. Have him question Wilford about the whereabouts of Olson and Summers after he searches the plane." Agent Monroe paced the room. He studied the storyboard on the wall and considered his next move.

"What about Olson's credit card? And Summers? We have a profile on Erick Olson. Why is there no mention of the Grangeville farm?" Monroe barked.

"I have something on that, Boss." Agent McCoy looked up from her screen. "There is no recent activity on their personal or company credit cards. I checked with the county clerk in Idaho, and it seems the farm is held in trust in Olson's maternal grandfather's name— Lars Karlson. Erick and his deceased brother are the beneficiaries. The brother died in a tractor rollover while still in high school, leaving Erick as the sole beneficiary when his grandfather passed. Olson apparently left the farm in the trust. He leases out the tillable land to a neighboring farmer. The trust has a bank account and Visa in the trust's name," McCoy paused. "I'm looking at the trust bank account for last year. It looks like the rental income is more than three times the property taxes and utilities for the farmhouse. The trust is self-sustaining and has its own tax ID number."

"What about the trust Visa card?" Monroe asked.

"I'm pulling that up now … here it is … on Thursday, the card was charged for two tickets on Aeromexico from Vancouver, BC to Cancun, Mexico. They were scheduled to arrive in Cancun at 10:15 p.m. last night," McCoy said.

"Cancun," Agent Monroe repeated, his mind racing. "Any other charges?"

"Nothing."

"I need to call the Chicago Director and get permission to fly to Cancun," Monroe paused and massaged his temples. "McCoy, contact our consulate office in Mexico City. Have them request cooperation from the state and local police … have an agent dispatched to Cancun."

"I'm on it," McCoy said, reaching for her phone.

Agent Monroe coughed, clearing his throat. "We're going to Cancun. McCoy and Polak will stay here to continue the investigation. Once I get the green light, we leave for Mexico. Agent Polak, get us a charter."

CHAPTER 69

HIS DESK PHONE rang Saturday afternoon, and Romano snatched the handset, "Michael."

"Joe, here. Our informant with the Chicago FBI came through. FBI agents are looking for Olson and Summers in Cancun, Mexico … We don't know exactly where, but we're putting out a bounty that should produce their location soon enough. Go ahead and get Gerald started."

"I'll take care of it," Romano spoke forcefully.

Romano placed the call to Gerald Carter on a prepaid cell phone to the assassin's number.

"Hello."

"I have a job for ya," Romano said.

"I'm available."

"It's the Whitman Company. We need you to take care of the CEO, Erick Olson, and his girl, Amy Summers. He's the tall blond guy you saw at the lawyer's office in Spokane."

"Anything else?"

"Olson stole twenty million from us. Persuade them to wire it back before you finish 'em. Play rough with the girl. Olson will cave. I'll email pictures and the rest of the file to you."

"Where are they?"

"Cancun, Mexico."

"It's a big city."

"We'll work to narrow it down. We're puttin' out a bounty for information leadin' to them. Someone will talk … shouldn't take long. You need to leave today."

CHAPTER 70

AGENTS MCCOY AND Polak rolled up the driveway to Betty Olson's Pullman home at 9 a.m. The house was a two-story white colonial. A large sunroom hung off the south end of the building with floor-to-ceiling muntin-paned windows on three sides. It was the sort of house Agent McCoy had dreamed of living in since she was a young girl.

The agents approached the front door, and McCoy reached out to press the buzzer. Chimes rang inside the home, the sound making its way to the front porch.

The windowed door opened, and Betty greeted them dressed in a purple jogging suit. "Good morning," Betty brushed a loose strand of hair from her eyes.

"Good morning. This is Special Agent Polak. He's working on the Whitman Communications investigation with me," McCoy said.

"It's nice to meet you. Please come in. We can talk in the sunroom."

"Thank you for meeting with us on a Sunday." Agent McCoy smiled.

"It's really not a problem. Would the two of you like coffee or tea?"

McCoy exchanged glances with Agent Polak, an unspoken agreement to stay focused on the business at hand. This was not a social call.

"We had coffee earlier, thank you," McCoy said.

Following Betty into the sunroom, they sat on rattan chairs with white cushions surrounding a round copper-topped coffee table. A white baby grand piano rested peacefully in one corner of the large room.

Agent Polak pulled a small notepad and pen from his breast coat pocket.

"So, what is it you'd like to talk about this morning?" Betty looked first at Agent Polak and then shifted her focus to McCoy.

"Ms. Olson—," Agent McCoy began.

"Please, Betty. Call me Betty," she interrupted and returned a closed-lip smile. "Have you found Erick?"

"Not yet," McCoy said. "We're here mostly about the money Summers and Romano wired to an offshore bank account in Hong Kong. Do you recall when Romano was placed on the Whitman bank records as a signatory?"

"I didn't know he was on them until after the wire took place. I mean, he's on our board, but I had no idea. I can check with the bank on Monday and see when he was added to the account," Betty's composure cracked. "Am I a suspect?"

Agent McCoy leaned back and crossed her legs, "No, you're a person of interest. Which means we believe you may have knowledge about what happened … that's what we're trying to determine. What exactly happened with Romano, Summers, Erick and the missing money?"

"I really know nothing. I was caught flat-footed when Erick and Amy disappeared. I mean, like I told you before, I know they have a romantic involvement of some sort. But stealing the money? I never would have dreamt such a thing possible. It's completely out of character for both of them." Betty shrugged her shoulders and gazed out the window.

"Betty, we would like your cooperation in our investigation. We'll recommend favorable treatment in exchange for your helping us."

"Why would I need that? I've done nothing wrong." Her tone sparked in anger.

"As a company officer, under federal statutes, you may be an accessory to bank wire fraud for the missing twenty million dollars," McCoy spoke in a clear and deliberate manner.

"Is that a threat?" Betty asked.

"No … we want you on our team. Will you work with us?" McCoy said in a soft tone.

"Of course. I want to get to the bottom of this more than anyone. What is it you'd like me to do?" Betty's eyes focused on McCoy.

"We know Romano called the other day looking for Erick. When he calls again, we'd like for you to engage with Romano and reassure him that all is well. You'll need a viable story about where Erick is."

"You mean something better than Erick took all our money and ran off with his girlfriend?" Betty's tone was defeated, and her eyes teared up.

"Continue whatever contractual arrangements are in place with Romano's company without interruption. You mentioned a contract with Romano's billing company. Keep that going. It should be business as usual with Romano," McCoy's eyes narrowed, and she leaned toward Betty.

"Alright, I can do that," Betty said, her brow creased in worry.

"I know this must be a difficult time, but try to put your personal feelings aside for a moment."

"Okay, I'll take his call. Honestly, the relationship with Romano was all Erick. I met the man once at one of our board meetings. He holds a non-voting seat and doesn't normally even show up ... What should I tell him about Erick's absence?"

"Is there a trip Erick has planned, or somewhere he's always wanted to go?" Agent McCoy relaxed on the edge of her seat.

"He often talks about going fishing up in Alaska."

"Perfect, he's in Alaska. Tell Romano he'll be back in a month. If he asks where in Alaska, tell him a river in the middle of nowhere fishing."

CHAPTER 71

SPECIAL AGENT MONROE paced the floor in the temporary workspace provided for his team by the Cancun Police Department. Pursuing Olson and Summers had become a complex game of strategy as if two masters played a chess match over the phone. Monroe needed to think several steps ahead, or he would always be chasing his two fugitives.

"Hey, let's take a break and get something to eat," Monroe announced to his team. Just then, his cell rang. "Agent Monroe."

"Boss, Agent Polak. They found Wilford at the ski resort."

"What did we learn?" Agent Monroe fell into his chair and grabbed a pencil.

"Wilford confirmed with our agent in Canada that Olson chartered the plane to Vancouver. Part of their deal was Wilford would spend a week in Canada after dropping them off. He claims to have no knowledge of where Olson or Summers are or where they were headed," Polak said.

"Do you think he's telling the truth?" asked Monroe.

"Yes, from what I can gather. Wilford's flown Olson and Summers routinely to business meetings. Olson would have no reason to tell the pilot his plans once he left the plane."

Monroe put the cell away and faced his team, "That was Agent Polak on the phone. Our agent in Canada found the pilot in Whistler, BC. He confirmed flying Olson and Summers to Vancouver but claims to have no knowledge of where they were heading after leaving his plane or what their future plans are," Agent Monroe shrugged. "We know they landed here, in Cancun, Friday night. So let's get on it and pick up their trail."

CHAPTER 72

SUNDAY AFTERNOON, ROMANO sat in his home study, looking for a path forward. He knew the money Olson stole would bring the regulators down hard on Whitman Communications if uncovered. The entire operation could blow up. Romano could temporarily cover the twenty million dollars with funds from Spokane Community Bank, but that required Tony's blessing. Romano's pulse quickened at the thought of having that conversation with Tony. Before the next regulatory review of Whitman's financial statements, Romano knew he must recover the money from Olson. There was no other way.

Romano's cell phone rang. He glanced at his watch, 2 p.m.

Flipping the phone open, Romano said, "Yeah?"

"Gino here, Boss. I'm checking to see if you still want me watching Whitman next week?"

"Probably no point, Gino." Romano exhaled deeply. "Erick Olson and Summers disappeared with a pile of our money. It doesn't seem like Betty Olson is a part of their plan."

"What's our next step, Boss?"

"Acosta got word that Olson and Summers are in Cancun, Mexico. We got a guy on the way down there. Tony wants to have Betty Olson run Whitman for now. I'm gonna set up a lunch meetin' with her for some time this week. You know, so she understands the score," Romano said through an evil smile.

She would have one chance to join the team. If not, she'd join her friend Skip in the afterlife.

CHAPTER 73

MONDAY MORNING AT 6 a.m., Erick and Amy stepped into the elevator on their way to breakfast at the poolside café. Amy pushed the button for the lobby. They had a busy travel day ahead of them, and Amy wanted a decent breakfast. The doors opened on the lobby level, and they walked off the elevator.

"Damn it," Erick said as he patted his back pocket. "I forgot my billfold … I need to run back to the room. I'll be right back."

"Okay, I'll wait for you in the lobby."

The lobby was deserted at this early hour. Amy headed toward a seating arrangement with a long sofa and a leather club chair at each end, turned at a right angle. She plopped onto the sofa and sighed deeply. The past week had been brutal, and she was exhausted.

A gentleman in his late forties, holding a folded newspaper, walked over and sat in the vacant chair beside Amy. She glanced at him and smiled warmly. He nodded politely.

It was nearly over, Amy reassured herself. In less than twenty-four hours, she and Erick would be sitting on the beach sipping fruity cocktails. Like a hot-air balloon releasing air and floating softly to the earth, relief flowed from Amy.

They were nearly home free. Amy closed her eyes and could almost taste the cocktails. As easily as she slid into the comfort of her imagination, her always-present anxiety burst to the surface. We have to stay focused. What had Erick said? 'Most shipwrecks occur within sight of the harbor. A ship crosses the ocean safely to be scuttled on the rocks a

short distance from her berth. Sailors can never let their guard down.'
Only a few more hours. A few more hours and she could relax knowing
they'd pulled it off. Escaped.

A half-minute later, the stranger leaned toward her. "Amy?"

She stiffened, startled. Instinctively, she leaned away from him. Her
throat thickened, and she swallowed her words. "Do … do I know you?"
Panic ran through her.

"We have mutual acquaintances." He stood from the chair and moved
next to Amy on the sofa.

"Who … who are you?" Her body trembled. She had never before
seen the slender man. His eyes were dark and soulless.

He cut his hardened eyes to his lap. She followed with hers. He held a
small pistol pointed at her. The gun had a long tube attached to the barrel.

"Not a word, or this ends badly," he growled. "You took something
from my employer. They want it back." He grabbed her elbow with his
free hand and held it firm.

"You're hurting me," Amy cried. "I don't know what you're talking
about."

"Sure, you do. It's green and has pictures of presidents on it." He
smiled with his lips shut tight. "We're going to wait here for Erick. When
do you expect him?"

Her heart pounded. "What?"

"Quit stalling. Where is he?" He pulled her arm down and pushed
the barrel into her ribs.

She moaned in pain. "We're meeting here for breakfast. I'm not sure
where he is."

CHAPTER 74

LEAVING THE ELEVATOR, Erick approached the lobby. Erick hadn't slept hardly at all. Relieved to be leaving Cancun, he was dead tired. Turning the corner in the hallway, Erick froze, startled by the sight of a stranger sitting next to Amy. Their backs were toward him. Erick could see the man gripped Amy's arm and pushed her tight against the armrest. No way was it the FBI. It had to be Romano's people.

Erick back-stepped to the elevator and rushed to their room. He knelt on the floor next to his suitcase and held his head in the palms of his hands. Unzipping the bag, Erick reached inside for the pistol Martin gave him. His hand touched the cool steel, and he withdrew the weapon. Erick's heart filled with fear. Fear for Amy and himself. All he knew for sure was that he must confront the man beside Amy. And, he must do it now.

Standing over the bag, Erick seated a magazine, released the safety, and pulled the slide, loading a round into the chamber. The sound of the gun's metal-on-metal action heightened his sense of danger and urgency. Erick's hand trembled with the weight of the weapon. He laid a sweater over his arm to conceal the pistol and left the room.

As he closed the thirty-foot distance to the sofa, Erick caught sight of the gun pressed against Amy's ribs. Taking controlled, measured breaths and short steps, lightly on the balls of his feet, Erick covered the distance in near silence. Standing behind the stranger, Erick pressed the barrel of his weapon against his back. Erick's heart pounded so loud he could hear it, and he watched his shirt move with each beat. Erick cut a glance to the front counter and found no one at the desk. The three were alone in the lobby.

"Hand me the gun, slowly," Erick's hand shook with fear.

"If you're not careful, something bad will happen," the guy said.

"You hurt her, and I'll kill you." Sweat loosened his grip on the pistol. He switched hands and wiped his damp hand on his slacks.

"Games over for you, pal. I found you this time. My replacement will find you next time. The game goes on—until you're out of it."

"Screw you. Give me the gun—now. Then we're going to the room to figure this out."

"Okay, chief." The man slid the base of the gun toward the back of the sofa. Erick reached down and grabbed it from him.

Erick leaned toward Amy and handed her the pistol. "Take this and hurry back to the room; cover it in that newspaper," he motioned to the morning paper. "Leave the door open."

"Get up, asshole. My finger's on the trigger."

"Take it easy," the man said in a gruff tone.

The man stood. Erick pushed the club chair with his foot to make room for the stranger to walk behind the sofa. Erick had no idea what they were going to talk about. This stranger was the final obstacle standing in the path of Erick and Amy's freedom. Could they tie him up and leave him bound in a closet? Would they have to kill him? This outcome hadn't been anticipated in their escape plan.

Amy left the hotel room door unlatched. Erick pushed the door open with one hand and held the gun pressed into the guy's back with the other. He applied pressure and began to guide him into the room.

As Erick entered the room, bam! The man shoved the open door into his face. The force threw Erick off balance. Blood covered his face. Pain seared through his head.

Amy screamed, "Erick!"

Erick struggled to recover his lost footing. Blood filled his eyes. He put his hands up in defense and waved them wildly.

The stranger spun around and snarled. He stepped toward Erick and punched him in the jaw. Erick dropped to all fours, still holding tight to the pistol. The former navy seal kicked Erick's arm, holding the gun, and slammed the door shut. The pistol dislodged and slid out of reach. Erick collapsed face-first on the carpet. His jaw ached. The man was on him in an instant. He held Erick in a choke hold, squeezing the life from him. Erick kicked and thrashed violently on the floor, waves of pain rolling through his body.

Erick watched Amy move toward him in blurry, slow motion, fading in and out of consciousness. Her mouth was moving, but he couldn't hear a sound. She raised the gun, and a flash of fire spilled from the barrel. Erick slipped into darkness.

A minute later, Erick's eyes blinked open to the total weight of the guy splayed on top of him. Amy stood next to them, a look of shock on her face. She held the assassin's gun loosely, dangling at her side.

"Are you okay?" she asked, the color gone from her face.

"Did you shoot him?"

Tears burst from her eyes, "I had no choice."

Erick struggled to find his bearings. "Help roll him off me."

Head pounding, Erick climbed to his knees and hovered over the unconscious man. He furiously searched the guy's pockets. "Who is he?" The man carried no identification."

"Is he dead?" Amy asked.

Erick felt for a pulse. "No … We need to finish him. Hand me the gun."

"You can't kill him, Erick. That's murder. Let's leave him tied up," Amy pleaded.

"He's the only one that can figure out our next move. It was self-defense," Erick wiped the blood from his eyes with his sleeve. "Look, Amy, you shot him in the back twice. He's probably going to die anyway. He's bleeding badly. Hand me the gun. I'll do it."

"No, it's not self-defense; you have a choice. Don't do it, Erick. *Please.*" Amy took a step back in disbelief.

Jumping to his feet, Erick growled and reached toward her, "Give me the damn gun." *Doesn't she get I'm doing this for us?*

Amy held her hand out with the pistol. Erick grabbed the weapon and pumped two slugs into the assassin's forehead at close range. Blood and tiny skull fragments covered in brain matter splattered on Erick's clean shirt. The moment he pulled the trigger, Erick had second thoughts. He felt sick to his stomach. Regret coursed through him. This isn't the way he wanted their story to end.

"Amy, I'm going to drag him into the closet. Can you give me a hand?"
Amy stood frozen in place, sobbing softly.

"Amy! Pull it together. We need to hide him." Erick stood and took
her in his arms, hugging her tight, "it's almost over, Amy," he whispered
softly, "it's almost over."

"Erick, you ... you shouldn't have done it. It's wrong," she sobbed.

"He was sent to kill us, Amy," Erick said matter-of-factly. "I don't
like it any more than you do. We had no choice." Erick's conviction grew
stronger each time she challenged him.

At noon, Erick leaned over the hotel balcony, scanning the vehicles parked
out front. Glancing down at his phone, he confirmed the minivan description Martin had texted.

"Time to go. Our ride's here," Erick said, stepping back into the room.
He glanced at the bedroom closet door. The man he killed hours earlier
was laid out on the closet floor covered with a sheet. The odor of blood
and death had overcome the room. Erick was beyond ready to leave
Cancun behind.

Amy frowned and shrugged in defeat.

They grabbed their bags and headed for the lobby.

A bellhop approached as Erick and Amy struggled through the lobby,
toting their luggage. Erick averted his eyes after catching the guy eyeing
Amy's legs.

"Checking out, sir? May I give you a hand?" the bellhop asked.

"We're good, thanks. We already checked out. Just taking our bags
now," Erick said as he pulled the brim of his ball cap down to disguise
his features.

They pushed through the revolving door. Sweating profusely, Erick
glanced back at the bellhop and a desk clerk watching them make their
way to the minivan.

Erick tapped on the half-open passenger window. "Martin, it's good
to see you."

"I hardly recognize you two." Martin smiled.

"Yeah, we needed a new look. Something to match the new passports." Erick grinned.

"Toss your bags in the back, and let's roll," Martin said.

As they pulled away in the van, Erick looked over his shoulder, saw the bellhop had moved to the sidewalk, and watched them drive off.

"What's wrong?" Amy asked.

"Probably nothing. That bellhop seemed awfully interested in us. I doubt he could get our plate, though."

"Let's hope it's nothing. He looked me over pretty good."

"You're probably right, Amy," Erick said.

"Don't worry, kids. They won't track this van. I put a *borrowed* plate on it."

Erick drew in a deep breath. "Martin, there's something I need to tell you." Erick cleared his throat.

Martin turned to face him, "what is it?"

"A guy came after Amy this morning with a gun. I killed him. His body's in the hotel room closet," Erick said shakily.

"Was the guy tied in with the people you're running from?" Martin's eyebrows pinched together.

"Yeah, he was. It was him or us. I had no choice," Erick said, still trying to justify the killing to himself.

"That will cause some commotion here, but the person who rented the room for me doesn't know anything. So she can't really help the cops. The police will run into a dead end. Honestly, if the guy is not a Mexican citizen, they won't try too hard to solve it. Thanks for telling me, though. You look like you've been in a bit of a scuffle."

"I feel like it too." Erick rubbed his sore jaw.

"Before I forget, here's your new passports with the appropriate stamp documenting when you entered Mexico. I want you to know I didn't look at either passport. So, if the police ever do happen to make it to me, I don't know your new identities."

"Thanks, Martin."

"Now, let's get you to the airport."

CHAPTER 75

ROMANO PICKED UP the phone and dialed Erick Olson's number. With Erick and Amy gone, the time had come to put the pressure on Betty Olson.

"Erick Olson's office, this is Candy. May I help you?"

"Candy, Michael Romano here. Can you transfer me to Betty?"

"She's in a meeting. May I take a message?"

"Tell her I'm on the line. She'll take my call." *Damn, well, better take my call.*

After a few seconds, "I'll transfer you now."

"Mr. Romano, this is Betty Olson. What may I do for you?"

"Where's Erick?"

"On a fishing trip in Alaska," Betty tripped over the words. "He forgot to let the front desk know so they could properly route his calls ... Erick and I bought Whitman Communications together. If you need anything, I should be able to help."

"You know about the contracts between our companies?" Romano hoped she did. He needed to keep the cash flowing to Chicago without interruption.

"In general. Is there a problem?"

"No, I want to make sure everythin' is still goin' accordin' to plan." Romano wondered if his new associate at Whitman would give him any trouble.

"As far as I know, it is."

"We're good then."

"If you have any questions, feel free to call me while Erick's out of pocket."

"We need to meet. How about one o'clock Wednesday at De Rosa's?" Romano said.

"I don't have anything planned for lunch that day. I'll put it on my calendar."

"I'll see ya then." Romano turned his hardened stare to the window.

"Good day now."

Romano sat the handset down hard. "Alaska, my ass." He spit the words in frustration.

CHAPTER 76

SPECIAL AGENT MONROE'S team searched Cancun through the weekend. The local police assisted his team in the hunt for Olson and Summers. They focused on hotels and motels near the beaches.

The team questioned hotel front-desk staff, maids, and bellhops up and down the waterfront. They visited upscale restaurants popular with yachtsmen and seedy bars frequented by merchant-ship captains. They always asked the same question, 'Have you seen these two?' and flashed pictures of a tall, blond, blue-eyed financial wizard and an exotic Asian beauty. Monroe believed someone seeing the two together would remember them. He bet his career on it.

Agent Monroe's cell rang, "Monroe."

"Boss, Agent Murphy here. It looks like we got a hit on the pictures at the Tipton Resort Hotel. A bellhop remembers them checking out. They had quite a bit of luggage and refused help. He followed them to the loading zone out front, and they got into an older style, silver Dodge minivan. He thought the behavior odd because it's a top-drawer hotel and all. He said the pictures are off. The woman was a real looker, though."

"It had to be them. Get over there and talk to the bellhop. I'll see if the local police have a facial artist they can send over. Figure out how their appearance has changed," Monroe said. "And show the pictures to the rest of the hotel staff, determine if anyone remembers what floor or room they were staying in.

"Have Agent Chesterfield get with the local police and see if they can search their database for an older, silver Dodge minivan. And compare the vehicle list to names on the hotel guest registry going back a week."

Monroe's mind spun with the possibilities. Are they still in town? Had they caught a plane or a boat somewhere? The permutations seemed endless.

"There's gotta be a ton of those vans, Boss."

"After the first cut, have them narrow it down to registration addresses in Cancun within two miles of the beach."

CHAPTER 77

SITTING IN A Panama City hotel bar at 8 p.m., Erick set his drink on the table. "Let's see where Monroe is." It was time to send Agent Monroe back to the States.

Amy held her laptop open on her thighs while she read an electronic version of the *Seattle Times*. She checked the obituaries daily and searched for Grandma's name. The doctor had said her grandmother could pass at any time.

Amy struck a few keys. "He's still in Cancun."

"Send him a note. Let him know we've left Mexico and are attaching the encryption key for all the emails and voicemail recordings we have on Romano." Erick sighed with relief. Their running from the law was nearly over.

Erick knew he could have used the evidence to get a deal with the Feds, but he would have had to testify against Roman in open court, a certain death sentence. Romano ruined Erick's life. Providing the evidence to put him away would even the score.

Amy clicked away on the keyboard, hit enter, and said, "Okay, I sent it. Anything else?"

"Yeah, look at the emails in Monroe's sent folder and see if there's anything helpful."

"Okay," Amy said and punched a few keys. "There's not much recent history. Here's one from this afternoon to the Chicago Field Director providing a status update. A bellhop identified us at the Tipton Hotel and observed us getting into a silver minivan. They have a facial artist working with the bellhop to get up-to-date images. And they're interviewing the hotel staff to see if anyone knows which room we were in."

"Well, they'll find the body soon. I suppose that's to be expected." Erick blew out a breath as his thoughts trailed off.

CHAPTER 78

WORKING FROM THE Cancun police department offices Monday evening, Agent Monroe wondered if Olson and Summers planned to make Cancun their home. A friendly city with white sandy beaches, the two fugitives could disappear into the tens of thousands of tourists and ex-pats for years without drawing attention. If they found a quiet residential development, he felt his odds of ever locating them were slim.

Agent Monroe's laptop beeped, notifying him of an incoming email. He clicked the email icon, revealing the sender: Amy Summers. "Summers, maybe she's ready to take the deal," he said quietly and clicked the email to open it.

> *Agent Monroe:*
> *We have left Mexico. Attached is the encryption key you need to unlock the evidence we have saved on the Whitman Communications email server.*
> *Erick Olson*

The Chicago office had approved Monroe's stay for three days. He would need compelling evidence to get an extension and wasn't optimistic. The Cancun police were busy distributing updated pictures of the two fugitives to precinct locations, ports of entry, and key transportation hubs across the city. What's the point if Olson and Summers are gone? They may still be here, but that's doubtful.

"Good evening, Special Agent Monroe." Cancun Detective Cruz stood next to his desk. "Something has come up that will be of interest to you. A body was discovered at the Tipton Hotel by the housekeeping staff. It appears to have been a US citizen."

"Who was it?" Monroe contained his emotions. The bodies of US citizens turned up routinely in Mexico.

"It's a bit odd. The body was found by housekeeping in the room of a local Cancun family that had rented it for a week. They wouldn't have normally entered the suite, but a strong odor was coming into the hallway. The deceased is Gerald Carter, based on identification we found in *his* room on another floor of the hotel. The room we found the body in had been occupied by the Americans you've been searching for. The housekeeper identified them from the artist renderings." Detective Cruz scratched his beard.

"Are you telling me Olson and Summers were staying in a room registered under someone else's name?" Monroe furrowed his brow.

"It does appear that is the case, Sir."

Monroe coughed on his coffee and stood. "Cause of death?"

"Carter had been shot several times. We found a twenty-two caliber pistol and spent casings in the room where we found his body and extra rounds in *his* room. He may have been killed with his own weapon."

"Is there any evidence Olson and Summers left behind in the room?"

"No. It appears they left after the murder. The room was registered to Maria Sanchez, a citizen of Mexico. She resides here in Cancun. We've dispatched a detective to interview her."

"I can't see Olson killing someone. He's an executive type." Monroe narrowed his eyes, confused. Murder didn't comport with the FBI profile on Olson.

"There looked to be a violent struggle."

PART V

Seeking Redemption

I run through the dark of night;
you follow me one step behind.

Your fingers fall free from my hand.
You slip silently into the crowd.
Tears fall from your almond eyes.

I reach, but you do not respond;
I shout, but you shy away.
Our eyes meet; I will you back to me.
A river of humanity holds you hostage.

And as the stream of strangers
dwindles and disperses,
you attempt to escape in earnest
on fragile wings of redemption.

—Erick Olson

CHAPTER 79

TUESDAY MORNING, SPECIAL Agent Monroe awoke early and ate breakfast alone in his Cancun economy motel's dining room. The sun had already warmed the morning air. He wished he had brought shorts instead of his usual G-man dark suits. Then again, did anyone really want to see his untanned legs? They hadn't seen the sun in years. He packed his travel bag and loaded the Whitman case files into his briefcase.

Monroc found a comfortable, easy chair in the motel lobby and composed a short email to his task force:

> Team – the trail has gone cold here in Cancun with no new leads on Olson or Summers. The Chicago director is pulling us back to Spokane. We're heading out on a charter later this morning, arriving in Spokane at noon. The encryption key unlocking the Whitman server is attached. The folder named Romano is hidden on the email server. Agent McCoy, take the encryption key to Betty Olson and have her make us an electronic copy of everything in the Romano folder. Begin processing the evidence immediately. Special Agent Monroe

Monroe wasn't happy with his superior's decision to pull him back to Spokane. His nose and thirty years of experience told him he was close to Olson and Summers. He needed another few days, but his request was denied. Ferrari was the bigger fish. The two fugitives Monroe chased would be left for another day and another agent. He popped an antacid pill and headed for the airport to join his team.

Special Agent Monroe and his team worked through the night. It seemed to Monroe that Erick Olson had handed them a case against the Ferrari crime family on a silver platter. They reviewed and categorized hundreds of pages of evidence Olson had saved encrypted on the Whitman Communications email server.

"Do we have anything showing fund transfers to Ferrari?" Monroe asked.

"I ran a search and didn't find anything," Agent Kramer said.

"The flow looks to be mostly from Whitman to Romano's companies, with a modest kick-back amount coming back to Whitman," Agent Polak added.

"Someone check out that supply company—Telcom Equipment Supply—in Chicago. It should have a registration on file with the Illinois Secretary of State listing the officers. Let's see if there's a connection."

"Boss, Romano, and Acosta are clearly discussing the money flow to Chicago on some of our wiretap recordings," Agent McCoy said.

"Good, stay on it. See if you can piece together a timeline with the conversations."

"According to the Illinois Secretary of State website, both Acosta and Romano are officers with Telcom Equipment Supply," Polak said.

"Bingo! Print that out," Monroe said. "I'm going upstairs to talk with the lawyers."

He spun around in his chair and looked at the storyboard. It had blossomed into a picture book like a caterpillar morphed into a butterfly. The team had rearranged the board to run chronologically from left to right. A picture of the LightPoint headquarters building in Charleston served as the starting point. Above the photograph, Monroe had written 'Ferrari' with a question mark. The storyboard flowed to the right through the barn explosion, the Spokane Community Bank loan to Olson, the initiation of the consulting contract with Local Exchange Billing, the vendor agreement with Telcom Equipment Supply, the murder of Skip Britain, and an unexplained bank wire transfer.

The extensive manhunt chasing Erick Olson and Amy Summers across the country and into Mexico had been dropped from the storyboard. The chase was over—for the time being.

Monroe hoped Amy would accept his offer of favorable treatment in exchange for returning the stolen money and leading them to Erick Olson. He clung to the belief that Olson had dragged her into the Whitman fraudulent activity. The soft spot he held for her had grown deeper through time.

CHAPTER 80

MONROE STOOD IN a dreary motel room Wednesday morning, peering out the window with his back to Betty Olson, Agent McCoy, and a female surveillance technician.

The DOJ lawyers were impressed with the evidence Special Agent Monroe presented to them incriminating the Ferrari Crime Family. Still, they required more substantive evidence to secure arrest warrants for the Ferrari Family principals. To ensure a rock-solid prosecution, Monroe needed more.

"How much do you know about the contracts with Romano's companies," Agent Monroe said through the drapes.

"I read them earlier this week. The agreement with LEB for software support seems like an awful lot of money for what little they do for us. I haven't got my arms completely around Telcom Equipment Supply yet," Betty shrugged her shoulders. "But it appears Whitman is purchasing all of its network equipment through the company.

"You need to understand that both of those agreements are designed to over-charge Whitman Communications to steal money from the FCC subsidy pool," Monroe sighed. "I imagine part of this meeting with Romano today is to ensure you continue the schemes. If he brings it up, try to draw more out of him. Get him talking about it."

"I don't know if I can do all of this. It's a lot." Betty frowned and looked at the ground.

Fear overcame Betty's countenance and reverberated in Monroe's chest. Romano would hear it, too. *She needs to calm herself,* he thought.

"You'll be fine, Betty," McCoy said. "We'll be with you the entire time."

Betty sat stiffly in a straight-back chair, with her blouse unbuttoned as though in a department store window display. Agent Monroe kept his back to the women and focused his eyes on the parking lot below through partially parted drapes. The technician hurried to attach wires, a tiny microphone, and a transmitter to Betty's skin with adhesive strips the size of small Band-Aids. McCoy sat on the edge of the bed across from Betty.

"How much longer," Monroe asked, his back still toward them. "She's got to be out of here in twenty minutes."

The technician spoke without lifting her eyes as she struggled to attach a miniature microphone a little below Betty's bra. "Almost done, then we sound test."

"Good. Betty, how are you holding up?" Monroe asked. Undercover surveillance was routine for Monroe, but he sensed she struggled.

"Nervous as hell, I feel like I'm in *Mission Impossible*."

"You'll do fine. Remember, you're doing this for you. Romano has nearly cost you everything you've worked for. As we discussed yesterday, Agent McCoy and I will be in the restaurant, and agents will be posted by the front and rear entrances. We'll move in immediately if we sense danger or you say the code word. Do you remember the code word?"

"Flabbergasted," Betty said softly.

"We're ready to test," the technician said. She stood and moved to an open foam-lined equipment case resting on the bed. The aluminum-clad transport trunk held communications gear and a digital recorder. "Betty, if you would please step into the bathroom for me. Close the door and start speaking in a normal tone. I should have everything calibrated and tested in less than five minutes."

"Of course, what should I talk about?"

"Talk about Romano. Or Erick," McCoy suggested.

Betty went into the bathroom and closed the door.

"Testing, testing, testing," Betty said.

"We can hear you fine, Betty," Agent McCoy said.

"God, I feel so stupid. But why, Erick? Why? You're smarter than Romano. You're smarter than the whole lot. Was it the easy money? Did they promise you riches? Was cheating the FCC your idea all along? And where are you now, asshole? You left me with a God damn mess!"

She pounded her fists on the bathroom countertop and yelled, "You son-of-a-bitch, I'll cut off your—"

"Betty, I think we've got it," McCoy interrupted through the closed door and exchanged a pleading look with Monroe.

McCoy doesn't believe Betty's up to it, Monroe thought. He squeezed the window drapes held in his hand tightly.

Betty opened the door and stepped into the room. Her face flushed. She locked eyes with McCoy and shared a moment.

"Are you alright," McCoy asked softly.

"Sorry for the tears. That was a lot of anger I needed to let out. I'll be fine." She rubbed her eyes. Mascara had run down her cheeks and left dark streaks in its wake like wax running down a candle.

"Why don't you fix your makeup, and then we'll head over to De Rosa's."

Agent Monroe locked eyes with a worried McCoy. *Yeah, we have to get her calmed down.*

Agents Monroe and McCoy drank iced tea at a window table in De Rosa's. They had a five-minute head start on Betty Olson. Their position commanded an unobstructed view of Romano's reserved table.

"How long do you think she'll be?" Asked Agent McCoy.

"Any time now." Agent Monroe glanced at his watch.

"She's pulling in now." The sound technician said through their earpieces.

Monroe adjusted his earpiece's volume and looked out the window toward the parking lot and the FBI surveillance van. "Copy that," he whispered into his microphone.

From his vantage point, Monroe watched Betty exit her car, walk down the sidewalk to a crosswalk, cross the street, and enter the restaurant. The hostess led Betty past Monroe's table. Monroe met Betty's eyes with a half-smile of encouragement. As she passed, she shifted from Monroe's field of vision into McCoy's.

"I heard our pigeon's conversation with the hostess clearly. All looks good. Recorders on," said the tech.

"Copy. Let's cut out the chatter so we can listen in," Monroe said. He focused on McCoy's facial expression—and tried to read her mind.

"She's at the table. Romano's standing and shaking her hand," McCoy said.

"It's good to see ya again, Betty." The sound of Romano speaking flowed clearly from Monroe's earpiece into his consciousness.

"Thank you for the invitation," Betty said.

"Please sit," Romano said.

McCoy tilted her head toward the floor and spoke softly into the microphone. "Romano motioned to a seat across the table from him ... So far, so good."

'It's nice to see you, Betty," Jimmy Delane said. "May I get you something to drink?"

"An iced tea with lemon, please," she leaned back and crossed her legs. "What exactly did you want to talk about, Michael?"

"The talk," he sat up straight, took a deep breath, and turned serious. "In our business, we call it the *talk*. I had it with Erick. Now he's gone, so you and me will have it."

"I told you he's in Alaska." She squirmed and re-crossed her legs.

"Pardon my French, but you can cut the crapola. I know he's gone with the girl."

Asshole, Monroe thought.

"Erick and I got off on a bad foot. He thought he was callin' the shots. It just ain't that way. When the Family invests in a business, we gotta have the final say—there ain't no other way. You follow?"

"I think so."

"You're an associate. You manage the business, but when I tell ya to do somethin', ya got to come through. Follow?"

Come on, there's the opening. Get Romano talking about the billing contract, Monroe thought. His heart pounded. They were on the cusp of a breakthrough. She needed to push a little harder.

"Are you talking about the consulting arrangement with your company? The *inflated* contract?" she blurted out.

No. You have to be subtle, Monroe thought. He exchanged glances with a startled McCoy. Monroe gripped the arm of his chair tightly.

Romano raised an eyebrow, took a sip of wine, and leaned over the table. He looked from side to side as if to ward off any wandering ears.

"That's mostly it, and the supply company. We need to keep that going, too," he said in a lowered tone.

"To get more FCC subsidy money?"

That's our girl, Monroe thought.

"Yeah. I'm told that's the money tree."

"The FCC will figure it out eventually, you know?" Betty reached for her iced tea. When she grasped the glass, Michael's large hand clasped over hers and squeezed hard.

"He grabbed her hand. This is not good," McCoy whispered frantically to the team. "He's not letting go." McCoy rose halfway from her seat.

"That's your job, honey. Make sure they don't," Romano growled.

He released her hand and leaned back as though nothing had happened.

"All clear, he let her go," McCoy said and dropped back into her chair.

Monroe's heart raced. He had the confession he came for.

CHAPTER 81

WEDNESDAY EVENING, AMY watched the sunset from a comfortable seating area in the Panama City airport terminal. She waited with Erick for the final leg of their journey to begin.

Amy studied Erick's face and wondered if he thought about the man he killed two days ago. The memory repulsed her—made her want to increase the distance between them. And yet, he had done it to save them. In a way, it was self-defense.

The intense look in his eyes when she handed him the gun had burned a fresh line between right and wrong deep in her mind like nothing else in her life experience. And when the light left Erick's eyes, in that moment, she caught a fleeting glimpse of her future with him. The fear or desperation in his face, she wasn't sure which, left her unsettled. Amy cringed at the thought.

"When was the last time Monroe pinged a location?" Erick asked. "Amy?"

Lost in thought, Amy startled when Erick placed his hand on her knee and gently squeezed.

"What?" she looked into his eyes and withdrew from his touch, "Sorry, I was daydreaming."

"We'll have plenty of time for that on the beach tomorrow. We're almost to the end of the rainbow," Erick smiled.

Amy met his eyes but did not respond. She had an uneasy feeling their journey faced additional hurdles. They were only now coming into focus.

"Can you check on Monroe to see where he is?"

Amy tapped a few keys on her keyboard. "Let's see. He pinged an hour ago from Spokane. Looks like he went home."

"You know, don't you? I'm sorry I got us into this mess." Erick locked eyes with her.

"I'm a big girl. I decided to help with the scam. I'm okay with all of it. As far as being with you, I wouldn't want it any other way."

In the next moment, his words from months before overwhelmed her with thoughts of betrayal, *'Don't do anything stupid. You're in this as deep as me.'* He had tried to reclaim the words after they spilled out in anger. Yet the threat lodged deep in her memory only to break loose and cloud her thoughts whenever he became angry. She never understood if he meant the threat or blurted it out loud from anger and frustration.

"I'm going to grab a coffee. Do you want anything?" Erick asked.

"A blueberry muffin would be nice if they have any. Thanks."

She watched as he strode across the concourse and took his place in line behind a dozen other travelers placing their beverage orders. Amy thought Erick projected an unwarranted sense of confidence at this point of their journey.

Returning to her laptop, Amy opened the email folder. A flurry of keystrokes later, an unread email from Agent Monroe lit up her screen. She glanced over the top of her laptop; Erick stood in line with his back to her. She read the email.

> *Amy Summers:*
>   *If you return the twenty million dollars and tell us where Olson is, the DOJ and Washington State's Attorney General are prepared to go easy on you. You can avoid serving time, perhaps community service instead. Don't sit on this.*
>   *Special Agent Monroe*

She closed the email and shut her laptop. The FBI offer would be her one chance for redemption. It was a lame offer, nothing in writing. The promise of leniency. Her heart sank in disappointment. Thoughts of her Grandmother, alone in the Seattle memory unit, pulled her toward home. However, Grandma was in the final stage of decline, and there was no rational reason for Amy to return to Seattle. Yet the thought of

Grandma dying alone saddened her. In her confusion about Erick and Grandma, Amy suddenly wanted to talk to Ali. She relaxed in her seat and breathed deeply. Yes, Ali can help me.

"Hey, I got your muffin," Erick said.

"Thanks." She took the muffin and set it on her laptop. "They called your flight for boarding. Looks like it's on time."

"Yeah, I heard. Guess I should wander up and take advantage of first-class early boarding," Erick feigned a frown.

Amy climbed from her seat, and they embraced. She took in his scent, wanting to hold on to it forever. Erick leaned into her, and she kissed him long and deep. His moist lips etched the moment in her memory for all of time.

"Wow," he said, "I miss you already," Erick grinned broadly.

"Good flight. I'll see you later tonight." She smiled, and something tickled inside her.

Erick had insisted she book them separate flights for the last leg of their escape—their first time apart since they left the Idaho farmhouse. When Erick insisted they fly the final leg of their escape separately, she wondered for an instant if his plan was to ditch her in Panama City and keep the money for himself. The money meant nothing to her. All she needed to be happy was Erick. In her heart, she knew he would never leave her behind.

Amy lingered in view of the gate, watching Erick board his flight. As he disappeared into the darkened jetway, her heart sank. She was alone. Amy wandered into an airport bar and took a table in a quiet corner. She had three hours to kill until her flight left.

Ordering a bottle of wine, she pulled out her laptop and reread the deal offered by Agent Monroe a dozen times. After a couple of hours and several glasses of wine, she dug out her burner phone and called Ali.

"This is Ali," her cheerfulness drifted from the cell phone into Amy's heart.

"It's Amy."

"Amy, where are you? I didn't recognize the number," Ali said, sounding surprised.

"I'm in an airport. I wanted to talk to you."

"Amy, the FBI came to see me. They found my car in the barn at Erick's farm. What happened? Is this because of the trouble Erick's in?"

"I'm sorry, Ali. You didn't do anything wrong; you only loaned me your car," Amy bit her lip.

"I know, but it's scary. The agents acted like they believed I was in on something."

"What did they ask you?" Anxiety cracked Amy's confidence.

"They wanted to know if I knew where you and Erick are. Of course, I don't."

"Did you get your car back?

"They said I should get it back later this week. The FBI impounded your car, too. I've been riding the bus," Ali's words trailed off.

"I'm so sorry. I should have never involved you in this," Amy's tears burst to the surface.

"I'll be okay. What about you, Amy? Is this what you want, to be on the run with Erick?" Ali said, her tone colored with concern.

"I don't know anymore," Amy paused. "It feels so right being with Erick. But, Ali, he murdered someone. A man sent to kill us."

"Oh my God, Amy. Murder? Where is Erick now?" Panic laced Ali's words.

"He's on a plane to our final destination. I'm supposed to follow in an hour," Amy felt weak and uncertain. She gazed out the window onto the darkened tarmac and wondered what to do.

"Amy, you can't follow him. You need to think of yourself," Ali's urgent tone sprang from the phone.

"The FBI offered me a deal if I return the money we stole," Amy paused. "But I have to lead them to Erick too. I could never do that to him." She took a sip of wine and closed her eyes, letting the warm buzz embrace her.

"You have to take the deal. Cut Erick loose; he's bad news. He's ruining your life."

"I've got to go, Ali." Overwhelmed, Amy's eyes filled with tears.

"I mean it, Amy. Leave him. Do it now!" Ali demanded.

"I've got to go. Love you."

Amy downed the last of her wine and left the bar.

CHAPTER 82

A S THE CLOCK approached midnight, Special Agent Monroe and his team waited across the street from Michael Romano's Spokane South Hill home. They wore black windbreakers with 'FBI' written on the back in twelve-inch-tall, yellow letters over Kevlar bulletproof vests. The team shivered in the cold. They were in constant communication with a companion team leader in Chicago. Agents were positioned outside the homes of Tony Ferrari, Joe Acosta, and a dozen other high-ranking family members. The Chicago field office would execute its raid, timed with Romano's apprehension.

The evidence Erick Olson stored on the Whitman Communications server, along with Romano's recorded confession during his lunch with Betty Olson, provided substantive evidence of the fraud conspiracy perpetrated between the Ferrari organization and Whitman Communications against the FCC subsidy pool. An unhappy Federal judge, roused from bed at 10 p.m. tonight, issued arrest warrants for Romano and a search warrant on Romano's Spokane home and businesses. They had a warrant for his arrest for violations of federal racketeering statutes.

The judge issued similar warrants for Ferrari, Acosta, and other operatives in the Chicago area. The DOJ lawyers believed they had sufficient evidence to put away the principals of the Ferrari crime family for many years and bring their widespread crime operation to an end.

"Are you ready, Chicago?" Monroe said. He popped an antacid. His stomach churned.

"Copy that," Chicago responded.

Monroe's watch flashed 12:00. He spoke into his cell. "Let's roll." He strode to the front door of Romano's lavish home with his agents in tow. Several of the team broke off and made their way to the property's backyard to foil any attempted escape.

Agent Monroe pounded on the door with the heel of his hand. "Michael Romano. FBI. Open the door! Open up now!" Monroe's hand stung from striking the door in the early morning cold. Standing on the brink of his greatest career success, his heart beat wildly.

CHAPTER 83

THE FBI INTERROGATION rooms were located in the Spokane Federal building basement, down the hall from a group of holding cells. Michael Romano sat in an uncomfortable chair at an ancient wood table. A fluorescent light fixture in the ceiling showered the small room in a harsh, unforgiving light. Romano's nerves were on edge. Agents Monroe and McCoy were seated across the table from him.

"What the hell is this about? Ya ain't got no right to do this," Romano said. He twisted in the straight-back wood chair.

"You know what it's about, Romano. Erick Olson turned on you," Monroe said.

"Olson? That's what the hell this is about, Olson?" He tapped his fingers nervously on the table.

"We've read the agreements between your companies and Whitman Communications. Colluding to overbill a telephone company is a felony," McCoy said. "Phone companies are federally regulated."

"Under RICO, you could do twenty years and a quarter-million-dollar fine for each count," Monroe added. "And we have multiple counts."

"My agreements are legit. Any fraud is on Olson. All the phone company regulatory shit is him." Michael leaned back in the chair with a smug look on his face as though he had it all under control. He was not new to the interrogation process. "I never trusted that guy."

"Yeah, we see how you structured this to implicate Olson—very clever. You can't run away from the twenty million dollars you wired from Cooperative Rural Bank to the numbered account in Hong Kong.

The bank's loans are federally guaranteed. That's wire fraud and carries a minimum five-year sentence for each count," Monroe said.

"I don't know nothin' about no wire." The pent-up rage within him began to surface. "It wasn't me. I got no access to Whitman bank accounts. That's all management crap." He gave them an arrogant smile. *I'm way ahead of you.*

"Really?" McCoy said. "How do you explain this?" She slid the bank wire confirmation for the Cooperative Rural Bank twenty million dollar transfer across the desk to him.

"What the hell's this?"

"It's the bank confirmation showing you authorized Amy Summers to wire the money to a bank in Hong Kong," McCoy said, leaning over the table.

"Bull shit. Like I said, I don't have access to their bank accounts."

"Show him the email," Monroe said.

McCoy pushed a single sheet of paper toward him.

"Read it," Monroe barked.

Romano picked up the email and read it to himself:

> *Amy,*
>
> *In my capacity as Vice Chairman for Whitman Investment Company, I need you to wire twenty million dollars from our Cooperative Rural Bank line of credit to the Hong Kong account that you have on file. Use this email as your authorization to initiate the transfer. I'll log on to the Cooperative Bank account and approve. This needs to be done today.*
>
> *Michael*

The blood boiled in his veins, flowing hot through his body and into his brain. Romano knew Olson had tried to frame him with the wire transfer, but this was the first time he had seen the forged email. Out of control, he jumped to his feet and shoved the table into McCoy. Romano couldn't see through his bloodshot eyes; his throat swelled, choking off his words. He dropped the email, grabbed the confirmation from the table, and read the account number again. Romano struggled desperately to process the information on the two sheets of paper.

"Bullshit, this ain't my email. Doesn't even sound like me."

"That's a good one, Romano. No one will believe you. Legitimate tax-paying companies the size of Whitman Communications don't have unreported offshore bank accounts," Monroe said.

"This is bullshit. It's a setup!" Romano yelled. He felt himself falling apart at the seams.

The agents grabbed him, one on each arm, and forced him back into the chair.

"Kind of stings, doesn't it?" Monroe leaned over the table and got in Romano's face.

"And there's the fake charges you've been putting on peoples' telephone bills for toll-free 800 services. And after Pacific Bell stopped billing for your company, you made up customer bills to look like Bell's and mailed them yourself. The phone bills go through the mail. That's one count of mail fraud for every one of those fraudulent bills you sent out." Monroe smiled in victory.

"That's bullshit," Romano said.

"Look, we know you aren't the brains behind the operation. Tony Ferrari and Joe Acosta are pulling your strings. If you testify against them, we'll recommend the DOJ go easy on you," McCoy said. "This is a one-time offer, Romano."

"No way, I'd be a dead man," Romano paused a beat, "this is entrapment."

"Unfortunately for you, the money wired into your account is real," Monroe said.

"I want my lawyer. I want my damn lawyer now. I ain't sayin' nothin' else." He folded his arms across his chest in defiance and locked his burning eyes on Monroe. Accepting nothing would be resolved until his lawyer arrived, Romano's blood pressure returned to normal. His head ached from the stress of the interrogation.

CHAPTER 84

STEPPING FROM THE San Jose Airport terminal onto the sidewalk, Erick breathed in the cool night air. *We did it. We're free now.* He picked up his reserved rental car and strode through the parking lot, car keys jingling in his hand. Amy would be hungry when she arrived at 10:00 p.m. this evening. Erick wanted to make her a late-night supper in their new home, something light, not too heavy.

Erick found a grocery store and grabbed a cart. Wandering through the aisles, he selected fresh produce: mixed salad, tomatoes, green pepper, and mushrooms. Turning into the dairy section, he saw the eggs. *Perfect, I'll make breakfast burritos for our first night in Costa Rica.* He laid a carton of eggs and a bag of tortillas in the cart. Then, a tub of butter and a gallon of milk. *What else? Sausage can't have a burrito without sausage.* Erick found the meat section and added sausage to his cart. *Oh, and potatoes, what am I thinking?* He found an inexpensive Styrofoam ice chest and a bag of ice and checked out. Erick used his Brian Sanderson credit card for the first time.

Back in the rental car now, Erick glanced at his watch, 9:15 p.m. His heart beat faster with excitement. Amy's flight would arrive in forty-five minutes. Turning out of the parking lot, Erick headed back to the airport.

Walking through the airport parking lot, a plane flew in low on its landing approach. The roar of its engines drowned out all other sounds. Erick checked his watch, 9:45 p.m. Amy's flight. *We did it. We'll be on the road to our new home and freedom in half an hour.* Erick found his way to Amy's gate and took a seat in the waiting area with a clear view of the jetway. He recalled the warmth of her body and the taste of her goodbye kiss in Panama City. Goosebumps rose on his arms.

Erick watched anxiously as the stream of passengers rolled off the jet-way. He missed her in the crowd. His chest tightened. When the flight attendant stepped through the door, he reached out and touched her on the shoulder. She turned and smiled.

"Is anyone still onboard?" Erick asked.

"The flight crew, that's it," she said.

"Thanks, I must have missed her," panic filled Erick's eyes. His stomach turned.

Erick ran frantically toward the baggage claim, his breathing labored. His eyes shifting from face to face as he fought through the crowd. She wasn't here. He checked his cell phone, no messages.

Erick sat on a bench by the entrance to the concourse and tried to calm his nerves. "Where are you," he whimpered softly. Panic filled his veins and clouded his mind. *Maybe they snagged her at the Panama City airport after I left. We should have stayed together. God, where is she?* His heart beat wildly.

Running to the rental car, Erick climbed in, and called her—voicemail. He didn't leave a message. She'd see who called. Hands shaking, he left the airport and turned toward Playa Langosta and their rental condo.

At 1 a.m., he arrived at the condo and unpacked the car. He tried her phone again—voicemail. Sitting on the sofa, Erick held his head in his hands, "where are you," he moaned. By the time 2 a.m. arrived, he had fallen fast asleep on the sofa.

The burner phone in his briefcase vibrated, awakening him a few minutes past 9 a.m. He fished it out and stared at the screen, an email from Amy. Erick's heart tingled with anticipation.

At last. Where are you? What happened?

Erick desperately fumbled with his passcode. Barely awake, it took him five attempts to unlock the phone. He clicked on the email, and a short message filled the screen. Erick skimmed quickly through the paragraph. Words from her email floated in his mind like alphabet soup. Romano. Killed. Love. Forsaken. Rationalized. The words made no sense to him. Confusion coursed through his brain.

"The money, what about the money. What have you done, Amy?" Erick said, panicked.

Flipping open his laptop, Erick logged into their Hong Kong bank account. Twenty million US dollars had been wired out this morning. The remaining account balance sat at less than five hundred thousand US dollars.

"No, Amy! No!" he cried out in the condo. The chill of betrayal rolled through his heart while his mind fought to reject the reality in plain view on his screen.

Erick turned back to the email on his phone. He focused on her note, this time reading slowly. He strained to understand how this could have happened. He searched for hidden meaning between the lines.

> *Erick –*
>
>   *When you dragged me into the Romano mess of your creation, I rationalized my hacking background made me no better than you. When you killed the stranger in our hotel room, you crossed a line I cannot get past. For that, my love for you is forsaken. I'm truly sorry.*
>   *Amy*

Erick's heart rejected the truth that she had turned on him. It had to be something else. He couldn't imagine going on without her. Maybe it was a trick by the FBI or Romano. But the words were hers; no one else could have written them. Raw emotion twisted and churned inside him. Tears washed his face, and shouted it was real.

"Son-of-a-bitch!"

Not knowing what treachery to expect next, Erick grabbed his bags, tossed them in the rental car's trunk, and drove south toward the Panama border.

CHAPTER 85

Five years later

ON THEIR LAST day in Panama City, one of Erick's t-shirts ended up in Amy's luggage. The fabric carried his scent, and though she tried not to, Amy slept with that old shirt every night for the past five years. Just like their last kiss in the airport, Erick's scent was burned into her memory for all of time. Amy's romantic connection with Erick was over. Yet his memory continued to cast a shadow over her future. The best she could do was trudge forward and hold tight, believing that someday she would meet someone special enough to fill the hole Erick left in her heart.

Closing the door to her apartment, Amy rushed through the drizzling rain to catch the 7:05 a.m. bus two blocks away. Her hair had grown silky-black again and swung to and fro as she jogged down the hill. She adored the salty smell of the ocean in the early morning. The light morning fog clung to her cheeks like a moist towel. Fifteen minutes later, the bus would drop her off at her job in the Tech Center.

Amy climbed the steps onto the bus and exchanged greetings with the driver and regulars she had come to know a bit through the years. She knew a little about some of them, like who was married and what school a passenger's children attended—the first names of some, the last of others.

But staying faithful to her reserved nature, Amy's commuter companions knew very little about her. She had dropped only enough hints about her past to maintain the mysterious image of the woman they saw each morning with an affinity for computers and numbers. Amy cultured the illusion of a successful young woman living in an affluent community at what appeared to be a very tender age. It was all a lie. She was now thirty-seven and struggling to make ends meet. A woman with a secret, she diligently guarded the gates to her past.

Amy grabbed a vacant seat on the half-empty bus and leaned her head against the rain-splashed window. She stared vacantly into city storefronts as the bus lurched through heavy traffic. As they often do, her thoughts turned to Erick. She questioned her decision to leave the *Financial Wunderkind* during quiet moments every day. Maybe Erick was right, and killing the assassin had been self-defense. After all, they were running for their lives. But the guy was still alive when Amy handed Erick the gun. That rationale played over and over in her mind like a vinyl record stuck in a groove. She often feared her heart may never recover.

The big decisions made in her life continued to haunt Amy. No matter how far she ran or how fast she went, the impact of her life choices were always with her. Amy often wondered what might have been if she hadn't drawn that hard line in the sand. On one side, all the crimes she had ever committed. Across the line, murder. Erick crossed the line, and there could be no forgiveness in her mind.

Amy rarely waxed philosophical. The line between murder and all other crimes was the exception. Society will forgive most crimes in time. Not murder, though. To commit murder is to carry a life sentence of moral judgment. Judgment that can never be redeemed. There is no societal redemption for murder. And that was the difference between Amy and Erick. The act of senseless violence repulsed her. The act that extinguished the undying love she carried for him.

Sitting in the Panama City airport bar talking to Alison years before, Amy's friend had nearly convinced her to return the stolen money and turn herself into the FBI. In the end, Amy couldn't bear the thought of going through life as a convicted felon.

After her phone call with Alison, the pieces fell into place. It all seemed so right. Amy booked a flight to Osaka, Japan, where most of her extended family lived. That decision came easy. The decision of what to do with the money came harder. Allowing Erick to keep it felt wrong.

He was a murderer and hadn't earned the money. Returning it to the FBI seemed like a bailout for the Mob. Amy never wanted the cash; she wanted Erick. And now she would have neither. Ultimately, she wired the twenty million dollars to an orphanage in South Korea and felt whole in doing so.

The bus rolled to a stop in front of the Tech Center. Amy grabbed her messenger bag and stepped onto the sidewalk and into the rain. The wind had picked up; she could feel her hair getting wet. Opening her umbrella, Amy took a moment to appreciate the building's grandeur and the people rushing in and out of the front entrance—they felt like her people.

Changing her name from Summers to Sanderson created hurdles when Amy first looked for a job in Japan. She couldn't use her transcript and degree from UW because they were in her former name. With her exceptional financial and computer skills, it didn't take long for her to persuade a cyber security start-up to take a chance on her.

Walking through automatic doors into the building, Amy shook off her umbrella. The rain reminded her of how much she missed Seattle. Thinking of Seattle, her heart ached for Ali's smile. The moment she decided to fly to Japan and make a fresh start rather than return to Spokane and turn herself in to Agent Monroe, Amy knew she would never see or talk to Ali again. And that may end up being the greatest tragedy in her life.

ABOUT THE AUTHOR

 Terence D. Robinson is an award-winning author and published poet. He is the Idaho Writer's League 2017 Poet of the Year. Terry splits his time between Priest Lake, Idaho and Colorado Springs, Colorado. He spends his days writing poetry and working on his next novel. When not writing, Terry can be found hanging out with his grandchildren or playing with his golden retriever Max.